The
MADAM

JAIME RAVEN

avon

AVON

A division of HarperCollins*Publishers*
1 London Bridge Street
London
SE1 9GF

www.harpercollins.co.uk

A Paperback Original 2016

2

Copyright © James Raven 2016

James Raven asserts the moral right to
be identified as the author of this work

A catalogue record for this book is
available from the British Library

ISBN-13: 978-0-00-817146-9

Set in Minon by Palimpsest Book Production Limited, Falkirk, Stirlingshire
Printed and bound in Great Britain by Clays Ltd, St Ives plc

MIX
Paper from
responsible sources
FSC C007454

The
MADAM

This one is for Catherine, with love.

PROLOGUE

Southampton: 2011

I was naked and covered in someone else's blood. It was smeared across my flesh and dripping from the tips of my fingers onto the carpet.

Around me the room seemed to be spinning slowly, like a fairground carousel. My vision was blurred, but I could make out various objects. A door. A sofa. A flat-screen television. A wall painting. A bed.

A man's body.

The body was lying on the bed, naked like me and face up. And there was more blood. It soaked the sheets and the rug of thick, grey hair on the man's chest. There were even splash marks on the wall above the wooden headboard.

I knew instinctively that he was dead. His eyes were bulging out of their sockets and he wasn't breathing. He was motionless.

The realisation that I wasn't dreaming hit me like a bag of ice. I made an effort to scream, but nothing came out. The shock of what I was experiencing had rendered me mute.

I tried to bring my thoughts to bear on what was happening.

Where was I? Who was the man? Why was there so much blood?

As I stood there, dazed and bewildered, the back of my head throbbing, it gradually came back to me.

A few moments ago I'd been lying on the bed beside the corpse. I must have been unconscious because suddenly I was awake and aware that something was wrong. So I'd rolled off the bed and onto my feet.

And that's when I looked down and saw the shocking state I was in.

Oh God.

The room stopped moving suddenly and my eyes focused on something on the floor. It glinted in the wash of colour from the bedside lamp.

A large knife. And there was more blood on the blade.

I backed away from it until I came up against the cold, smooth surface of the wall. From here I could see the whole room. The full, horrific scene of carnage.

I felt my legs wobble. A wave of nausea washed through me. I reached out and grabbed the back of a chair for support. The chair stood in front of a dressing table, and there was a big square mirror in which I caught sight of my reflection.

There was so much blood. On my face, my breasts, my shoulders. It even trailed down across my stomach into my pubic hairs.

As I stared at myself the rest of it came back to me. I realised who the man was. I recalled what had happened in the room before I lost consciousness. The raised voices. The violent struggle. The drunken haze that smothered everything.

And it was these mental images that finally dislodged the scream from deep inside my throat.

'I've got some bad news for you, Lizzie.'

They were the first words out of the governor's mouth when I was escorted into her office. Maureen Riley had only been in the job for a few months so I'd never had a one-to-one meeting with her before today. I'd assumed she was going to read me the riot act, tell me that under her stewardship I would have to change my ways and become a model prisoner. But I could tell from the solemn expression on her face that I'd been summoned for a different reason.

'I think perhaps you should sit down,' she said, waving to an empty chair across the desk from her.

But I just stood there, rigid as a tent peg, my blood racing in anticipation of what was to come.

She had her back to the window, through which I could see a fierce afternoon sun beating down on the streets of North London. The stark light accentuated the lines around her eyes and mouth, and I found myself momentarily distracted as I wondered how old she was. Mid-to-late forties? Early fifties? It was hard to tell. Her brown hair was liberally streaked with grey and she had a fleshy, nondescript face.

'I really think you should take a seat, Lizzie. What I'm about to tell you will be extremely upsetting.'

Everything inside me turned cold. My heart started thumping, thrashing against my ribs.

'Has something happened to Leo?' I said, my voice thin and stretched. It was the first fearful thought that sprang into my mind.

She clamped her top lip between her teeth and leaned forward across her desk. Her eyes were steady and intense, and I could see the muscles in her neck tighten.

'I'm afraid your son had to be rushed to hospital this morning,' she said. 'He was taken ill suddenly at his grandmother's.'

An awful stillness took hold of me. I tried to speak but the words snagged in my throat.

The governor rearranged her weight in the chair, took a long, deep breath and then uttered the words that every parent dreads to hear.

'Leo passed away, Lizzie. It happened several hours ago. I just received the call.'

It took a couple of seconds for it to sink in. It can't be true, I told myself. How can my little boy be dead? He's only three years old, for Christ's sake.

But then it hit me and a sob exploded in my throat.

'No, no, no,' I cried out.

I clenched my eyes shut and the world tilted on its axis. I felt myself falling, but the screw who had brought me to the office grabbed me before I fell to the floor. She managed to lower me onto the chair as the tears poured out of me.

The governor waited a few minutes before she spoke again.

'I've been told that your mother was with him at the end, Lizzie. He was very ill, apparently. Viral meningitis.'

I felt a darkness rise up inside me. Not in my wildest dreams could I have imagined this. My darling son was everything to me. He gave meaning to my life, a life that had been twisted out of shape by bad luck and mistakes.

And now he was gone.

'I'm so very sorry, Lizzie,' the governor said. 'I know this is a terrible shock and I wish there was something I could say that would soften the blow. But of course there isn't.'

Images of Leo cartwheeled through my mind. I saw him in my arms just after I'd given birth, and when he took his first steps across

4

the living room carpet at nine months old. And then there was the very last time I saw him, not long after his first birthday. His bright blue eyes and curly fair hair. The smile that never failed to melt my heart.

Oh God how could he be dead?

I continued to sob hysterically. The governor got up and came around her desk. She placed a hand on my shoulder and spoke in a soft voice. But I didn't take anything in because the shock and grief were all-consuming.

When finally I recovered my composure she gave me a tissue to wipe my eyes and said she would arrange for a bereavement counsellor to come and see me.

'And of course I'll keep you informed about funeral arrangements,' she said. She then told the screw to take me back to my cell.

As I was led out of the room I broke down again, and through the deluge of tears I heard my mother's voice in my head from long ago.

'*You've ruined your son's life as well as your own, Lizzie,*' she told me after I was charged with killing a man. '*I hope God can find it in his heart to forgive you, because I know I can't.*'

Those words had tormented my soul for three long years. The weight of guilt was a burden I'd been forced to endure ever since they locked me up.

And now it was going to be much, much heavier.

I stopped crying on the way back to the cell block, but I could feel the scream building inside me.

It seemed odd that all around it was business as usual. The daily grind of the prison continued uninterrupted. Raised voices. Stilted laughter. Doors slamming shut. Small groups of women engaged in furtive conversation.

5

None of them knew about my loss yet. But they soon would. Holloway houses more than five hundred female prisoners, from murderers to petty thieves. When something like this happens the news spreads like wildfire.

I knew I could expect a lot of kind words and sympathy from most of the inmates. But a good few wouldn't give a toss. They were the druggies and bullies and psychopaths who cared only about themselves.

And as sod's law would have it a bunch of them were gathered in the corridor close to my cell. When they saw us approaching they fell silent. Then they stood aside to let us pass.

I lowered my gaze so that I didn't have to look at them, but not before catching the eye of Sofi Crane, the undisputed leader of the pack. She was a large woman with a hard face and a fierce reputation. I was one of the few inmates who weren't intimidated by her and that had always got under her skin. It was why she hated my guts and took every opportunity to wind me up.

She'd never seen me upset before, though, and I just knew that my obvious distress would delight her. But wisely she chose not to make any snide remarks as I was steered towards my cell.

The door stood open, and as I stepped inside the screw let go of my arm, told me again how sorry she was, and then retreated. I had no doubt that she'd tell Sofi and her mates what had happened. But that didn't matter. Nothing did any more.

As soon as Scar saw me she leapt up from the bed and dropped the book she'd been reading on the floor.

'Jesus, babe,' she said. 'What the bloody hell has happened?'

I looked at my cellmate, my lover of two years, and I realised that even she wouldn't be able to ease the pain of my loss.

'It's Leo,' I said, my voice cracking. 'He's . . . dead.'

Scar rushed over and wrapped her arms around me. She held me tight as the grief pulsed through me in waves.

'I don't see how I can go on,' I said. 'Not now that I've lost everything.'

'You've still got me, Lizzie,' she replied, and I felt her sweet, warm breath on my neck. 'I'm here for you and always will be.'

The tears returned with a vengeance and I cried into her shoulder, great wrenching sobs that shook me to the core. I wanted to die too at that moment. I wanted the ground to open up and suck me under. But I knew I wouldn't be that lucky.

Scar's body stiffened suddenly and someone else's voice came from behind.

'Just heard about your son, Lizzie. What a bummer. Still, it's not as if you've had anything to do with the poor little bugger these past few years.'

I pushed Scar away and spun round. Sofi Crane was standing in the doorway, her lips curled back in a malicious grin. I choked back a sob and a smouldering rage ripped through me.

'What did you say you bitch?' I shrieked at her.

'Oh sorry,' she said. 'Did I strike a nerve?'

Scar grabbed my arm but I jerked it free. I felt something primal take hold of me. The grief turned to anger and I launched myself at Sofi Crane with a ferocious bellow.

Before she had time to react I drove a fist into her face. The blow caused ribbons of blood to spurt from her nostrils. She let out a horrific grunt and stumbled backwards into the corridor.

I lunged forward, grabbed the front of her sweatshirt, shoved her hard against the wall. She lost her balance and collapsed in an untidy heap on the floor.

But I didn't let up. Instead I aimed a kick at her stomach with everything I had. She gave an anguished cry and rolled on her side. I then kicked her in the small of her back and she curled up like a hedgehog to protect herself.

I was still kicking and screaming when two screws pulled me away and dragged me back into my cell. And that was where I remained until the commotion died down and my anger subsided. But it took a while because I was in such a state. My lungs burned with every intake of breath and my thoughts swam in feverish circles.

But I didn't regret what I'd done. Sofi Crane had deserved it, and I was glad I'd hurt her. But her suffering was nothing compared to the pain I was going to inflict on the bastards who had wrecked my life and taken away my only son.

I was now more determined than ever to track them down and make them pay. It would just have to wait until I was finally released from this rat-infested hell hole.

1

Present Day

Three years and eleven months. That's how long I spent behind bars for a crime I didn't commit. Almost the entire sentence imposed by the judge. Some people said I should have got life and been banged up for a minimum of fifteen years. But they didn't get their way, so in that respect I was lucky.

Inside I met four lifers who claimed they were innocent, and two of them convinced me that they were telling the truth. They were dead inside. You could see it in their eyes. No hope. No future.

Three years and eleven months had been just bearable. If I'd been a model prisoner I would have got out sooner on licence. But sheer anger and frustration caused me to make too many mistakes and too many enemies. That burning sense of injustice gave me a reason to live, though. Served as a constant reminder that one day in the not too distant future I'd get out and be free to find the bastard or bastards who had destroyed my life.

Well that day had finally arrived.

It was a warm, grey Thursday in late July. A light drizzle greeted me as I walked out of Holloway Women's Prison just after midday.

I was wearing faded jeans, a white Gap T-shirt and a denim jacket that was a size too big. I was carrying a canvas holdall containing all my worldly possessions.

This first taste of freedom felt strangely hollow, like sucking on a joint that's slow to take effect. Maybe that's how it is for everyone. A bit of an anti-climax until it truly sinks in.

The sky over North London was the colour of the walls in the cell I'd just vacated. It had been the same on the day I arrived. As grim and lifeless as a cancer ward.

The farewells had been short and sweet. I'd embraced a few of the inmates I'd come to regard as friends. They all got a pack of Marlboro Lights as a parting gift. The governor gave me a little pep talk and said I had to get on with my life and forget about the past. She then wished me well and told me she didn't want to see me back inside again.

I raised two fingers to the large, red-brick building just for the hell of it. I felt I had to make some sort of gesture. As feeble as it was I felt better for it. Then I walked along the access road to where Scar was waiting.

She'd parked the car with two wheels on the kerb and was standing with her back against the nearside wing. The sight of her sent my heart racing and I felt the sting of tears in my eyes.

She'd had her hair dyed and cut short, and it made her look younger than her twenty-six years. It was black now, instead of auburn. She'd also splashed out on a new leather jacket that she wore over a red cotton blouse and tight beige trousers.

As I closed the distance between us she gradually came into focus. Five foot five. Narrow face, high cheekbones. Body tight and toned. She was slender, but with not a hint of fragility. Her eyes were cerulean blue, same as the water colour that's cool and opaque, and a tiny silver stud glinted in the left side of her nose.

Her most striking feature was a two-inch-long scar that ran from just beneath the lobe of her left ear to the middle of her cheek.

'Hi, beautiful,' I said when I reached her and it was all I could do not to let the emotion of the moment overwhelm me.

We embraced, and it felt good to feel her warm breath against my neck again. It had been a long time. Too long. I'd missed her so much and the thought of snuggling up in bed with her tonight filled me with a sense of well-being. We clung to each other for a full minute and the lump in my throat got so big I couldn't swallow.

Scar and I had formed a relationship after we started sharing a cell towards the end of my first year inside. For me it provided a much needed distraction, a way to make the banality of prison life bearable.

'I'm taking you to a pub first,' she said, when we finally moved apart. 'We'll celebrate with a bottle of champagne. Everything else can wait. So get in the car, sit back and relax.'

I sat back in the front seat of the ageing Fiesta, but I couldn't relax. Too much to see and too many thoughts to process.

For one thing I had to remind myself that I'd got my identity back. I was Lizzie Wells again, Twenty-seven. Light brown hair. Dark brown eyes. Almost perfect teeth.

In prison the screws had labelled me a troublemaker because I found it hard to control my temper and would always answer back. That was why I didn't get released any earlier. But then they were constantly trying to rob me of my self-respect. They were still at it even up to a few days ago.

'You were a looker when you came in here, Lizzie,' one of them had said. 'But you look like shit now. I doubt that blokes will still want to pay you for sex. Good job you're now a dyke.'

She was right about the way I looked, but the jury was still out on the other thing. In prison Scar and I had become soulmates and sexual partners. The bond between us was strong and intimate. But freedom gave me the option to return to being straight, so my sexuality was among the issues that I would need to address. I would, of course, but in my own time.

And time was something I'd become far more conscious of. In prison it passed slowly. I counted the hours and days and often my head was filled with nothing but the loud ticking of an invisible clock.

Now time was going to burn like a fuse. I was sure of it. There were things to do, people to see. The monotony of prison routine was behind me. The pace of my new life was set to blast me into orbit.

For the first time in years I felt glad to be alive. But my newfound freedom was already filling me with trepidation. A lot had changed since I'd been banged up and I was fearful of not being able to cope. I realised suddenly that I hadn't really prepared myself mentally for the chaos of life on the outside. I'd been too wrapped up in what I planned to do.

Scar turned into Parkhurst Road. It was heavy with traffic and noisy as hell. The wail of a police siren made me jump and set my teeth on edge. We stopped at some lights. A party of primary school children in bright red uniforms started crossing the road. Their animated chatter made me smile. We then continued along Parkhurst Road and swung left into the much busier Holloway Road. Here the pavements were lined with shops and packed with pedestrians.

As we drove on I took it all in. Cars crawling by in a welter of exhaust fumes. A young mum pushing a pram. A couple of teenagers holding hands and laughing. An elderly woman struggling with two heavy Tesco bags.

Normality. The everyday things that you take for granted until they're taken away from you. I'd missed so much of everything, and I felt bitter about that.

'There's a pub on the corner,' Scar said. 'The champagne is on me.'

I reached out and touched her knee.

'Thanks for being so thoughtful,' I said.

'It's no more than you deserve, babe. Life's been a bitch to you, and it makes me want to cry just to think about it.'

The boozer was called The Red Lion. It was just off the high street and more than a little drab on the outside.

I couldn't remember the last time I'd been inside a pub, or who I'd been with. It was a long time ago, though.

Before that fateful night my favourite tipple had been vodka, lime and lemonade. But I was also partial to bottles of potent German lager. For a time back in those days binge drinking had been a problem, along with class B drugs. It was no wonder that I got into such an awful mess with my life and ended up in Holloway.

The champagne tasted strangely medicinal, and the bubbles tickled my nose and made me sneeze. Scar laughed and poured herself a glass.

'Just a small one for now because I'm driving,' she said. 'We can let rip tonight when I don't have the car.'

The pub was small with a clean floor and dimpled copper tables. A few people were propping up the bar, office types mostly, on early lunch breaks.

We sat in a corner and attracted a bit of attention, but only because the cork made a loud pop when Scar extracted it from the bottle.

13

I'd half expected people to stare at me because I was an ex con. But that was stupid. It wasn't as if I had it written across my forehead in large black letters.

'Here's to your new life,' Scar said, raising her glass to mine. 'May it be long and happy.'

'Right on,' I said.

We clinked our glasses, and I felt a wave of affection for my former cellmate. She was the most considerate person I'd ever known. Her real name was Donna Patterson, but inside she was nicknamed Scar for obvious reasons. She told me that she didn't mind because it gave her an air of mystery. But I knew it was a lie. In truth the scar bothered her, just like it would any woman. It disfigured an otherwise beautiful face, and unfortunately no amount of make-up could conceal it.

I drank some more champagne and savoured the chill that swept through my insides. For a brief moment I felt like crying. It welled up suddenly, and I had to fight it back. Now wasn't the time to react to the emotional impact of what was happening.

So I cleared my throat and said, 'So tell me what you've got.'

Scar, bless her, had come prepared. She had known that I'd want to get straight down to business, that any celebration would be muted and short-lived.

She took a notepad out of her handbag and flipped it open. But before reading from it she cocked her head on one side and looked at me. The scar was more pronounced as the light through the window set off the ridge of red, gnarled skin.

'Are you sure you want to go down this road?' she said.

'We've had this discussion,' I pointed out.

'I was hoping you might have changed your mind.'

'Well I haven't.'

Scar took a deep breath, and said, 'Fair enough. Just don't tell me later that I didn't try to stop this madness.'

The thing was I had to start somewhere. There was no game plan as such. No obvious clues to follow up. I only had a bunch of names and a list of unanswered questions. But it would have to be enough. If I could just stir things up then maybe I'd get a result.

I'd spent four years going over it in my mind. Bracing myself for the day when Lizzie Wells would embark on a new career as an amateur sleuth.

Scar was right, of course. It was madness. I really had no idea what I was doing, but I wasn't going to let that stop me doing it. I'd waited too long for this.

'Let's start with the flat you asked me to rent,' Scar said. 'As you know I've taken a one-bedroom place on a six-month lease, all paid up front. It's in a part of Southampton called Bevois Valley. Nothing fancy, but it's tidy and decently furnished.'

'That's good,' I said. 'I know the Valley. It's where I used to live.'

'I've also made a reservation for tonight at The Court Hotel. Room eighty-three. The one you wanted. Check in any time after two o'clock today. I didn't tell them we'll only be popping in and out.'

She reached into her handbag and took out a mobile phone.

'As requested. It's a pay-as-you-go smartphone. High-end model.'

I took the phone from her. It was slim and metallic grey.

'Your number will show up in the display window when you switch it on,' she explained. 'I've put my own number in the contacts list.'

She then flipped over the first page of her notebook. 'I checked up on the four names you gave me. They're all still living in Southampton, which is what you suspected.'

'Right, so let's start with Ruby Gillespie.'

Scar took a sip of champagne and leaned forward across the table. Her breath smelled yeasty and sweet.

'Ruby is still doing the same old shit,' she said. 'But I gather business is not as brisk as it used to be. There's more competition from other escort agencies in the city and she's found it hard to recruit new girls. That's partly because the drink problem you told me about has got much worse. Word is she's now an alcoholic and taken her eye off the ball.'

'It was on the cards,' I said.

'The address you gave me near the Common checks out,' Scar said. 'She's still living there by herself, and the house doubles as a brothel at times.'

I'd first met Ruby Gillespie at that very house after responding to one of her newspaper ads. A curvy brunette with dark Mediterranean features, Ruby was actually more attractive than most of the girls who worked for her. She exuded a charm that was natural and an air of sophistication that was not. I liked her at first and I was taken in by all the talk of being part of 'a big happy family' and having her full support if ever I got into trouble.

But when I did get into trouble she threw me to the wolves like a piece of stale meat. She refused to answer my calls while I was being held, and then in court she appeared as a witness for the prosecution. She claimed I'd once told her that I always carried a knife in my bag for protection. It was a lie, but the judge believed her.

She was on my list as I wanted to know why she said that.

16

'Who's next?' I said.

Scar flipped over another page.

'Detective Chief Inspector Martin Ash. He's still with Southampton police.'

'And he's been promoted since he put me away,' I said. 'In those days he was a lowly DI.'

'Well he's an ambitious bastard,' Scar said. 'It didn't take me long to find that out. People don't mess with him. Or like him much.'

Ash and DCI Neil Ferris had been the arresting officers in my case. I remembered Ash as being a snappy dresser in his early forties, with a pot-belly and a florid complexion. He was also an arrogant bully.

DCI Ferris was a sinewy figure who was less arrogant and more sympathetic. I wondered if that was because he was the father of two teenage daughters. He mentioned them a couple of times during those gruelling interview sessions. Said he prayed they wouldn't turn out like me.

'I don't believe your story about what went on in that room,' he'd said just before they charged me. 'But I also don't believe that you're a cold-blooded killer. Therefore I'm willing to accept that you got involved in a brawl with Benedict. So if you cop a manslaughter plea we won't pursue a murder conviction.'

Ferris had made it sound like they were doing me a favour. My lawyer had urged me to go along with it. Told me I faced a stark choice. Plead not guilty to murder and face an almost certain conviction based on the evidence. Or plead guilty to manslaughter and claim that I stabbed Benedict in self-defence when he got violent, even though I couldn't recollect how it had happened.

'Look at it this way,' Ferris had said. 'If a jury finds you guilty of murder it'll be life. If you go down for manslaughter you could be out in four or five years. That's not the end of the world. And having got to know you a little I'm sure you can handle it.'

He'd been right. I had managed to cope. But ironically the period after my trial had proved more of a struggle for Ferris.

Something happened to make him kill himself. My lawyer sent me a copy of Southampton's local evening newspaper, *The Post*. On the front page was a story about how detective Neil Ferris had jumped off a railway bridge into the path of a train. His wife, Pamela, was quoted as saying that she had no idea why he did it, and he didn't leave a note.

That night I lay on my bunk feeling sorry for his wife and daughters. But I wasn't able to dredge up any sympathy for the man himself.

'Do you plan on seeing Ash?' Scar said.

'Of course.'

'What makes you think he'll talk to you?'

I shrugged. 'No reason why he shouldn't.'

'So what do you think he can tell you that you don't already know?'

'Maybe nothing, but he might be able to shed light on a few things that have bugged me.'

I drank some champagne and glanced out of the window. The rain had stopped, and the sun was trying to force itself through the cloud cover. A lump rose in my throat again. I still couldn't believe I wouldn't be sleeping in that dingy cell tonight.

'Anne Benedict has moved house,' Scar was saying. 'I gather it happened soon after the trial. She's now living in Eastleigh on the outskirts of Southampton. Both her sons have moved out so she's by herself.'

Anne Benedict. The distraught wife of the victim. As she'd stared at me across the courtroom the thing that had struck me most had

18

been her blank expression. What I'd expected to see were eyes filled with hate, but instead they were just devoid of life. That, I thought at the time, seemed strange. *The Post* – for whom her husband had worked – had described them as a close and happy family. But of course that was crap. Happily married men don't pay for sex with prostitutes. I was keen to talk to the widow to find out what, if anything, she knew about what had happened.

'Finally we come to Joe Strickland,' Scar said. 'He is a prominent Hampshire businessman with a few million quid to his name.'

Strickland's name had come up during the investigation because a few weeks earlier he had made threats against Rufus Benedict. The reporter had made an official complaint to the police, and Strickland was given a verbal warning.

There was no question that Strickland would have been the prime suspect if the evidence against me hadn't been so overwhelming. Benedict, *The Post*'s long-serving investigative reporter, had been probing Strickland's business activities and was apparently close to publishing a story about him involving large-scale criminal activities, including corruption of local government officials. But the article was never written because Benedict was stabbed to death.

'I've got Strickland's address,' Scar said. 'He lives in a big detached house in an upmarket part of the city.'

'Is he married?'

'He's got a wife and daughter. The wife's name is Lydia and she runs one of his companies. The daughter lives with her boyfriend in London. He made his money as a property developer and now has his hand in lots of local pies, some of them illicit by all accounts.'

'I'm looking forward to talking to him,' I said.

Scar furrowed her brow. 'Do you really think he'll be up for it? He'll probably tell you to fuck off.'

'But I won't,' I said.

'Then he'll have you arrested.'

'I doubt it.'

'Then maybe he'll have you killed.'

'Now that would be an admission of guilt.'

Scar rolled her eyes and filled my glass. I swigged back the last of the champagne and said, 'Thanks for helping me out on this. You've been a gem.'

'To be honest it's been fun,' she said. 'It beat looking for a full-time job as soon as I got out. And it's put me back in contact with some old friends on the coast.'

Scar had been released from prison two months earlier after serving four and a half years inside for cutting off the testicles of the man who raped her and disfigured her face. It was yet another example of cock-eyed justice, and it made my blood boil. The judge took a dim view of the fact that she went to the man's house, broke in and attacked him while his wife was out shopping. But he accepted there were extenuating circumstances and was lenient when it came to sentencing.

Scar was no stranger to Southampton, having lived most of her life in neighbouring Portsmouth, where she long ago established a reputation as a bit of a tearaway. So when I'd told her what I planned to do she'd offered to help – after first trying to talk me out of it.

She got a part-time job serving behind the bar in a club and agreed to do some legwork for me when she wasn't working. I gave her access to one of my accounts in which I had some money stashed. That in itself was a mark of how much I trusted her.

'So are you ready to head south?' she said.

20

I put my glass down and stood up unsteadily.

'You've got me drunk,' I said. 'But it feels good.'

Scar smiled up at me and reached for my hand. Hers was soft and warm.

'Do you want to go straight to the hotel?' she said.

I shook my head. 'First I want you to take me to the cemetery.'

The champagne had gone straight to my head, but I was determined to stay awake during the ninety-minute drive to Southampton. The sun finally penetrated the cloud cover, turning it into a glorious day.

Fields rolled away into the distance on either side of the M3. Traffic whooshed and hummed and the sound of it was strangely soporific. Lorries the size of small houses. White vans weaving from lane to lane. Brake lights flashing on and off. Overhead gantries issuing threats and warnings.

It all became a blur to me as I sat back and listened to Westlife oozing out of the car's speakers. As we drove past Basingstoke, Scar asked me about some of the inmates we'd left behind, especially Monica Sash who, like me, was serving time for a crime she didn't commit.

'She wants me to clear her name after I clear my own,' I said. 'Eh?'

I shrugged. 'Told me her family will pay me a pot of money to get her out.'

'Jesus. Was she joking?'

''Fraid not. I told her she was being daft, that there wasn't anything I could do.'

I recalled the conversation and couldn't help but smile.

'*I'm not a private detective, Monica,*' I'd said. '*I'm a convicted killer and former prostitute.*'

21

'*But you're going after the people who framed you, Lizzie. And I think you'll find them. You've got what it takes. And when that's sorted you can do the same for me.*'

She'd been serious too. Had managed to convince herself that I was her last chance. I shook my head at the memory of those pleading eyes and turned to Scar.

'So what's it like to be free?' I asked.

She said she'd felt lost on her own at first. After the years inside it took time for her to feel comfortable and safe again in the big, wide world. We talked about the bar work she'd been doing in Southampton. The money was poor but at least it meant she didn't have to sit around by herself in the evenings.

'I'm not working tonight or the rest of the week,' she said. 'So we can party.'

We didn't talk about our relationship and where it would go from here because we weren't ready for that. I needed time to adjust to being on the outside and Scar needed to be patient. She knew I was confused so she wouldn't push me into making a decision. She'd want me to be sure about my feelings and about what I wanted. Scar meant the world to me and it was going to be tough when and if the time came to break her heart.

As we neared the south coast I began to experience a flutter of nerves in my stomach. It felt strange to be heading back to my home town when I no longer had a home there. Before I lost my freedom I'd rented a two-bedroom flat close to my mother's house in Northam. That was gone along with the furniture I'd managed to accumulate.

I didn't bother asking my mother if I could move in with her and my brother, Mark. She would only have said no. Ours had always been a tumultuous relationship, and what happened while I was in prison had made things worse. It was a shame as I missed my little brother, and I knew he missed me. He didn't visit me inside, but he did write me letters. They were short and sweet and barely discernible, but they meant a lot, and I'd kept every one of them.

We reached Southampton in the middle of the afternoon. The city lies between Portsmouth and Bournemouth and is just a few miles from the New Forest. It has several claims to fame, including the fact that the *Titanic* sailed from its huge port on its first and last voyage. Strangely, the good people of Southampton find that something to be proud of.

The cemetery was on a hill overlooking the Solent, that stretch of wind-lashed sea so loved by yachtsmen that separates the mainland from the Isle of Wight.

We parked at the entrance and Scar said, 'I'll wait in the car if you want to be by yourself.'

'I'd like you to come with me,' I said.

We strolled up the path with the Solent on our right and the city sprawled out on our left beneath the warm afternoon sun. Much of the cemetery was overgrown. It looked abandoned. A jungle of rampant weeds had grown up between the headstones. There were dead flowers on top of dead people.

Leo's grave lay in the shadow of a willow tree. The headstone was small and simple. The inscription read: *Here lies Leo Wells – a much loved son and grandson who left our world before his time.*

My baby died just over a year ago, and they let me out for the funeral. It was a devastating experience. I remembered standing at the graveside between my mother and brother as the coffin was lowered into the ground.

'This is your fault,' my mother spat at me. 'If you hadn't chosen a path of debauchery my little Leo would still be alive.'

Her words had burned into my heart and added to the weight of my loss. And I couldn't really disagree with her. It might have been cruel of her to point it out to me at the funeral, but she'd been right nonetheless. Leo died after contracting meningitis. Two months before his fourth birthday. I was sure that if I hadn't been locked up it wouldn't have happened. I wouldn't have let the doctor send him home after deciding he had nothing more than a simple headache and prescribing Calpol. The inquest was told that if he had been admitted to hospital and put on antibiotics he would have survived.

The guilt was an agonising pain I had to live with, and I bore a heavy sense of shame and self-loathing.

But Leo's death wasn't entirely my fault. Whoever framed me was, as far as I was concerned, even more culpable. He, she or they had killed my little boy. And I wasn't prepared to let them get away with it.

'Are you all right?' Scar said.

'I'm fine,' I lied.

There was a bunch of pink roses on the grave. They were slightly wilted, but still vibrant, and had no doubt been put there by my mother. I knelt down and told my son that I was back and that I was sorry I'd been away for so long. Hot tears welled up then, and this time I didn't try to stem their progress.

I sobbed uncontrollably for several minutes while clinging to the headstone. I wanted to dig down into the earth to be closer to my son. I wanted him to feel my warmth. Instead I just let the grief work its way through me.

Eventually I got to my feet and dried my eyes. I felt Scar's hand on my shoulder.

'This was always going to be tough, babe,' she said. 'But you have to be strong if you want to find the bastards who were

24

responsible for what happened. And I want you to know that I'll be with you all the way.'

The Court was a four-star hotel that catered mostly for business types. It was less than ten years old and had been built overlooking a park in the city centre. The reception area hadn't changed much. It was still cold and colourless.

We checked in and made our way up to room eighty-three on the third floor. Scar held my hand going up in the lift. She could tell I was anxious. My breathing suddenly became laboured and my stomach began to curl inside itself.

The corridor had a new carpet. The walls were lined with sepia prints of Southampton before German bombs ripped into it during World War Two. They too were new additions.

Scar inserted the key card in the lock, stood back to let me go in first. The moment I stepped through the door it all came flooding back with alarming clarity.

The room had been refurbished since that night, but everything was familiar. Bed, TV, sofa. All in the same places. The colours and shapes were different, but not the feel of the place.

Scar closed the door behind me and I had a sudden vision of Rufus Benedict lying on the bed. Blood everywhere. The knife on the floor.

I rushed into the bathroom and threw up into the toilet. The regurgitated champagne made my eyes water. I stayed there for a few minutes retching into the pan, sweat prickling my face. When I went back into the main room Scar poured me a glass of bottled water from the mini bar.

'Drink this,' she said.

It was cold and refreshing, but it failed to wash away the taste of vomit.

'It must be weird coming back here,' she said.

I sat on the edge of the bed and looked around. Saw myself in the mirror above the dressing table. Not a pretty sight.

I'd had to come back. Reliving that night was part of the process I knew I had to go through. It was necessary to remember as much as possible.

'Talk me through it,' Scar said.

She was sitting opposite me on the sofa, a can of Diet Coke in her hand. She'd removed her jacket, and I noticed she had a new tattoo. The name Lizzie was scrawled across her right forearm, and there was a red heart beneath it.

'I got a call from Ruby that evening,' I said, casting my mind back and feeling at once the sharp stab of bitter memories. 'One of her regulars wanted someone new. I had to turn up at the hotel at eight and come straight up to the room. That was pretty much how it worked most times. All very straightforward.'

'And businesslike,' Scar said with a hint of sarcasm in her voice.

'Yes,' I said. 'And businesslike.'

I'd actually been an escort for five months by then and I told punters to call me The Madam because I thought it had a saucy ring to it. The money was good and having sex with strange men wasn't as bad as I'd feared it would be. It was usually over very quickly, and the guys were mostly decent and polite. There was the shame and guilt, of course, but it was something I was prepared to live with.

After all, I'd started selling my body out of desperation, not because it was a chosen vocation. I was a single mum with a pile of debt and an addiction to soft drugs. It was an easy way to resolve my problems, or so I thought. The plan was to save enough money to pull myself out of the mire and secure a better life for myself and my son. But that's not how it worked out.

26

'Rufus Benedict opened the door in a hotel robe,' I said. 'He was a middle-aged guy with bad breath and a big belly. But he seemed harmless enough. We talked for a bit and just as we were about to get started there was a knock on the door. Benedict put on his robe and answered it. Outside the door there was a bottle of chilled champagne with a note saying it was with the compliments of the hotel.'

Benedict was all smiles as he popped the cork and filled two glasses. He told me to undress and sat there sipping at his drink as he watched me remove my clothes to soft background music. I'd developed a well-practised routine that was designed to tease and titillate. My clothes came off with slow precision as I licked my lips and ran my fingers gently over every inch of uncovered flesh.

'It all gets a little hazy after that,' I said. 'He took off the robe and asked me to get him aroused, which I did.'

Scar was trying not to show her revulsion. I'd told her the story before, but never in so much detail. She looked away briefly and bit into her bottom lip.

'We eventually moved to the bed,' I said. 'But nothing more happened because Benedict was suddenly struggling to stay awake and couldn't even keep it up. I felt tired too and a little giddy. Then I heard someone's voice and realised we weren't alone in the room. I turned round and saw that two men had let themselves in.'

'So what happened?'

'Well, everything was distorted so I couldn't make out their faces. Then I saw one of them attack Benedict and when I started to scream the other one put a hand over my mouth and pulled me down onto the floor. I could barely breathe. It was terrifying.'

Scar put down her Coke and came and sat beside me. She placed an arm around my shoulders. I was trembling.

'Take it easy, babe,' she said.

I downed some more water and said, 'I took a blow to the forehead then and everything went blank. When I came to I was covered in blood and Benedict was lying here on the bed. He'd been stabbed once in the chest and he was dead. The murder weapon was a knife I'd never seen before and my prints were on it.'

I closed my eyes and recalled the awful sense of panic that had consumed me.

'What did you do?' Scar said.

'I couldn't stop screaming. Before long there were people knocking on the door. When I finally managed to open it I was so worked up that I fainted. The cops arrived and I was arrested. As far as they were concerned it was an open and shut case.'

'Jesus.'

'There was no evidence to suggest that anyone else had been in the room. The security cameras hadn't picked anything up, and the only prints on the knife belonged to me. I couldn't convince them that someone had come into the room while we were having sex.'

'What about the champagne?' she said. 'Did they check to see if it was drugged?'

'There was no champagne. Whoever killed Benedict took the bottle and glasses away. The hotel's room service claimed they hadn't delivered anything to the room.'

'But what about the post-mortem? They do toxicology tests, don't they? That should have shown up any knock-out drugs in your system.'

'Well, it didn't. My lawyer said not all drugs can be detected during an autopsy.'

I got up and walked around, touching things, while letting the memories crowd my mind. Benedict's blood had been spattered across the sheets, the walls, the carpet. It was smeared across my

28

own breasts and face and even now it was the dominant theme of recurring nightmares.

'The police were certain that I murdered Benedict, but my lawyer put up a convincing argument that I was defending myself,' I said. 'There was the head wound and some other bruises. There'd obviously been a struggle, so the CPS agreed to drop the murder charge to manslaughter to make sure they got a conviction, provided I pleaded guilty.'

'You were lucky you didn't get life, Lizzie.'

That was true. But I was unlucky to spend time behind bars for something I didn't do.

'Come on,' I said. 'Let's get out of here. I need some fresh air.'

A few minutes later we walked out into the car park. As we approached the Fiesta I noticed something white under one of the windscreen wipers. I thought it was a leaflet or a flyer. But when I pulled it out I saw it was a piece of lined paper from a notebook. There were two short sentences scrawled on it in black felt tip ink.

Let it rest, Lizzie. Open up old wounds and you'll regret it.

2

Southampton central police station. An eight-storey building near the city's enormous port complex.

Scar waited in the car while I went into reception and asked for DCI Martin Ash. I gave my name and explained that I didn't have an appointment. The duty officer ran his eyes over me like I was something nasty that had been blown in from the street. He probably knew instinctively that I was just out of prison. Maybe it's something that cops can tell simply by looking at you.

Eventually he picked up the phone and called the Major Investigations Department. After a brief conversation he cradled the receiver. 'The DCI's out. But DS McGrath got back a few minutes ago and is coming down to see you.'

And with that he returned to whatever he was doing before I arrived. I sat on a bench and thought about the note. Back in town for less than an hour and already I'd been warned off. But that was cool because it meant that someone was worried. They knew – or suspected – that I was going to stir things up and they weren't happy about it.

DS McGrath stepped out of a side door into the reception area after about five minutes. He was mid-to-late thirties and looked vaguely familiar. In fact I was surprised that I couldn't immediately place him because he had the kind of looks that a girl doesn't easily forget. Dark wavy hair, sharp distinctive features. Handsome in a rugged, natural way. A Holloway pin-up for sure.

'Hello, Miss Wells. I'm Detective Sergeant Paul McGrath.'

He thrust out his hand for me to shake, but I ignored it as a matter of principle. Despite his good looks and obvious sex appeal he was still part of the establishment that had put me away.

'I just talked to DCI Ash on the phone,' he said, withdrawing his hand a little self-consciously. 'He's on his way back to the office and he's happy to see you. He wants me to take you upstairs and give you a cup of coffee.'

'I'd prefer tea,' I said.

He flashed a thin smile, showing a gap in his front teeth. 'That's no problem. Just come and make yourself comfortable while you wait.'

The corridors were familiar. I was led through them after I was arrested. Very little had changed. The posters that adorned the walls issued the same old warnings about drugs, knives and casual sex.

We walked through an empty open-plan office to a small room at one end. There was a desk and several chairs. View of a bus stop.

'Take a seat and I'll fetch you that tea,' McGrath said.

I sat and stared at the wall behind the desk. More posters were pinned to it, along with memos and newspaper cuttings. On the desk was a photo of Martin Ash with his family – a plump wife and two young sons. There was another framed photo on the grey filing cabinet to the right of the desk. It showed two men together

– Ash and Neil Ferris. They were wearing suits and smiling for the camera. I thought back to the hours they spent interviewing me in a tiny windowless room. Playing good cop, bad cop. Trying desperately to get a confession. Pumping me with tepid tea and false reassurances.

God knows how many times they made me recount what had happened in that hotel room. They wanted to know exactly what Benedict and I had got up to before he was killed. Did we have intercourse? Did he pay me in cash before we got started?

They asked me time and again why my fingerprints were on the knife if I'd never seen it before. And why the hotel staff knew nothing about the bottle of champagne I said had been delivered to the room.

It was a tough time for me. I was confused and disoriented. And angry because they refused to accept that I'd been the victim of a well-planned stitch-up.

McGrath returned with tea in a plastic cup. I couldn't help but notice how tight his trousers were. They showed off a narrow waist and well-toned ass. It was the kind of thing that used to turn me on, and if I was honest with myself it still did. It was a stark reminder of how hard it was going to be to decide which path to follow in respect of my sexuality.

'Careful,' he said, as he handed the cup to me. 'It's hot.'

I thanked him and drank some. He was right. It was scalding, but it tasted pretty good.

McGrath sat on the edge of the desk and folded his arms. I could smell his sweat and aftershave. After four years without a man it was difficult to ignore.

'Do you know how long Ash will be?' I asked.

'Any minute now,' he said. 'He's probably pulling into the car park as we speak.'

I sipped some more tea and met his gaze. His eyes were pale blue and alert. He seemed to be searching my expression for something.

After a beat, he said, 'You probably don't remember me. But I was one of the officers who brought you in. I was a DC then.'

'That so?'

'You were in a bit of a state. I don't think I've ever seen so much blood.'

I was suddenly conscious of my appearance. I knew I looked pale and drawn. My clothes were ill-fitting and my hair was a mess. I couldn't help wondering if he'd already given me marks out of ten.

'I can barely believe it was so long ago,' he said. 'It's flown by.'

A bolt of anger shot through me. 'I'm glad you think so. But then you weren't locked up in some poxy cell for most of the time.'

He looked mortified.

'Shit, I'm sorry I said that, Miss Wells. It came out wrong. It was insensitive.'

'Too fucking right it was,' I said.

'I wasn't thinking. Please accept my apology.'

'That's the trouble with you coppers,' I said. 'You're brainless fucking twats who don't think.'

He was about to respond when DCI Ash walked into the room wearing a broad grin that revealed sharp little teeth.

'What is it with you, McGrath?' he said. 'I leave you alone with a lady for ten minutes and you've already managed to upset her.'

McGrath looked from me to Ash and then back to me. His face reddened and for some reason I felt sorry for him.

'I've got a big mouth, guv,' he said.

'So tell me something I don't already know.'

Ash came further into the room and looked down at me. He was wearing a blue suit and white shirt with a starched collar. The creases in the trousers were razor sharp. His thinning hair was slicked back with gel. He'd put on weight since I last saw him and had a more generous paunch.

'Good to see you again, Lizzie.'

I arched my brow at him. 'Really?'

'For sure. It's not often that someone I put away looks me up the day they get out. It is kind of freaky, though. Should I be concerned?'

'Only if you're a lying bastard with something to hide,' I said.

The smile became a hearty chuckle which stayed with him as he walked behind the desk and folded his bulk into the chair.

'Very funny, Lizzie,' he said. 'I can see you're still a spirited little madam even after a few years in the slammer.'

I never did like Ash. There had always been an arrogance in his tone that angered me. From the moment he took me into custody he treated me like slime. His favourite put-down line back then was: 'So how should I describe you, Lizzie? Or should I say Madam Lizzie? What are you: a brass, a tom, a whore or a prossy?'

'Try escort,' I'd responded that first time, but he thought it was funny and told me not to be ridiculous.

'Escort implies that you're sort of respectable,' he'd said. 'When in fact you're anything but.'

I could tell he hadn't changed. Still arrogant, obnoxious and judgemental. And that made him dangerous.

'I've actually been expecting you to show up,' he said. 'Soon as I got wind that your girlfriend was in town and asking lots of questions.'

I stared at him. 'How the hell did you know that?'

'Come off it, Lizzie. We're not stupid. Some strange bird looking like Al Capone suddenly appears on the scene and starts pumping people about things that are none of her business. Didn't it occur to you that we'd get suspicious, especially when she began touting for information on a killing that happened years ago?'

'How did you make the connection?'

'It wasn't difficult,' he said. 'She has a few contacts down in Portsmouth. One of them happens to be a snout for me. He alerted me that she was snooping around and we did some checking.'

'So why didn't you talk to her?'

'No reason to. She hadn't done anything wrong. And besides, we guessed that she was sniffing around for you. I'm assuming you're here to tell me why.'

'In a second.' I took the folded note from my jeans and leaned over the desk to hand it to him. 'First look at that.'

'What is it?'

'Someone put it on my girlfriend's windscreen after we left the car for a short time.'

He held the note between his fingers as though the paper might be radioactive.

Then slowly he unfolded it and read aloud, '"Let it rest, Lizzie. Open up old wounds and you'll regret it."'

He grunted and dropped the note onto the desk.

'So what do you make of it?' I asked him.

He looked at me quizzically. 'What am I meant to make of it?'

'Well, if I'm not mistaken that's a threat. And aren't the police supposed to protect people who are threatened?'

'This is a joke, right?'

Did I expect any other reaction? Probably not. Scar had told me the cops wouldn't take it seriously. But, at least the note had

35

given me an excuse to drop in on Ash, and that was good enough for now.

'I want to know who wrote it,' I said. 'And I'd like to know if I should be scared.'

He threw a glance at McGrath. 'So what's your take on it, detective? Do you think we're in the business of protecting confessed killers?'

To his credit, McGrath chose to ignore the question. He said, 'Where was the car parked, Miss Wells?'

'At The Court Hotel,' I said. 'We were inside for about half an hour. My girlfriend picked me up from Holloway and we drove there.'

'Are you sick in the fucking head or something?' Ash snarled. 'What were you doing going back to that place?'

'I wanted to see the room again,' I said. 'I wanted to refresh my memory.'

'Why, for fuck's sake?'

'Because now that I'm out I intend to find out who stitched me up.'

The room got quiet. Both coppers stared at me as though I'd suddenly broken out in huge red welts.

Ash eventually broke the silence. 'So prison turned you into a raving lunatic then.'

'I didn't kill Rufus Benedict,' I said. 'Someone went to a lot of trouble to make sure I got the blame for it.'

'That's bollocks,' Ash said, his voice filled with agitation. 'There's no question that you stabbed that poor, pervy bugger to death. You even pleaded guilty to manslaughter, for Christ's sake. But, hey, you served your time so move on. Go back on the game or wash dishes in a curry house. I don't care. Just don't piss around trying to be a detective.'

36

'I'm serious about this,' I said.

'You're insane more like.'

'That note suggests otherwise,' I pointed out. 'Someone is worried enough to try to warn me off.'

'How do we know you didn't write it yourself?'

'Check the CCTV cameras in the hotel car park for starters,' I said.

'That'll prove nothing. You might have got someone to plant it.'

'Why would I do that?'

'Because you're a nut. Because you want attention. Because you've decided it'd be fun to waste our time. There are a hundred and one reasons.'

'Get real,' I said. 'I'm telling you it was put there.'

He took a deep breath and exhaled it through his nose.

'Well, there's nothing I can do about it. No crime has been committed, and I don't intend to divert resources to helping a lowlife killer like you.'

I let that one pass and said, 'So how about answering some questions about Benedict's murder. There were things that didn't come out at the trial.'

He'd already started to get up from the chair. Now he stopped and looked down at me, his big hands resting on the desk.

'You've got a fucking nerve, Lizzie. I'll say that for you. But no way am I going to encourage you to make a nuisance of yourself. You're clearly mad to even think you can pull this crap. So listen carefully. I don't want you or Scarface to go around upsetting people. It'll just cause a heap trouble for everyone, including me.'

'You can't stop me asking questions,' I said.

He stood up and drew in a lungful of air. At the same time his stomach flopped ungraciously over his belt.

'Don't cross me, Lizzie. Just count yourself lucky that you're not going to spend the rest of your life in prison. You're out now because we let you get away with a manslaughter plea. So I suggest you make the most of your freedom. In fact I share the sentiments of whoever wrote that frigging note. So don't go stirring things up because it won't take much to put you back inside.'

I held his gaze. 'Does that mean you won't investigate the threat that's been made against me?'

He glared at me, the veins in his neck swelling.

'Just get the fuck out of here before I really lose my temper.'

McGrath was instructed to escort me down the stairs and out of the building. He didn't say a word until we got to the exit, and I sensed he was a little embarrassed by his boss's outburst.

Out in the sunshine, he said, 'I'm sorry about that. The governor isn't known for his good nature and even temper.'

I shrugged. 'I shouldn't have expected anything else from him.'

'Well, we're not all like Ash. As far as I'm concerned you committed a crime and you served out your punishment. Therefore, you're once again a regular member of the community with the same rights as everybody else.'

He handed one of his cards to me. 'I don't for a minute condone what you're doing, Miss Wells, but if you receive any more threats then give me a call. My mobile number is on the back.'

I mumbled my thanks, slipped the card into my back pocket.

'It might be useful if you gave me your number,' he said.

I turned on the phone that Scar had given me and read out the number.

'Ash was right, though,' he said. 'You shouldn't go raking over old coals. The last thing you want is to get into trouble again and wind up right back in the clink.'

38

'Thanks for the advice,' I said.

'I'm serious, Miss Wells. If you're not careful you could get into serious trouble again.'

I pressed out a grin. 'Don't see why. As you just said I served my sentence so like everyone else I'm now free to make an arse of myself as long as I keep it legal.'

I walked back to the car. Scar was puffing on a menthol and blowing the smoke out the window. She waited until I was strapped into the passenger seat.

'Didn't go well, did it?' she said.

'Is it that obvious?'

'You look fit to explode.'

'Ash is a bastard.'

'So I gather.'

I told her what had transpired in his office.

'I did warn you that it wouldn't be easy,' she said. 'I just can't see anyone helping you out, especially the Old Bill. I mean, why would they?'

It was the same question I'd been asking myself for ages, and I still didn't have an answer.

'Let's go to the flat,' I said.

Scar gunned the engine. 'Bevois Valley here we come.'

I lowered the side window and breathed in the familiar tang of salty sea air. It beat the smell of prison piss and disinfectant.

'By the way, the Valley is close to the town's red light district,' I said. 'Is this your way of trying to make me feel at home?'

Scar gave me a look. 'It was the cheapest pad I could find. And it's within walking distance of the bar we're going to tonight.'

'That so? What kind of bar is it?'

'It's big, dark and noisy. You'll love it.'

'Really? Let me guess – it's called the Mercury Club?'

'Hey, that's right. You know it?'

'Everyone knows it. It used to be the town's biggest gay venue.'

'Still is,' she said cheerfully. 'And you know what? I can't wait to show you off there.'

We drove along the dock road. A cruise ship was berthed in the port terminal, waiting to transport hundreds of well-heeled passengers to exotic locations. Maybe one day I'd be among them. It was something I used to dream about when, as a child, I'd watch the QE2 heading out into the Solent, its bow cutting through the water like a knife through jelly.

The city was much as I remembered it, except there were more flats, more speed cameras, more students and more cars. It was the Southampton I'd grown up in. A vibrant community with a colourful ethnic mix; where ugly new buildings nestled beside stone walls and ramparts from bygone eras; where women were gobby and people spoke with an accent that fell somewhere between cockney and west country.

My father had worked in the docks before he succumbed to bowel cancer at the age of thirty-five, leaving my mother to take care of my brother and me. Life was never the same after that. My father and I had been very close. He was the one who read me bedtime stories and paid me the most attention. I was a daddy's girl for sure and his death left me bereft.

My mother took it really hard and she never really came to terms with her loss. His death carved a hole in her life that couldn't be filled. She was forever searching for a meaning to her existence, and unfortunately for me she eventually found it in religion.

And there, just up ahead, was St Mary's church where she did all her praying. It's the largest church in the city, and my mother was fond of telling me that the sound of its bells had inspired the words of the song *The Bells of St Mary's*, which was sung by Bing

Crosby in the film of the same name. I was never sure why she thought I was interested.

She used to drag me to the services, but I hated it. I hated the smell of the polished wood, and I hated the hypocrisy that permeated the air like toxic fumes. When I was fifteen I called a halt to it, stood my ground. My mother had given up on me by then anyway and didn't go to war over the issue.

'Your mother and brother live near here, don't they?' Scar said. 'You want to go see them?'

The prospect of seeing my mother did not fill me with joyous anticipation.

'Tomorrow,' I said. 'There's no hurry.'

We drove on into Bevois Valley, a run-down inner city area full of student flats, live music venues and grubby takeaways. It's a few minutes walk from the decrepit flat I used to live in with Todd, the loser who fathered Leo. He stuck around long enough to realise a child meant cost and commitment. Then he disappeared, leaving me to cope by myself. He never saw his son, and the last I heard he'd moved up north. Even the cops couldn't trace him to tell him little Leo had died.

The flat that Scar had rented was just off the main drag opposite a small motorcycle repair shop. It was on the first floor of a scruffy terraced house. Peeling paint on the window frames. Chunks of brickwork missing. An overflowing wheelie bin out front.

It might have been a grim place in a grim part of town, but to someone who had spent nearly four years in a poky cell it wasn't half bad. Even when I saw the flat's interior I didn't flinch, though I was sure most people would have.

The carpet was grey and threadbare throughout. Wallpaper clung precariously to the walls. Some of it had peeled away to reveal rough, brown surfaces beneath. The ceilings were smoke-ravaged and lumpy and the net curtains were the colour of wet sugar.

There was a living room, bedroom, bathroom and small kitchen that barely held two people.

But amazingly it felt like home. Maybe that was because the finer things in life had always eluded me. Money had always been scarce. I got used to second-hand furniture, Primark clothes, same-day loans and fake jewellery. Real cash only came my way when I started turning tricks, and all that money went into paying off debts and building society accounts for Leo's future.

'I've stocked up the fridge,' Scar said. 'So we've got plenty of food and drink. I've kept a tally of everything I've spent.'

Scar was excited. Could barely keep still.

'Why don't you unpack your bag?' she said. 'I'll pour us a couple of drinks.'

The bedroom looked crowded with a double bed. Scar had bought a duvet and cover-set in black. She'd placed candles on the tiny bedside tables and there was a bunch of fresh flowers in a vase on the dressing table.

I threw my holdall onto the bed and unzipped it. Took out everything I owned and it didn't amount to much. A few T-shirts, another pair of jeans, sweater, papers, some jewellery, a small photo album filled with pictures of Leo, my brother's letters. I planned to go shopping soon to buy whatever I needed. There was at least five thousand pounds in the accounts, assuming Scar had spent a couple of grand on the flat and various other expenses. We'd cope on that for a few months, then decide what to do and where to go.

Back in the living room, Scar poured us beers and lit a couple of spliffs. The beer went down a treat and the spliff helped ease away the tension in my bones.

It all seemed so unreal. Like it was happening to someone else and not me. I was out. No more lockdowns. No more crappy food. No more shit from the screws. No more mind-numbing boredom.

I had my life back, but even so I didn't feel there was any real cause for celebration. I just felt like I had things to do, an objective to achieve. Until that was sorted I felt I had to hold back.

'Chill out, babe,' Scar said. 'It's time to scream from the rooftops, for pity's sake. You're back in the land of the living.'

She was right and it made me feel stupid. There was no harm in enjoying the moment. The other stuff could wait. I owed it to myself to relax a little and savour the glorious buzz of freedom.

And then I felt Scar's fingers in my hair. She came up behind me as I was staring out through the window at the bright blue sky above Southampton. Her touch was soft and gentle, and it set my body on fire.

It was the first time we'd made love on a double bed, and it was as good as I knew it would be. The sheets were soft and clean and we didn't have to worry about the cell door being thrown open by some pervy screw.

Scar lit a few scented candles and the heady mix of jasmine and coital sweat was quite intoxicating.

We pleasured each other in ways that only women know how. Gently. Expertly. Homing in on exactly the right spots.

For a brief moment it took me back to my first girl-on-girl encounter some years before. I was eighteen and in between boyfriends. Natalie Boyd was a good mate with a firm body and fake tan. We were at a house party and more than a little drunk. Teamed up with two guys whose names I'd forgotten. Mine was an electrician whose parents owned the house and were away on holiday.

After everyone else had gone home, the four of us ended up naked in the garden jacuzzi together. Playful banter and a bit of groping before the guys egged Nats and me on to snog each other. And why not? I was horny as hell and curious to boot. Nats was wet and sexy and clearly up for it.

So we kissed, much to the delight of the two blokes who sat in the churning water stroking themselves. We then went on to explore each other's bodies with our hands and tongues and quickly got carried away on a tidal surge of passion.

The lads continued to watch until they couldn't contain their excitement any longer and we all partied well into the early hours.

It was my first lesbian experience and although it was great, it wasn't life-changing. In fact, I wasn't desperately keen to repeat it, preferring instead to continue steering a straight course where sex was concerned. Even when I became an escort I didn't go for the girl-on-girl thing.

But that changed when I went inside and met Scar. We became firm friends and one thing led to another as it often does in prison. It was fair to say that she opened my eyes to a world of new and exquisite experiences.

But this time the sex was something else entirely. I got completely lost in the swell of desire and emotion, to the extent that I felt tears trickle onto my cheeks.

It was clear that our feelings for each other were undiminished. And I was overwhelmed by the fact that Scar was still there for me, despite the hassle I'd heaped upon her.

She was in her element, sucking and kissing every inch of my body, her tongue probing and teasing until I could stand it no longer and let out a high-pitched scream from deep inside my chest.

I shut my eyes tight as I came, then savoured the deep, rocking sensation that carried me all the way to a full, mind-blowing orgasm.

3

For a long time after our love making we just lay on the bed entwined in each other's arms. A portable fan offered some relief from the heat of the afternoon.

Being with Scar again after a couple of months apart made me realise how right it felt. And it wasn't just about the sex. We'd been drawn to each other because of an emotional empathy, a shared capacity to talk about our feelings. It was something I'd never had with any of the men in my life.

'Come on, gorgeous,' Scar said, rising from the bed. 'Let's go to town and do some shopping.'

After we showered, we drove to the West Quay retail complex in the city centre where I got my hair done and then went in search of some new clothes. I'd lost weight in jail and was now a size ten. That was one good thing to come out of my incarceration, I supposed.

Shopping had never been so much fun, even back in the days when the agency work meant that I had cash to spare. I bought a pair of jeans, a couple of skirts and blouses, sandals, shoes and a light summer jacket in beige with big brown buttons.

We spent an inordinate amount of time choosing sexy underwear, and to round it off I treated us to a couple of interesting looking toys in Ann Summers.

A few hours later we hit the town. Powdered, painted and reeking of perfume. It was my first night of freedom and I was determined to enjoy it.

Scar was dressed to kill in a short black leather skirt and lemon halter. I wore my new slinky jeans and a blue blouse that revealed maybe a bit too much of my pert breasts.

We had a tankful before leaving the house, so by the time we got to the Mercury Club we were both gobby and giggly and hot to trot.

The music inside was thunderous, and everywhere you looked there were same-sex couples. But I didn't feel out of place or uncomfortable. The atmosphere might have been heavy and electric, but it was also friendly.

Scar seemed to know half the people there and introduced me to them as her girlfriend. I wondered how many knew that I had only just been released from prison. I was glad it was too noisy for conversation. It meant I didn't have to answer awkward questions and could concentrate on having a good time.

I stuck to vodka, lime and lemonade, fearing the consequences of mixing my drinks. But Scar had no such concerns and was knocking back Tequila shots, Southern Comfort and the occasional wine. She got me in a clinch at one point and told me that she loved me.

'I hope we can hold on to what we have, Lizzie. I know it won't be easy for you now that you're out. But promise me one thing – you'll be totally honest about how you feel.'

I cupped her face in my hands and made a solemn promise which I knew I might not keep. Then I gave her a long, lingering kiss on the lips that coincided with a slow Jenny Read number that happened to be one of my favourites. So we continued clinging to each other as we moved around the crowded floor until the DJ upped the tempo and the club was once again shaking to the heavy beat of an R and B group.

It was 1 a.m. when we left the club and joined the parade of revellers heading home. The air was warm and muggy and filled with a cacophony of familiar city sounds – drunken laughter, loud swearing, the distant wail of police sirens.

We were both unsteady on our feet as we walked hand in hand through the dingy streets of the grimiest part of Southampton. Drunk, but not paralytic. It was a good place to be. Tomorrow life was going to get a lot more complicated. Maybe even dangerous. But tonight I was relaxed and enjoying the feeling.

We stopped at a mobile snack bar. Bought burgers and chips. Lots of salt and vinegar and tomato sauce. Sheer bloody bliss.

We were crossing the road towards our new home when the roar of an engine suddenly seized our attention. We stepped quickly onto the kerb as a car screeched to a halt right in front of the house about fifteen yards ahead of us.

Then the rear nearside door was flung open, and to my astonishment a man's body was pushed out onto the pavement by an outstretched arm.

The car then revved up and lurched forward, the door slamming shut as it screeched away along the street, before turning out of sight.

Scar and I rushed over to the figure lying on the pavement. He was on his back and his blood-covered face was bathed in the glow of a street lamp. Blood frothed around his mouth so we knew he was breathing.

I dropped to one knee to take a close look. And that's when my heart exploded in my chest and I almost fainted.

'Oh my God.'

Scar lowered herself to a squat beside me.

'Calm down, Lizzie. The guy's alive. We'll call an ambulance.'

I shook my head. 'You don't understand. This is Mark. This is my fucking brother.'

The sight of my brother lying there on the pavement instantly sobered me up. I yelled for Scar to call 999, then leaned over him.

'It's me, Mark. Lizzie. Can you hear what I'm saying?'

He was conscious, thank God, but I couldn't tell how badly hurt he was. There was a large dark swelling beneath his left eye and his bottom lip was cut and oozing blood. But most of the blood was coming from his nose, which was red and inflamed.

He was wearing a short-sleeved shirt and tight trousers. The shirt was intact, very little blood, and I couldn't see any knife wounds. That was a relief.

He opened his eyes and his lips parted as though he were about to speak. But blood pooled in his mouth, making him cough.

'I'm here, Mark. We've called for an ambulance. You'll be okay.'

He scrunched his face up in pain.

'What's happened to you? Who did this?'

He swallowed with difficulty, squeezed his eyes shut. I felt the panic rising inside me and fought to control it. Stay calm, Lizzie. He's not seriously hurt by the look of it. Just battered and bruised. Could have been much worse. At least he hasn't been knifed or shot.

'An ambulance is on its way,' Scar said, kneeling back down beside me. 'How is he?'

I shook my head. 'I'm hoping he looks worse than he is.'

My breath grew patchy. I could feel my whole body shaking.

'So what the fuck is going on, Lizzie?' Scar said. 'Why'd they dump him here in front of the flat?'

It was the obvious question and one that had flashed through my mind already. But I was too traumatised to dwell on it right now. I couldn't concentrate on anything but my brother's face.

I recalled seeing him like it once before and shivered at the memory. We were kids then and a couple of boys had picked on me in the street, pulling my hair and calling me names. Mark was four years younger than me and about half the size of the boys. But that didn't stop him wading in to protect me. Trouble was he took a savage beating, during which he hit his head on the kerb and suffered minor brain damage as a result. That was why he had learning difficulties and why my mother stopped loving me.

Now he was twenty-four and fourteen years on I was looking at his damaged features and wondering once again if it was down to me.

He tried to speak, but it was clearly painful, so I told him to stay quiet and stroked his wavy brown hair until the ambulance arrived. Scar wanted to come with us to the hospital, but I told her to go to the flat and get some sleep. She kissed my cheek and squeezed my hand and before I knew it I was in the back of the ambulance watching a paramedic tending to my brother.

'He'll live,' she said matter-of-factly. 'Wounds are superficial. Fist damage, I'd hazard.'

Her words were meant to reassure me and I suppose they did to a degree. Even so, for the next hour my nerves were stretched to breaking point. I was worried sick about my brother and I couldn't shake the image of him being hurled out of that car onto the pavement.

50

At the hospital, Mark was treated in a cubicle in the emergency department. After he was patched up I was allowed to see him. There were stitches in his top lip and his left eye was swollen almost shut.

He was sitting up on a bed. His face had been cleaned, but he still looked a mess.

He was able to smile, though, and this lifted my spirits. I gave him a cuddle and kissed him on the forehead. I wanted to cry, but managed to hold it in. It wasn't easy. Emotions were churning inside me like a storm in a bottle.

'I didn't know you were out before tonight,' he said, his speech slow and slurred like always. 'Why didn't you call or come to see us?'

'I was planning to. Tomorrow.' It was a lame excuse, and I felt the guilt wash over me. But typically my brother did not hold it against me. His smile widened.

'It's good to see you, sis.'

I took a deep, stuttering breath to hold the tears at bay. 'I've been trying to phone Mum, but there's no answer.'

'She'll have switched the phone off,' he said. 'Always does when she goes to bed. I told her I had a key.'

'So where were you tonight? And what happened?'

The smile vanished and he stared at a point beyond me, his swollen features taut suddenly.

'I was at Tony's,' he said. 'He's a friend. Lives up the road near Iceland. We watched a film and I went home late. I'd let myself in and was pouring a glass of milk when someone knocked on the door.'

He stopped to wipe sweat from his brow.

'When I answered the door there were two men standing there,' he said. 'One had a big tattoo on his chest. I could see it because

51

his shirt was open. They asked me if I was Mark Wells and I said yes and then they grabbed me and pulled me out of the house. Their car was parked in front and they pushed me in the back. The one with the tattoo sat next to me while the other one drove. And as soon as we were moving he started punching me in the face.'

He started sobbing so I handed him a glass of water and told him to drink it.

'Did you know these men?' I asked him.

He gulped the water, spilling some of it down his chin.

'I've not seen them before,' he said.

'So why did they do it? Did they tell you?'

He looked at me and blinked away more tears. 'The one with the tattoo told me it was another warning to you, Lizzie. Said if you don't stop dredging up the past then next time they won't be so . . . merciful.'

'Oh fuck.'

'He also said if you go to the police again he'll come back and kill me.'

4

The hospital kept Mark in for observation, and I stayed with him. I did my best to extract descriptions of the two men, but all he could remember was that they were both big and mean looking.

'Like those blokes in black suits who stand outside pubs and clubs in the town centre.'

Heavy dudes in other words. The type who carry out the dirty work for someone else. Someone with the means to pay them well and keep them in check.

Was this the first real sign that I was way out of my depth on this and should heed the warnings that were coming at me thick and fast?

Mark did have a clear recollection of one thing though – the tattoo on his attacker's chest. And no wonder. It sounded pretty distinctive. A dog baring a set of sharp teeth. It was just the head, he said, peering out from the opening in the guy's shirt.

'It was really ugly, sis. The way a dog growls at you as it gets ready to attack.'

It was an unsettling aspect. The man sounded like a scary bastard, just the sort of psycho you don't want on your case.

The doctor did his rounds at seven. Checked Mark over and gave him the all-clear. No broken bones, no sign of concussion and no internal injuries. Just a few cuts, a couple of bruises and a loose front tooth.

But before he could be discharged a uniformed cop arrived to take a statement. I let him know that Mark had learning difficulties, and he made a note of it. Mark told him exactly what he'd told me and answered all the officer's questions as best he could.

I then explained my situation and mentioned the note left on the windscreen at the hotel.

'I want you to inform DCI Ash,' I said. 'He'll want to know about this.'

At nine o'clock a taxi dropped us off outside my mother's house. I saw her at the kitchen window as we piled out of the cab. The front door was flung open long before we reached it and when she set eyes on her son I thought she was going to have a fit.

'Marky, Marky. What in the Lord's name has happened to you? I thought you were in your room.'

She grabbed his shoulders and looked closely at his face. The swollen eye and stitched-up lip. The large plaster on his forehead. Her own face drained of colour and she started to shake violently.

'Have you had an accident? Are you badly hurt?'

'He was attacked, Mum,' I said, 'but his wounds are not serious.'

She turned to me, and a frown quickly turned to a scowl.

'What are you doing here? Shouldn't you be in prison? How come you're with your brother?'

'Let's go inside and I'll explain everything,' I said.

She pondered this for a second, then put her arm around Mark and led him into the small, cluttered kitchen that was dominated by an ugly pine table with more craters than the moon.

My mother told Mark to sit down while she put the kettle on. He caught my eye and smiled. I smiled back and winked at him.

'Lizzie stayed with me at the hospital, Mum,' he said. 'She took care of me.'

My mother turned away from the sink, kettle in one hand. She looked from Mark to me and pressed her lips together. That was usually a sign that she didn't know what to say.

'I tried to call,' I said. 'But Mark told me you take the phone off at night.'

She stared at me, pink, watery eyes full of doubt and confusion. I wanted to cross the room to embrace her, tell her not to worry, that everything was going to be fine. But I didn't because I knew she'd only pull away. So I just stood there, knowing that what had happened to Mark was going to be another nail in the coffin of our relationship.

The last time I saw her was at Leo's funeral. She'd lost weight since then from her short, stocky frame. Her face had hollowed out and the harsh lines and bloodless lips made her look older than her fifty-four years. The hair didn't help. She'd stopped putting colour on it and it was now grey and lifeless.

Ours had always been a strained relationship. I was convinced that to begin with it was because my father doted on me, and she resented not being the centre of his world, even for that brief period. After he died she retreated into herself and what little affection she demonstrated towards me dried up completely. Then came Mark's head injury, which she blamed on me. She said I'd attracted the attention of the boys by wearing a disgracefully short skirt and heavy make-up. I was fourteen at the time and wanted nothing more than to be like the other girls. But my mother didn't see it that way.

Having found God everything to her was black and white. She became boorish and intolerant. She never took into account my raging hormones and teenage insecurities. And as I got older nothing changed. Whatever I did she disapproved of. And that had a good deal to do with why I went off the rails.

I stopped caring about what she thought of me. I ignored her advice and became more and more argumentative. Sometimes when she lectured me from her invisible pulpit I'd laugh in her face. If I was high on drugs I'd scream and swear at her. A couple of times she reacted by crying, but mostly she'd just shake her head and tell me I should be ashamed of myself.

Whenever I did try to be nice she would become suspicious because she'd assume I was only doing it because I wanted something. And most times she was right.

Her motherly instincts did kick in for a while, though, when my sorry excuse for a boyfriend walked out on me three months before Leo was born. She even invited me to move back in, but I couldn't see that working so I stayed put in the flat, gave birth to Leo and tried to hold down a succession of dead-end jobs from barmaid to cleaner. It was hard and depressing and the money, even with tax credits, was barely enough to live on. That's when the debts piled up and I tried to blank out my woes with drink and drugs.

I knew my life had spiralled out of control when I arrived at my mum's one night to pick up Leo. I was rat-arsed. There was a scene, and she slapped my face. I deserved it too and it made me realise that I had to do something. The next day I saw Ruby Gillespie's newspaper ad for escorts. I thought it would be a way out. Do it for a time to get on my feet, like a lot of women do. Some hope!

My mother came to see me in the police cell after I was arrested. Until then she didn't know I'd become a prostitute. She was appalled, told me I was the devil's child, whatever that meant. And she made it clear that she thought I was guilty of murder, which really hurt.

She took care of Leo when I went inside but refused to bring him to see me. She just couldn't let go of the grief and the shame. When I demanded to see him she threatened to have him put into care. But I couldn't allow that because I knew she loved him and would care for him even though I was dead to her. I did ask the authorities if I could have him with me in the prison's Mother and Baby Unit, but my application was rejected on the grounds that my crime was so serious and I was a known drug user.

I vowed to emerge from the pit of despair a changed woman. I set myself objectives. Hold down a proper job. Make things right with Mum. Ensure my boy had a good life.

But then he got a headache and all my plans and aspirations died with him.

'So are you gonna tell me what happened or are you just gonna stand there and stare at me all frigging evening?'

My mother's voice wrenched me back to the present. The trip down memory lane had shaken me. I took a deep breath and told her everything.

I was standing in Leo's bedroom, which used to be mine. The last time I was here was that evening when I dropped him off before going to the hotel and my session with Rufus Benedict. I told my mother I was going to work in the club, and I told Leo I'd see him in the morning.

I remembered how I tickled him and he got the giggles. And then how he waved at me as I walked out the door. My head was full of such memories and I cherished them even though they upset me from time to time.

His room looked no different. My mother had decided to leave everything as it was. Bright pink walls and matching carpet. Paddington Bear curtains. A shrine to her dead grandson, something tangible to sustain the hatred she felt for me.

The bed was made and I choked up at the sight of the Donald Duck duvet cover. My mother bought it in the Disney store in Southampton along with the bedside lamp and some of the cuddly toys lined up on the shelves.

On one wall was a large framed photo of my son on that first Christmas. He was sitting in his high chair stuffing peas into his mouth. His round blue eyes stared out at me, full of love and trust and it was all I could do not to collapse in a heap on the floor.

There were things in here I wanted to take with me to my new home when I eventually found somewhere permanent to live. But that would have to wait.

I backed out of the room, too emotional to stay any longer. I could hear my mother in the kitchen, still crying. That was why I'd come upstairs. She'd lost her temper and had shouted at me. But I felt she had good reason to lay into me. This time I *was* to blame for what had happened to Mark. They – whoever *they* were – had used my brother to get at me. A crude and cowardly threat, but one that was nonetheless prompted by my determination to find out who had stitched me up.

'I think you should move out for a while, Mum,' I'd said. 'You and Mark might not be safe here. Can you go to Aunt Glenda's?'

That was when she exploded. Said I was a worthless, troublesome daughter and God would punish me. She broke down in tears and I walked out, knowing she'd dig her heels in and expect me to change my mind. And that created a dilemma for me because I didn't want to. Seeing that Christmas picture of Leo had only strengthened my resolve. I couldn't stop thinking that if I hadn't gone to prison he'd still be alive.

I stood on the landing listening to my mother and wondering what was unfolding here. I must have put the fear of God into someone by coming back to Southampton and making my intentions known. Hence the note on the windscreen, and the attack on Mark. But why did they fear me? Was it because they thought I might actually find out who really killed Rufus Benedict?

My mother was still crying when I left the house. She refused to talk to me except to say that she was staying put and that she would never forgive me if those men did further harm to Mark.

I gave my brother my new mobile number and told him to be careful.

'Stay indoors for a few days and call me if you see those men again,' I said.

'Will we be all right, sis?'

''Course you will, bruv. I won't let them hurt you again.'

I phoned Scar and told her I was walking home, but she insisted on picking me up. She already knew what Mark had told me because I'd phoned her from the hospital, and she'd listened without comment. But once I was in the car it was a different story.

'So there you have it,' she said. 'This insane quest has to stop. You're putting the lives of your family in danger.'

'It was probably an empty threat,' I said.

'You can't be certain of that.'

'No, but surely if these people are prepared to go to such extremes then they'd come after me. Why bother with my brother?'

'Isn't that bloody obvious? They don't want to draw attention to themselves. If you turned up dead or in hospital then the police might start asking some serious questions and maybe even reopen the original case. But that's unlikely to happen if your brother is the victim – even if you insisted it was a warning to you. Think about the reaction you got from Ash. He'll just say you're making it up.'

She had a point, and it wasn't something I could just ignore. But neither could I ignore the fact that my 'insane quest' might actually produce results.

'I can't walk away from it even before I've got started,' I said. 'That would be crazy. I've planned it for too long.'

'You haven't planned it, Lizzie. You've obsessed over it. There's a big difference.'

'Not to me.'

'But these men are seriously dangerous. The consequences of ignoring their warnings could be dire.'

I let her words hang in the air as she brought the car to a halt outside the house. For a moment I saw myself in her eyes and understood why she was vexed. What I was doing was fraught with risks that in her mind were unnecessary.

She switched off the engine. 'Look, even if you get to the truth it's not going to change the past. You served time in prison. Those are lost years. Put them behind you and get on with your life.'

I turned to face her. 'And what about Leo? Don't I owe it to him to find out why he died?'

'He died because he contracted meningitis. Not because you were behind bars.'

I shook my head. 'I know that if I'd been there he'd still be alive.'

60

'You know nothing of the sort. It's just part of this crushing guilt trip you're on.'

'So what if I feel guilty? Wouldn't you?'

'Of course, but that's not the point.'

'Then what is?'

'Your future. That's what you should be focused on now that you're out. You have to accept that neither guilt nor revenge will bring back your son and those years spent in prison.'

'Actually I do accept that. But what I can't accept is that if I do nothing then whoever is responsible for the carnage will never be punished.'

'Get real. What are the odds on you finding out who the real perps are? You're not a copper. You don't have the necessary skills. You're stumbling blind into a world you're not familiar with. A dangerous world at that.'

'If I don't at least try I'll never forgive myself,' I said. 'If I walk away I really don't think that my life will be worth living.'

I was worked up now, verging on tears. Scar reached across the seat, brushed a tendril of hair away from my forehead.

She sighed. 'Okay, babe. I can see you're as determined as ever. And I want you to know that I'll stick by you and continue to help.'

I managed a smile. 'Thanks.'

A beat.

'There's this guy I know,' she said. 'For a few quid a day I think he might be persuaded to keep an eye on your mum and brother. Would you be up for that?'

'I suppose. If he can be trusted.'

'He can. We go back a long way, and it so happens he lives down the road in Portsmouth. He's also on the dole right now.'

'What's his name?'

'Craig Decker, but everyone calls him Tiny on account of the fact that he's built like a brick shithouse.'

'So how do you know him?'

Scar blushed. 'He happens to be my ex-husband.'

In prison Scar had never mentioned that she'd ever been interested in men, let alone married to one. The revelation left me speechless.

'I should have told you,' she said. 'The thing is it was a long time ago. I was young and I went with boys because I was in denial about my sexual orientation. At seventeen I met Tiny and the first time we did it I got pregnant. So we got married. But our baby died while I was giving birth. The marriage lasted another year, and then we went our separate ways.'

'But you stayed in touch,' I said.

She nodded. 'He was a family friend so yeah, we did. But that was okay because there was never any animosity. He even came to see me in prison once.'

'And did you tell him about yourself?'

'If you mean did I tell him that I wasn't straight, I didn't have to. He guessed it when I stopped going with guys. I came out when I was nineteen. By then I'd had enough of pretending I was someone I wasn't.'

It was hard for me to imagine Scar with a man and harder still to imagine how difficult it must have been for her before she came out of the closet.

'I came close to telling you about Tiny a few times,' she said. 'But you know what it was like in prison. Nobody wants to open up completely. You all feel the need to hold something back about yourself. Usually it's a part of your life you find difficult to share.'

I knew exactly what she meant. There were things about my

own life I hadn't mentioned to Scar. Secrets. Things I were ashamed of. Some of the stuff I got up to while on drugs.

'So what do you think?' she asked me. 'Shall I get Tiny over so that you can suss him out?'

'Would he be able to cope with being a minder?'

'Oh, sure. Last I heard he was a bouncer and he knows how to look after himself. Just so you know, he served a short prison sentence for causing grievous bodily harm to a bloke who picked a fight with him in a pub.'

'He sounds like a charmer.'

'He is, believe me.'

'What makes you so sure he'll be up for it?'

The corners of her mouth slipped into a smile. 'Because he's skint and because he's always said that if I ever need a favour I only have to ask.'

On the way back to the flat I used my mobile to call DS Paul McGrath. I got his number from the card he gave me.

'I was actually just about to give *you* a ring,' he said. 'The DCI has asked me to look into the attack on your brother. I'm going to see him in a bit and then I'd like to get a statement from you.'

'And there was me thinking that Ash wouldn't take it seriously.'

'The boss might not have the best people skills on the force, Miss Wells, but he's a good copper. He'll do all he can to catch those responsible for assaulting your brother.'

'It wasn't just an assault,' I said. 'They kidnapped him. They dragged him out of his own home and then put him into a car before beating him up.'

'I've been briefed by uniform,' he said. 'So I'm aware of the circumstances. Am I right in saying that your brother has learning difficulties?'

'That's right, but it doesn't mean he's brain dead. He'll be able to tell you exactly what happened.'

'Will you be there?'

I wanted to, but I knew that if I did go straight back my mum would only kick off again.

'No, I've just left,' I said. 'But our mother will be.'

'Then I'd like to get a statement from you later.'

'No problem. In the meantime you should know I'm really worried about Mark and my mum. The men said it was another warning to me and that if I went to the police they'd come back for him.'

'It doesn't mean they will, Miss Wells. It was probably just an idle threat.'

'Like the note that was put on my windscreen, you mean?'

He didn't respond and I heard him draw a breath.

'I want you to provide protection for them,' I said. 'Station an officer outside the house or something.'

'I'm not sure that will be possible, Miss Wells, but I will talk to DCI Ash and see what he thinks.'

'And what about *you*, detective? Do you think someone is desperate to stop me poking around in case I uncover the truth?'

'What's happened does make that a distinct possibility,' he said. 'All the more reason not to play at being a detective. You're putting yourself in danger.'

'But if I stop now nothing will happen and the truth will never come out.'

'We're involved, Miss Wells. You can rest assured that we'll thoroughly investigate these threats.'

'And what if you don't get anywhere? Will you then reopen the case into Rufus Benedict's death?'

After a moment's hesitation, he said, 'We can talk about that later.'

I snorted. 'Yeah, right. Well, tell Ash that I'm sticking with this. There's a good chance the men who killed Benedict attacked my brother last night. And that makes me even more determined to make them pay.'

Before hanging up I agreed to drop by the central police station at about two o'clock so that McGrath could take a formal statement from me.

I didn't kid myself that the cops were suddenly sympathetic to my cause. It was just that they had no choice but to investigate the attack on my brother. But at least McGrath was not as dismissive of me as his boss was. And that was maybe something I could work on.

Perhaps I could even woo him with my feminine charms. That was assuming I hadn't lost my touch.

5

It was a relief to get back to the flat. I felt bone-numbingly tired, but too hyped up to go straight to sleep. I undressed and had a shower. The jets of hot water blasted the sludge from my brain and I felt much better.

When I emerged from the bathroom wrapped in a towel, Scar handed me a mug of steaming tea.

'Would you like me to make you breakfast?' she asked.

I shook my head. 'I'm not hungry. You go ahead.'

'I had something before I came to pick you up.'

I sipped the tea as I walked over to the window and looked out. Dark clouds were scudding across the sky, and the streets were a sombre shade of grey.

'I called Tiny while you were in the shower,' Scar said. 'He's coming over later.'

I turned and felt my eyebrows pull together.

'So what did he say?'

'He said he'd be happy to help out because he's got nothing better to do. For fifty quid a day he'll watch your mum's house and keep an eye on her and your brother when they go out. And he understands that it's not a done deal, and that you'll want to see him first.'

'I'm looking forward to it,' I said. 'I take it he knows about us.'

'Of course. That's another reason he's keen to get involved. He wants to meet his ex-wife's girlfriend.'

I sat down on the sofa to finish my tea and think through the day ahead. Scar lowered herself onto the armchair opposite me and crossed her legs. She looked tired and drawn. And worried.

'Are you all right?' I said.

She hunched her shoulders. 'This is all a bit scary, Lizzie. I still can't believe what those fuckers did to your brother. We shouldn't need to be recruiting a minder for them.'

I chewed my lower lip and looked her squarely in the eyes.

'I won't blame you if you decide to move out,' I said. 'It wasn't fair of me to get you involved in the first place. If anything happens to you I'll never forgive myself.'

'Don't be a bloody drama queen, Lizzie. I've told you, I'm in this with you all the way despite the fact that what you're doing is crazy.'

I felt warm tears well up in my eyes. I'd never had someone in my life like Scar. Someone who was prepared to stick by me no matter what. It was a strange, but comforting feeling.

'I don't deserve you,' I said.

She clucked her tongue. 'Don't you think it's time you stopped putting yourself down? Okay, so in the eyes of the law you're a killer as well as a retired whore. You bite your nails and grind your teeth when you're sleeping. And you're so stubborn it's infuriating. But believe it or not you do have a few redeeming features.'

I tried not to grin. 'And what are they?'

She pretended to think about it. 'You have nice eyes. Your cheeks dimple when you smile. You've got a kind heart and soft hands.' A pause, then: 'Oh, and you make me very happy.'

I had to force myself not to cry. They were the kindest words anyone had ever said to me.

I put the mug of tea on the carpet and stood up. Scar raised her brow as I shed the robe and let it drop to the floor.

'You deserve a treat for being so kind,' I said, holding out my hand.

Another smile spread across her face and her eyes lit up. She got to her feet and took my hand. I gave her a gentle kiss on the lips and led her into the bedroom.

We made love for almost an hour and then we lay on the bed reminiscing about what it had been like inside. Before we eventually dozed off we talked about our fellow inmates, the ones we liked and the ones we didn't like. And we reminded each other of the many times we'd had sex on the floor of the cell and in the showers. And how on several occasions the screws had walked in when we were doing it.

We had each occupied single cells before they put us together. Neither of us had wanted to share but from that first day we hit it off and it wasn't long before we realised we were physically attracted to one another. I was the one who actually made the first move. Scar was upset over something and she was lying on her bed and sobbing. So I sat next to her and started massaging her shoulders and then her neck. When she turned on her back I felt an overwhelming urge to kiss her. And so I did, and she responded by pushing her tongue into my mouth. It was as though we'd both been waiting for it to happen.

In the dream it's Christmas Day and Mark is bouncing little Leo on his lap. We're at my mother's house and for once she's in a good mood. The festive spirit has encouraged us all to make an effort for Leo's sake. It's his first Christmas and we all want to make it a special one.

Mark loves his little nephew and he used his disability welfare payments to buy him a giant panda that sings nursery rhymes. Mum's bought him more toys than I can be bothered to count.

She's been able to spoil him because I've paid for everything else, including all the food and wine and their new 42-inch flat-screen television. The money from the escorting has made it all so much easier. Before I started whoring we were living hand to mouth and life was a struggle. What little I received in benefits I squandered on fags, booze and drugs because it was the only way I could relieve the pressure. My choices were limited and my prospects were grim. And the longer it carried on the worse I felt about myself. But after swallowing my pride and seizing control of the situation, I'm now flush with cash and the future's looking much brighter for Leo.

Of course, my mother has no idea what I really do when she's looking after Leo. She thinks I'm holding down two jobs – one in a restaurant and the other in a bar. It accounts for the odd hours I work. I hate to think how she'd react if she ever found out the truth. But as far as I'm concerned that's never going to happen.

As I look at my kid brother playing with Leo a great wave of sadness rolls over me. I'm reminded of what happened to him all those years ago when he came to my rescue. The damage to his brain from hitting his head on the kerb has blighted his entire life. He's never had a girlfriend and he'll almost certainly never have children. It's such an awful shame.

My mother has thankfully stopped telling me that it was my fault, but I know she still thinks it. I can see it in her eyes sometimes when she looks at me. It makes me wonder if she wishes I was the one cursed with a disability.

'Well merry Christmas everyone,' I say in order to banish the negative thoughts from my mind. 'And let's hope we have many, many more.'

I get up from the sofa and walk over to my brother to give him a kiss on the cheek. Then I turn to my mother and give her a hug.

She pats my back affectionately and says, 'Thank God you're getting your life together at last, Lizzie. That little boy has changed you for the better. For his sake you have to follow a righteous path from now on. No more drugs and drink. No more consorting with unreliable men. Stay on the path and all will be well.'

I woke up with my mother's words ringing in my ears. The memory of that Christmas Day was still vivid and I often dreamt about it. We all had such a great time and we were like a normal family again.

I'd been full of optimism back then, and I'd even dared to hope that my mother was beginning to think I wasn't such a wretched daughter after all.

But, of course, I should have known better than to believe that things would turn out well for me, especially given the fact that I never did stick to that righteous path.

I didn't want to get out of bed. I would have been content to lie there for the rest of the day, making love to Scar and slipping in and out of sleep.

But there were things to do. People to see. So I forced myself up and into the bathroom for another shower.

It still felt weird to have freedom of movement. In my head I'd been conditioned to the monotonous routine of prison life. Not having to ask for permission to do things would take some getting used to.

I wondered what it was like for lifers when they were tossed back into society after so many years inside. How the hell did they cope? Did they ever settle back into a normal rhythm? Or did they struggle to adjust until the day they died?

In the shower I reflected again on how lucky I'd been not to have been convicted of murder and given a life sentence. Three years and eleven months had been bad, but I still had a strong sense of who I was and what I wanted out of life. And the sense of injustice within me had not been replaced by a grudging acceptance. In fact it now burned more fiercely than ever.

The threats and the attack on my brother had only served to fan the flames inside me. They'd also made me realise that I wasn't wasting my time.

Whoever had murdered Rufus Benedict and stitched me up was already running scared. And that was even before I'd got started.

6

Scar offered to come with me to see Ruby Gillespie, but I told her that I thought it best if I went alone.

'How do you know she'll be in?' Scar said.

'I can't be sure, but in all the time I knew her she hardly ever left her house.'

Scar offered to give me a lift, but since Ruby lived only about half a mile away I said I'd walk.

'So what do you want me to do?' she asked.

'Wait for me to call you,' I said. 'You can pick me up and take me to the station to see Detective McGrath.'

'Please be careful, Lizzie,' she said. 'I heard a lot of bad things about that Gillespie woman. She sounds really unpleasant.'

'Don't worry. I'm sure I can handle her.'

It was warm but gloomy outside. The clouds had thickened above the city and there was moisture in the air. But I was conscious of a spring in my step as I walked along Onslow Road with its colourful shops and takeaways. Last night I'd been drunk so I'd failed to appreciate how liberating it was to be walking the streets again. One thing that prison teaches you is to never take such things for granted.

I tried not to reminisce as I walked, but of course it was hard to keep the memories at bay. I passed a Tandoori restaurant and the flat above it where I'd lived for a time, and then the Aldi supermarket where I used to take Leo shopping. I could see him in my mind's eye as he sat in the trolley while I pushed him around the aisles.

He was a happy and contented little boy, full of life and always smiling. He'd be five now if he'd lived, and at primary school. And I would no doubt be a proud, doting mother. But all I had were memories. I would never see him leave school, fall in love, marry or have children of his own. I'd never see him ride a bike or start work or pass his first exam.

It was easy for people to say that the meningitis would have claimed him even if I hadn't been locked up. But I was convinced otherwise. I would have known instinctively that there was something seriously wrong with him and I would have taken him straight to the hospital.

I didn't blame my mother for not having the same maternal instinct. But I did blame those who had robbed my son of his own mother when he needed me most.

Ruby Gillespie lived just north of Bevois Valley close to Southampton's vast city centre park known as the Common.

I was shocked to see the state of her house. Before I went to prison it had been a smart semi with a cream-coloured façade and a neat little front garden.

But over the last four years it had fallen into disrepair. The paint was chipped and stained and the garden colonised by hardy weeds. There were two overflowing wheelie bins in front of the downstairs window and a dead pigeon lying on the path.

It was hard to believe the place still doubled as a brothel. Would punters really want to be entertained in such a dump?

On the third ring of the bell the door was opened and there was Ruby. She was wearing a black top and beige skirt that must have taken an hour to squeeze into.

She looked older than her forty-odd years. She'd grown thicker round the middle, and her plump face was made heavier by a double chin. The sight of her unleashed a deluge of memories, all of them unpleasant.

'Hello, Ruby,' I said.

Her mouth hardened and her bloodshot eyes tightened as she studied my face.

'What the hell are you doing here?' Her voice was hoarse and croaky.

'Looking up an old friend,' I said.

As she sized me up, I noticed the lines on her face through the heavy make-up. She'd lost her looks and was trying hard to disguise it.

'I heard you got out,' she said. 'But I didn't expect you to turn up on my doorstep.'

I shrugged. 'I thought I'd surprise you. Aren't you going to invite me in?'

Her jaw stiffened. 'What do you want?'

This time when she spoke I smelled the booze on her breath.

'I want to ask you some questions,' I said. 'I didn't get a chance to ask them four years ago, and they've been playing on my mind ever since.'

She shook her head. 'I've got nothing to say to you, Lizzie. So bugger off and don't come here again.'

She started to close the door in my face, but she wasn't quick enough. I put my hand against it and pushed past her into the hallway.

'What the fuck?' she yelped. 'You can't . . .'

'Shut up, Ruby,' I said. 'Close the door behind me and let's go talk.'

Inside it smelled like a giant ashtray. The stale, cloying air reached into my throat and made me cough.

I stomped along the hallway and into the kitchen. My last visit here had been two days before Benedict's murder when I'd come to pay Ruby her share of a night's cash takings. Back then the large kitchen had been spotlessly clean, with newly fitted cupboards and polished surfaces. Now it was a mess. Unwashed plates and cutlery were piled in the sink and the worktops were cluttered. There were dark, sticky stains on the lino flooring and damp smudges on the ceiling. Through the rear window I could see an overgrown lawn and a slatted wooden fence that was missing a couple of panels.

'If you don't get out of here right now I'm calling the police,' Ruby said as she entered the kitchen behind me.

I spun round to face her, and a surge of fierce anger whipped through me.

'You're a callous fucking bitch,' I yelled. 'I was banged up for four years because of you.'

She bared teeth that were stained with nicotine and coffee.

'I didn't tell you to kill Benedict,' she said. 'You did that all by yourself.'

The red mist came down and I lunged at her. She jerked her body backwards and hit the wall. I grabbed hold of her top with both hands and fought the urge to smash my forehead into her puffy face.

'You lied in court, Ruby,' I said through gritted teeth. 'You said that I carried a knife around in my bag for protection. You know that wasn't true. And you must have known how it would play with the police and the judge. So why did you say it?'

75

Her eyes grew wide and her lips trembled. I felt a fire ignite in my belly. All the anger and grief that had built in prison was threatening to explode.

'Please stop, Lizzie,' she pleaded. 'You're hurting me.'

I came close to losing it completely, but her words pulled me back from the brink. I let go of her top and felt the tension leave my shoulders.

'Sit down,' I said. 'And start talking.'

As she shuffled across the kitchen to the table, I took a couple of deep breaths to slow my heart as it beat furiously against my ribs. For a moment it was like being back in prison where confrontations with other inmates were an almost daily occurrence. There I'd learned that the best way to handle bullies and troublemakers was to be aggressive and physical. That way they thought twice about picking on you.

Ruby pulled out a chair and sat down at the table with a heavy sigh. She reached for a pack of cigarettes, extracted one and wedged it between her lips. Her hands trembled as she lit it with a cheap throwaway lighter.

I stood with my back to the sink and stared at her. She avoided my gaze, and her eyes seemed to go out of focus as she watched the smoke from her cigarette curl upwards towards the ceiling.

'You must have known I'd come here,' I said. 'Or did you actually believe that I'd just forget that you stitched me up?'

She sucked at her lower lip. 'The police warned me that you might turn up, but I thought you'd have the good sense not to.'

'And why did you think that?'

She gave a one-shouldered shrug. 'Because there's nothing for you any more in this city except bad memories and people who hate you.'

'There's my son's grave,' I said.

She looked at me then and turned down the corners of her mouth.

'I heard about that. I'm really sorry.'

'If I hadn't gone to prison there's a good chance that Leo would still be alive,' I said. 'Which is why I'm holding you partly responsible for his death.'

Panic seized her face, and her breathing suddenly became laboured.

'You can't be serious. It wasn't just my testimony that got you jailed. You were caught red-handed in that hotel room. There was a mountain of evidence proving that you killed Benedict.'

'But the main thing was the knife, Ruby. I'd never seen it before, but the police didn't believe me because of what you told them.'

She swallowed hard and started to say something, but then stopped herself and drew on her ciggy instead.

'So come on,' I said. 'You at least owe me an explanation.'

I expected her to remain defiant and dare me to cross the line. The Ruby of old would have brazened it out, knowing that I wouldn't want to risk going back to prison for assaulting her.

But four years on she was no longer the woman she was then. The drink had made her weak and vulnerable. So instead of fixing me with a steely stare her face twisted into an uneasy frown, and tears began to form in her eyes.

Then, much to my surprise, she started to sob, her cheeks streaming with rivers of black mascara.

I watched and waited, saying nothing. It was obvious to me that the tears were genuine. It wasn't an act. But even so the only emotion they evoked in me was one of complete contempt.

After about thirty seconds she wiped her eyes with the back of her hand and said, 'I had to do it, Lizzie. I was given no choice.'

'What's that supposed to mean?'

She drew a shaky breath. 'I was told that if I didn't tell the police that you kept a knife in your bag then this house would be burned down with me in it.'

Ruby's words put a hard knot in my stomach and sent my pulse racing.

For nearly four years I'd wondered what had possessed her to lie in court. And now I knew. She'd received a death threat.

I had a sudden, intense flashback to the trial. Saw her telling the court that I'd boasted of carrying a knife in my bag for protection. The prosecution claimed I'd used that knife to kill Rufus Benedict in the hotel room during a struggle.

It had been the perfect set-up and Ruby Gillespie had played a pivotal role.

'I'm so very sorry, Lizzie,' she said, her voice now thin and fretful. 'I was too scared not to do what they said.'

'So who are *they*?'

She pinched her eyes shut to stop more tears from falling. 'I don't know. Honest. Three nights after you were arrested there was a knock at the door. When I answered it there were two men standing there. They were wearing balaclavas, and they forced their way in and roughed me up. They told me what they wanted me to do and said that if I didn't do it or went to the police they'd kill me.'

'And you have no idea who they were.'

'None at all.'

'Were they white? Did they have accents?'

'They were wearing gloves so I don't know if they were white, black or brown. But they didn't have accents. At least I don't think they did. It's hard to remember.'

'So what about their ages?'

'I don't know. Thirties, forties, I suppose.'

'Did they say why they wanted you to lie?'

'They said that you'd murdered Benedict, and they wanted to make sure that you didn't get off.'

'And you believed them?'

'It was hard not to. At the time everyone was saying you must have done it. You were alone in that room with him, and his blood was all over you. What was I meant to think?'

'Well, I didn't kill him, despite what I said at the trial,' I snapped. 'Two men came into the room and attacked us. That's why they got you to lie. I was framed.'

Her eyes glazed over with tears and her hands rested in her lap, clenching and unclenching.

'Those men,' I said. 'How often have they been here?'

'Just the once. But I had threatening phone calls in the months leading up to the trial. And since you went down they've called about a dozen times. They've told me they're watching me and that if I ever go back on what I said they'll come for me.'

'You have to go to the police, Ruby. There's no way they'll do anything to you now that I'm out.'

She studied her smouldering cigarette for a moment, then shook her head. 'I'm not doing that. I'll be done for perjury at the very least.'

'But what you did to me was fucking evil,' I fumed. 'I went to prison for a crime I didn't commit and lost my only son. You owe me, Ruby.'

'I've suffered too,' she said. 'I became a nervous wreck because of what happened. I lost business and got into debt. Why do you think I started letting myself go? It's been a nightmare.'

'Poor you,' I said sarcastically. 'But I can tell you it was no picnic for me inside.'

'Well, at least you've served your sentence and can begin over again. You're still young enough to start a new life. If I confess and go to jail my life will be over.'

'Well, you can't stop me telling the police what you've said.'

'Jesus, Lizzie. Are you so stupid that you think they'd believe you? I'd just deny it. Say that you came here to harass me.'

I felt a bolt twist in my gut. The bitch was right. No way would the cops take my word against hers.

'Just forget it, Lizzie,' she said. 'Be grateful that you're out and move on. You'll only get more grief if you go down this road.'

A cold breath of air flooded my lungs, and my chest heaved. I had to suppress a powerful urge to hurl myself across the room and beat the shit out of her.

I sensed that her contrition was half-hearted, probably because she wasn't convinced of my innocence despite what I had told her. But at the same time I wasn't entirely sure that she was telling me the whole story. Instinct told me that she was holding something back. But what?

'For your information I'm not letting go of this,' I said. 'I'm going to find out who those men are and why they framed me. I don't care how long it takes or how much trouble I stir up.'

Ruby exhaled a slow, stilted breath. 'Just keep me out of it. Please. I don't want them coming back.'

'Then tell me what else you know,' I said.

'I've told you everything.'

'I don't believe you. What about Benedict? He was a regular agency client. You must have known something about him. Like who might have wanted to kill him.'

'Of course I didn't. All my dealings with him were on the phone, except on two occasions when he came here.'

'So why did you set me up with him that night? Were you told to do that?'

She hesitated, cleared her throat. 'Nobody told me. It was just bad luck on your part. You see, Benedict only ever wanted one girl. He was infatuated with her, and when she suddenly disappeared from the scene he stopped calling. I didn't hear from him for a while. Then he phoned out of the blue and asked for an escort. You happened to be on call so you got the job.'

'So who was this other girl?'

'Karina Gorski. She was with me for about nine months.'

I nodded in recognition. 'I met her once when I came here. We arrived at the same time to give you money, and you shared a bottle of wine with us. She was Polish.'

'That's right. She was also a gobby cow, and there was something about her I didn't trust.'

'So where can I get in touch with her now?'

Ruby shook her head. 'I've no idea. She just stopped calling, and I assumed she decided to give up the escort business.'

I recalled Karina as being a pretty brunette in her twenties who, like me, had turned to prostitution after falling on hard times. I made a mental note to enquire into her whereabouts since it was possible she might know something about Benedict that hadn't been revealed at the trial.

'Where was Karina living back then?' I asked.

Ruby rolled her eyes. 'Derby Road. But Christ only knows if she's still there. She might well have buggered off back to Poland.'

I spent another fifteen minutes trying to persuade Ruby to come clean with the police. But she was having none of it. And the more I pleaded with her the less of a threat I seemed to pose. The tears dried up and she flexed her shoulders. Her voice became stronger, more assertive. She even got up from the table and took a swig from a half-empty vodka bottle.

I knew that if I dragged it out much longer I'd lose my temper and do something I'd regret. I couldn't afford to be up on an assault charge just a day after being released.

But before leaving I told the bitch in no uncertain terms what I thought of her, and once again she uttered an apology for what she had done to me.

But I really didn't think she meant it.

7

Ruby's confession had hit me hard. As I walked away from her house my stomach churned and my head filled with desperate questions.

Who were the men who had threatened her? Were they the same pair who had murdered Benedict? And had Ruby known what was going to happen when she sent me to the hotel that night?

I was more determined than ever to seek out the answers and identify those responsible for what had happened to me four years ago. I knew I couldn't just let it go. That would be a sure way to blight whatever future I might be able to carve out for myself.

But for the first time I think I realised just how difficult – and potentially dangerous – it was going to be.

The killers had gone to extraordinary lengths to claim their victim and incriminate me. It was unlikely they would hold back from stopping the truth getting out.

It was a chilling thought, and it caused my scalp to prickle.

The clouds had drifted away and the sun was pulling shadows from the street. A light breeze had started blowing from the south, bringing with it the smell of the sea. I stopped to light a cigarette, drew the smoke deep into my lungs.

And that was when I realised I was being watched. I saw him when I happened to glance across the road. He was on the other side, standing in front of a boarded-up shop.

He was maybe six feet tall and bulky, with hair that was shaved to a whisker. He looked to be in his thirties and was wearing jeans and a tight-fitting black T-shirt.

He was staring right at me with an unsettling intensity. When he saw me catch sight of him he didn't avert his gaze. But he did shake his head and make a cut-throat gesture with his right hand.

My spine went rigid, and I dropped the ciggy on the ground. I instinctively looked around to see if by chance he was signalling to someone close to me. But the nearest other pedestrian was about fifty yards away.

When I turned back to him, he'd moved away from the shop and was walking along the pavement in the direction I was heading.

For a second I didn't know how to react. Should I follow him? Was he just a mental case who made threatening gestures to passers-by? Or had he followed me to Ruby's house and now wanted me to know that I would regret it?

Adrenaline surged through my veins and my heart started to beat like a trip-hammer.

I was still trying to decide what to do when he looked over his shoulder and gave me another hard stare. And this time I could have sworn he smiled.

A moment later he turned to his left and disappeared into an alley tucked between a Thai food store and a vacant shop.

84

I decided to go after him. Find out who the hell he was. I couldn't believe his appearance was a coincidence.

I hurried into the road without looking and a white Transit van had to swerve to avoid me. The blast of the horn battered my eardrums, but I didn't stop or even bother to acknowledge the irate driver.

I ran at full pelt along the pavement, and when I reached the alley I stopped and peered into it. There was no sign of him. The alley was narrow and strewn with litter. It ran between the sides of the buildings for perhaps fifteen yards before veering to the right.

I felt a tightening in my chest as I stepped into it. The walls seemed to close in on me, and a voice in my head told me to tread carefully.

I walked past two closed doors and a window covered with tarpaulin. Stepped over crushed beer cans and discarded takeaway food cartons. I reached the bend and saw that beyond it the alley ran for another five or six yards before it came up against a high wrought-iron gate.

In front of the gate stood the man I'd been following. He was facing me with his arms crossed, and his mouth curled into a thin smile.

I halted and sucked in a deep breath. Dread swelled up inside me when I realised I'd been lured into a trap.

'Nice of you to join us, bitch.'

It wasn't the shaven-headed man who spoke. The voice came from behind me. I spun round and a sudden panic caused my stomach muscles to contract.

Another man was standing not five feet away. Tall, square-jawed, in his late twenties. He wore dark trousers, an open-neck shirt, wraparound sunglasses.

And he had a tattoo that was just visible on his exposed chest. A dog baring a set of sharp teeth.

'*It was really ugly, sis. The way a dog growls at you as it gets ready to attack.*'

That was how my brother had described the tattoo on the chest of the man who had beaten him up. The same man who was no doubt planning to do the same to me.

Shit.

I felt a flash of heat spread through my body and cursed myself for being a complete fucking moron.

The tattooed man narrowed his eyes, stabbed a rigid finger at me.

'You were warned to leave it alone. You should have listened.'

Before I could react I was seized from behind by the other man who clamped a hard, sweaty hand over my mouth, stifling a scream. He used his other hand to grab my left arm and pushed me roughly up against the wall.

Then his tattooed friend stepped forward and rammed a fist into my gut. The pain was excruciating, and I felt my legs buckle. As I collapsed onto the concrete my mouth was freed up and the air exploded out of my lungs. But before I could cry out the tattooed man flipped me onto my back and dropped himself on top of me.

I couldn't move. He sat across my pelvis and held my arms against the ground. I felt the spray of his words on my face as he spoke.

'This is your final warning, bitch. Stay away from Ruby Gillespie and don't approach anyone else involved in the Benedict business. You've made certain people very angry and if you carry on you'll end up dead. Is that clear?'

I squinted up at him and adopted an expression of defiance that earned me a fierce slap around the face.

'You might think that you're a tough little tart,' he said. 'But you're really just a stupid bitch who doesn't know what she's doing.'

'So people keep telling me,' I screamed back at him. 'Who the fuck are you?'

His tongue flicked briefly across his lips.

'We're your worst nightmare,' he said. 'And believe me when I say that you need to make us go away.'

He let go of my arms and heaved himself off me in a quick, fluid movement. At the same time his partner grabbed my hair and pulled hard. The pain brought nausea bubbling to the surface and made my eyes water.

'Get up,' he shrieked at me.

I tried to struggle free as he dragged me to my feet, but he was too strong, and I was too dazed and disoriented to resist.

When I was upright I opened my eyes and found myself staring at the growling dog tattoo. I had to lift my gaze to see his face. His lips were drawn back, revealing crooked teeth the colour of tired ice.

'Think yourself lucky that we're in a public place,' he said. 'Otherwise we'd be taking turns to rape you.'

He gave me another hard punch in the stomach. The other man released his grip on my hair, and I doubled over in agony.

The next blow struck me on the right side just below the rib cage. The one after that was to the back of my head.

I was still conscious as I hit the ground for a second time and aware of their receding footsteps as they ran back out of the alley.

I wanted desperately to leap up and give chase, but my head was spinning and my body felt like it was on fire.

So I curled up in a ball, trying to hold back the tears of anger and frustration that were threatening to overwhelm me.

8

Pain and shock conspired to make me throw up on the concrete floor of the alley. After that I hauled myself to a sitting position and tried to regain my equilibrium.

My head and body were throbbing, and my vision was blurred. I was shaking all over.

I'd been well and truly mugged. But even as I sat there I realised it could have been much worse. At least I was still alive and I hadn't been raped.

I was guessing they'd hit me in the stomach and on the back of the head because they hadn't wanted to leave any visible injuries. That way the police might not even believe I'd been attacked.

Jesus.

I struggled to my feet and fought another wave of nausea. I was still alone in the alley, which extended beyond the iron gate and gave access to a deserted yard cluttered with wheelie bins.

There would be no witnesses to what had happened. So no one would be able to corroborate my story.

But that wasn't going to stop me calling the police. I pulled my mobile from my jeans pocket and punched in 999. Told the operator I'd been attacked and gave my location.

Then, clutching my aching stomach, I dragged myself back along the alley to the street, which was still almost deserted. There was no sign of the two men who had attacked me.

I stood in the mouth of the alley with my back against the wall. While I waited for the cops to arrive I looked around in the hope of spotting a CCTV or traffic camera. Much to my disappointment, I didn't see any. This part of the street didn't appear to be covered, which was just my rotten luck. There would be no video of me or my attackers entering or leaving the alley.

I heard the siren before the squad car appeared and screeched to a halt at the kerb. It was five minutes after I'd called them.

An ambulance arrived while I was telling the uniforms what had happened. The paramedics wanted to take me to the hospital, but I said there was no need. So they checked me over and decided that I wasn't seriously hurt, which I already knew.

The cops searched the alley, found no evidence of an attack, and expressed dismay that there were no street cameras. Then, at my request, they put in a call to DS McGrath who wanted me to go straight to the station.

But I insisted on stopping off at the flat on the way.

Scar was beside herself when I arrived in the squad car. Shock quickly turned to anger as I explained what had happened while the officers waited outside. That anger was directed at me as well as the thugs.

'You said you were going to call me to pick you up,' she ranted. 'Why didn't you, for Christ's sake?'

I gave a weak shrug. 'I wanted to walk back.'

She drew in a sharp, audible breath, and her voice trembled in her throat.

'My God, this can't go on. First your brother and now you. This is ridiculous.'

She had a point, of course, but I didn't want to hear it right now. All I wanted was a little sympathy and a hug.

'Are you sure you shouldn't be at the hospital?' she said. 'I'll get the police to take you.'

'The paramedics checked me over,' I said. 'I'm okay.'

But that wasn't strictly true. My head felt like it was stuck in a beehive, and hot tears were stinging my eyes. What had happened in the alley had shaken me up more than I cared to admit.

'I have to go to the station,' I said. 'I want Ash and his team to know exactly what happened.'

Scar shook her head and the edges of her mouth tightened into a grimace.

'You could have been killed, Lizzie. Do you realise that? These are dangerous people you're going up against.'

I lost control then and the tears gushed out. Scar's response was instinctive. She wrapped me in her arms and squeezed me as I cried into her shoulder.

'Let it out, babe,' she said. 'There's no need to bottle it up. You've been through a terrible experience.'

I didn't think I would ever stop crying. It was like a tap I couldn't turn off. My body trembled. My nose ran. And blood pounded in my ears.

It was only when one of the police officers appeared in the doorway and asked me if I was ready to go that I managed to pull myself together.

Scar told them I needed to freshen up, and she led me into the bathroom where she helped me to rub away the smeared mascara and streaky foundation. She then insisted on going with me to the station, and I told her to follow in the car.

'Don't take any shit from those detectives,' she said. 'They need to start appreciating that the lives of you and your family are at stake here.'

At the station Scar waited downstairs while I was taken up to an office next to the open-plan operations room. A young woman in civvies appeared and asked me if I wanted a drink.

'I'd like a coffee,' I said. 'Strong, with plenty of sugar.'

McGrath arrived at the same time as the coffee. He was out of breath, a little flustered.

'Jesus, Lizzie. Are you all right?'

'What do you think?' I said. 'I've just been duffed up in an alley and had my life threatened by the same two thugs who attacked my brother.'

He pulled over a chair and sat next to me in front of the desk. He was wearing a sharp blue suit and open-neck white shirt. My eyes were drawn to the hairs that were revealed high up on his chest and I had to make a conscious effort not to stare at them. This in turn made me feel guilty because I suddenly thought about Scar.

'I know the gist of what happened,' he said. 'But I need you to go through it in detail.'

As I started to speak, he took out a pen and pad and made notes.

'So let me get this straight,' he said. 'You had only just left Ruby Gillespie's house when it happened.'

I nodded. 'And for your information the bitch told me she lied in court about the knife used to killed Rufus Benedict. Two men paid her a visit and told her what to say. They made threats against her life.'

He arched his brow. 'Is she prepared to say that to us?'

I shook my head. 'She's too scared. Maybe she would if you put her under enough pressure.'

I laid it out for him then. Everything Ruby had said. But it was hard to gauge his reaction because his face remained impassive.

'Why did you simply take her word for it that I carried a knife around in my bag?' I said.

He shifted in his chair and tugged at his earlobe. 'Because back then we believed she was telling the truth.'

'And we still do,' boomed a familiar voice behind me.

I turned. DCI Ash was standing in the doorway, his features rigid, his eyes small and fierce.

'You should not have gone to see her,' he said. 'I warned you.'

'She confessed,' I replied. 'She told me she lied to you.'

He shook his head. 'Well she told me you tried to make her change her story. I've just had her on the phone. She said you turned up at her house and harassed her. And she's not happy. Neither am I for that matter.'

'The bitch is lying again,' I said. 'I just went there to talk to her.'

'Is that right? Well, she's all shook up and considering making a formal complaint.'

'I don't believe this,' I said. 'I'm here because I was beaten up in the street by the yobs who assaulted my brother. But all you're concerned about is that I've upset a low life madam who wouldn't know the truth if it came out of her arse.'

He gave a short, caustic laugh. 'You're a fine one to talk about the truth. I've spoken to the patrol officers who brought you in. They're not convinced you were even attacked. I gather you don't have any wounds.'

Anger coursed through my body. 'Why would I make it up, you stupid fuck?'

He bristled. 'To get attention and lend weight to your story that you're the victim of some ridiculous conspiracy.'

'Are you saying my brother made it up too – even though my girlfriend and I saw him being pushed out of a car?'

Ash threw a glance at McGrath. 'What's your take on it, Paul? You just interviewed the brother.'

McGrath didn't appear to be intimidated.

'Mark Wells claims he was beaten up by two men, guv,' he said. 'And he says they told him it was a warning to his sister.'

Ash turned back to me. 'So did you or your girlfriend get the car's registration number?'

I had to admit that neither of us had. 'It happened too quickly. The car sped off as soon as my brother was pushed out.'

He stepped further into the room and stood right in front of me, glowering. I could smell his aftershave and see small hairs poking out of his flared nostrils.

'That's a real shame,' he said. 'Just like it's a shame that nobody saw you being attacked and that it took place at a spot where there are no street cameras. It means all we have is your word and that concerns me.'

He stared down at me, his eyebrows arched inquisitively. At the same time he put both hands into his pockets and started jangling some loose change.

I had to fight down the urge to leap out of the chair and throw myself at him. The arrogant sod was baiting me. He would have liked nothing better than for me to lose it and strike him. I'd be back in a cell in the blink of an eye.

'I know what your problem is,' I said. 'You don't want me to find out who really killed Benedict because if I do it'll mean you got it badly wrong. You'll look like a twat. So you're going to rubbish everything I say and do and use pathetic threats to shut me up. Well, it won't work. If you don't properly investigate both attacks I'll get onto the papers and the Police Complaints Commission.'

He clenched his jaw and struggled to control the tremor in his voice.

'I never said we wouldn't investigate,' he said. 'DS McGrath here has been put in charge of both inquiries and he's one of my best detectives. But let me tell you this, Lizzie Wells. If it turns out you're lying about the attack, or if you upset any more people, then I'll come down on you so hard you won't know what's hit you.'

He then stepped towards the open door, but before walking through it, he turned and said, 'And if you know what's good for you, you'll never call me a stupid fuck again.'

It wasn't the first time I'd called Ash a stupid fuck. I'd said it four years ago, when he and Neil Ferris were questioning me in this very building.

He'd reacted then by grabbing the collar of my blouse and yelling into my face that he was going to put me away for a long time. If Ferris hadn't urged him to calm down I was pretty sure that Ash would have given me a slap.

Ferris had always been more patient and less volatile than Ash. My rants and insults seemed to just bounce off him. I'd got the impression that he hadn't regarded me as pond life, even though he'd believed I'd killed a man. But Ash had been a bully from the start, which had only served to ignite my fiery temper.

On one occasion I threw a cup of water at the wall because he called me a filthy whore and a rotten mother. My reaction had probably had as much to do with the truth of his words as the fact that he had hurled them at me.

'Are you all right?' McGrath said, breaking into my thoughts.

I let out a sigh and nodded. 'I was just thinking how much I hate that man. Is he always so obnoxious?'

McGrath started to answer, but thought better of it. Instead, he asked me to describe my two attackers.

Their faces were still etched on the back of my retinas so it wasn't difficult.

'The descriptions match those given by your brother,' he said. 'The tattoo is especially significant. It might turn up on our database.'

'They told me that I'd made certain people very angry,' I said. 'And that if I carry on asking questions, I'll wind up dead.'

'So are you intending to carry on?' he asked.

'Too bloody right I am,' I said. 'I'm not letting those thugs or your dickhead boss stop me. I've been thinking about this for too long and I'm not giving up at the first hurdle.'

The bravado was for his benefit. I didn't want him or anyone else to think that I could be so easily intimidated. But in truth I could feel the nerves bunching up inside me, the fear growing. I was sure that any sensible, level-headed person would have decided that now was the time to call a halt and accept that carrying on would be bonkers. Maybe even suicidal. But then I'd never been sensible or level headed. That was why my life had become such a train wreck.

'So what if anything are you going to do to find these men?' I said.

He sat back in the chair and crossed his legs.

'We'll trawl the system and with your help work up some photofits,' he said. 'Officers are on their way to Bevois Valley to see if any of the shopkeepers saw anything. The lack of CCTV footage is really unfortunate.'

'You should talk to Joe Strickland. It wouldn't surprise me if he's involved.'

He raised his brow at me. 'I take it you mean Mr Strickland, the prominent Southampton businessman.'

'Who else would I mean?'

'But what would he have to do with it?'

I gave him a disdainful look. 'You've got a short bloody memory, detective. Or else you're pretending for some reason you don't know that Rufus Benedict was investigating corruption involving Strickland in the weeks before his murder. My lawyer told me Strickland made verbal threats against Benedict and Benedict went to the police. He would have been prime suspect if the evidence against me hadn't been so convincing.'

'But Strickland was cleared of any involvement,' McGrath said. 'He had an alibi for that night and Benedict's investigation didn't turn up anything sinister. His editor at *The Post* confirmed this and told us that Benedict's suspicions were unfounded. And as for the threat – well Strickland apologised, said he overreacted.'

'All very convenient,' I said. 'Unlike me, Strickland had a motive for killing Benedict. And unlike me, he had friends in high places. I'd love to know how many strings were pulled to keep him out of it.'

McGrath looked uncomfortable suddenly and I wasn't about to let the subject drop.

'You know as well as I do that Strickland is a shady character,' I said. 'He's been involved in all kinds of shit in this city for years. For every legit business he runs there are two as bent as a nine-bob note. The only reason he's not behind bars is because he's got enough money to grease plenty of palms.'

'I don't imagine Joe Strickland is as honest as the Pope,' McGrath said. 'But we have no reason to believe he has anything to do with these attacks.'

'Well, if you won't talk to him I will,' I said.

'I wouldn't do that, Lizzie. If you go anywhere near the man he'll be straight on the phone to us and there'll be consequences.'

'Is that another veiled threat?' I said. 'You're starting to sound like your boss.'

He gave an exasperated sigh. 'Wise up, Lizzie, for pity's sake. I'm just giving you some sound advice. I for one don't want to see you back in Holloway.'

His concern sounded genuine, which made me warm to him. So I flashed him a wide smile to let him know I was grateful. And I kept it in place for a touch longer than was necessary. It went against the grain to flirt with a copper, but I wanted at least one of them on my side. I knew he was married from the ring on his finger, but that didn't mean he didn't fantasise about getting into my knickers.

'What about camera footage from around the flat and my mother's house?' I said. 'Surely the car the attackers were in would have been picked up.'

'We're on it,' he said. 'But there are no cameras in those streets and the roads around them are very busy. It would help if we at least knew the make and colour of the vehicle.'

'It was a dark car,' I said. 'That's all I can remember.'

'At least it's more than your brother can recall,' he said. 'So we can only hope we get lucky.'

'What about cameras at The Court Hotel? Are there any covering the car park?'

'There's one,' he said. 'In fact, I've just looked at the footage and I can confirm that a man is captured on video walking into shot and placing a note on the windscreen of your girlfriend's car. But he's some distance away, and his face can't be seen because he's wearing a cap. So identification isn't possible, even when we enhance the image. We're now checking other cameras in the area to see if we can pick him up on one or more of those.'

'He must have followed me from Holloway,' I said. 'How else could he have known I'd go to the hotel?'

'Well, your friend Donna knew that you were planning to go there, so perhaps she mentioned it to someone.'

'She didn't.'

'How can you be so sure?'

'Because she told me so and I believe her.'

McGrath then asked me if I'd sit with a police artist and work up a couple of photofits of my attackers. I said okay but called Scar first to tell her I didn't know how long I'd be. She told me she'd go back to the flat and wait for me to call her.

In the event it took just under an hour to complete two pictures of the thugs who'd mugged me. The images were not bad likenesses, and they looked like a pair of Mafia gangsters.

The artist also produced a picture of the growling dog tattoo.

'It's a pit bull terrier,' McGrath said. 'They're the most common image for a dog tattoo and are meant to symbolise toughness and fearlessness. That's why they're popular with street gangs and hardened criminals.'

'And murderers,' I said 'I came across two women in Holloway who had them on their arms. Between them they'd murdered five people.'

9

Scar picked me up after my session with McGrath and the police artist.

'I need a drink,' I said.

She took me to the one of the city's best-known pubs, The Titanic in Upper Bugle Street. It used to be one of my favourite watering holes back in the day.

I gulped down a pint of lager and scoffed a bag of cheese and onion crisps. I hadn't eaten all day, but they seemed to fill me up.

I gave Scar a fuller rundown of what had happened to me, and her face went stiff with concern.

'So what did the coppers say?' she asked.

I told her about the Q and A with DS McGrath and DCI Ash.

'I've no reason to believe that McGrath won't carry out a proper investigation,' I said. 'He seems a decent bloke and I'm sure he knows I'm not lying to him about the attack. But Ash is a different matter. He's a nasty piece of work and he doesn't want me making waves.'

'You need to be careful, Lizzie. All he needs is an excuse to put you back inside. He's probably just as dangerous as those thugs.'

'I think I know that,' I said. 'I wouldn't put it past him to encourage Ruby to make an official complaint. If she does then things could get difficult.'

'There must be some way to get her to come clean,' Scar said.

'I doubt it. She's either too terrified to speak out or she's lied to me about the threats against her.'

'Why would she do that?'

I shrugged. 'I'm not sure. I just had this gut feeling that she wasn't being honest. Maybe she was a willing participant in what happened. Maybe she did send me to that hotel knowing what was going to happen.'

A quiet moment settled between us before Scar said, 'Did you manage to get anything useful out of the detectives?'

I shook my head. 'I didn't really get a chance. I did tell McGrath to talk to Joe Strickland but he said that wasn't going to happen.'

'No surprise there then.'

I shrugged. 'But I have a feeling that McGrath might be inclined to open up a bit – and maybe even help out – if only I can convince him that I didn't kill Benedict. I just need to spend some time with him. Try to win his confidence.'

Scar flashed me an insipid smile. 'Sounds to me as though that detective has made quite an impression on you. Please tell me that he's a fat, ugly bloke with bad breath.'

I felt the blood rush to my cheeks. 'As a matter of fact he's fairly good looking. A bit like Brad Pitt.'

'Does that mean you're attracted to him?'

I grinned. 'Why would I be? He's a man and I'm well and truly spoken for.'

Scar chuckled. 'Right answer, my dear. You've just earned yourself a bucketful of brownie points.'

When we left the pub we went straight to my mother's house. Her face dropped when she opened the door.

Her first words were: 'Why didn't you tell me the police were going to come here asking questions?'

'I didn't know myself until I left here this morning,' I said.

'Well, it came as an unpleasant surprise. Marky was scared and confused.'

'That's why I'm here,' I said. 'I've come to see how he is.'

My mother glanced at Scar, who was standing next to me.

'And who's this?' she said.

'This is my friend, Donna,' I said. 'Donna – meet my mum.'

Much to my surprise and relief, my mother produced a smile of sorts and gave a slight nod.

'I'm pleased to meet you, Mrs Wells,' Donna said, laying on the charm as thick as cement. 'Lizzie has told me a lot about you.'

My mother lifted her brow. 'Really? When was this?'

That was the thing about my mother. She was as sharp as the tip of a dagger. She knew I didn't have any close friends before I went to prison, so she'd no doubt guessed that Scar was another ex-jailbird.

'If you must know, Mum,' I said. 'Donna was my cellmate inside as well as my soulmate. She was released a while ago, and we're now sharing a flat not far from here.'

My mother fixed her with a curious stare.

'So who did *you* kill then?' she asked, her voice dripping with sarcasm.

It could have gone horribly wrong at that point if Scar had taken offence. But instead, she gave a brittle laugh and said, 'I didn't actually kill anyone, Mrs Wells. I just cut off a man's balls because he raped me. I'm sure you would have done the same in the circumstances.'

I felt my breath shorten and my heart spike. But my mother's response took me completely by surprise, no doubt because Scar had obviously wrong-footed her.

A smile split her features and she said, 'Nowhere in the Bible does it say that a woman can't defend herself, my love. So I've no doubt that God has forgiven you.'

I stood there open-mouthed as my mother stepped back and ushered Scar inside the house.

She then turned to me, and the smile vanished.

'So are you coming in as well or are you planning to stay out there all afternoon?' she said.

There's no denying my feelings were hurt. My mother had simply accepted that Scar had told her the truth – and that what she had done was deserving of forgiveness. What else would one expect from a church-going Christian?

And yet I'd never been believed or forgiven. My mother had chosen to believe instead the falsehood behind the conviction of her own daughter.

I tried hard not to let my feelings show as I closed the front door behind me and trailed my mother along the hall into the kitchen.

Mark was sitting at the table with a mug of tea in front of him.

'It's your sister and her friend,' Mum told him as she walked across the room to put the kettle on.

Mark looked much better than he had this morning, and he beamed at me as he jumped up from the chair, as excited as a puppy dog.

He gave me a hug and then did the same to Scar, even though he'd never met her before. I could tell that she immediately warmed to him. But then most people did. My brother's disarming personality shone through despite his mental impairment.

'So how are you, bruv?' I said.

He touched his forehead. 'My head still hurts a bit, sis. And my nose.'

My mother poured the teas as Mark explained how two police officers had come to talk to him.

'The one named Paul was very nice,' he said. 'He promised to catch the men who took me away.'

So despite what my mother had suggested, it was clear that he hadn't been further traumatised by the experience. And that was a huge relief. In fact he was back to his old perky self.

I decided not to reveal that the same two thugs had attacked me. It would only have made my mother worry even more. She poured the teas and stayed silent as Mark turned his attention to Scar, bombarding her with questions. It was a sign that he liked her, and she responded with good grace.

When he said he wanted to show her his own little flower bed in the back garden, she was happy to follow him outside.

The moment they were gone my mother said, 'A man phoned here for you this morning. He said he worked for the local paper.'

'Did he give a name?'

'Kevin Dewar.'

'He's the editor of *The Post*,' I said. 'I remember his name.'

'He heard you got out apparently and wants to talk to you. I told him you weren't living with me and that I didn't know how to contact you.'

'I'll call him. Did he leave a number?'

She picked up a piece of paper from the worktop and placed it on the table in front of me.

'Why don't you sit down, Mum?' I said. 'Tell me how you've been.'

She hesitated, and I thought she was going to blank me. But after a couple of beats she pulled out a chair and eased herself into it.

They say that time heals, and I wondered if that would ever be the case with our relationship. Or was the damage that had been done irreparable?

I leaned across the table and tried to get her to look at me. But she refused to make eye contact and stared instead at a spot on the wall.

'I haven't seen or heard from you since the funeral,' I said. 'Have you been okay?'

She took a deep breath. 'Mark told me that he wrote to you regularly.'

I nodded. 'He did and it was great to hear from him. He said you had a job for a while, but got made redundant. He also wrote that he kept begging you to bring him to see me in prison.'

She chewed on the inside of her cheek and said nothing.

'So why didn't you come and see me, Mum?' I said. 'And it upset me when you refused to bring Leo in.'

Now she looked at me, and her gaze made me feel uncomfortable.

'Do you really need to ask that question, Lizzie? On that day the police came here my world was shattered. Not only did I learn that you had stabbed a man to death, but also that you had done it while working as a prostitute. Can you even begin to imagine what that was like? The shock, the shame.'

'But when you came to see me at the police station I told you that I didn't kill him,' I said. 'Why didn't you believe me?'

'Because it was obvious to me that you were lying. The police told me about the knife and the blood. They said there was no question you stabbed that man.'

'I was stitched up, Mum. I really want you to believe that. Why do you think I'm determined to get to the truth now that I'm out?'

'I don't know, Lizzie. All I do know is that you betrayed your mother and your son. You sold your body for money and then you killed a man. And because of what you did you weren't around to take care of Leo.'

'And you blame me for the fact that he died?'

Her eyes sparkled with tears and she drew her lips together in a thin line.

'Of course I do. But I also blame myself for what happened to Leo. I should have suspected that he had more than just a headache. I shouldn't have simply accepted what the doctor said. If I'd taken him straight to the hospital I'm certain he would still be alive. And that's why I can't forgive you. I'll carry the burden of guilt around with me until my dying day. That's thanks to you, Lizzie. You weren't here because you gave yourself to the devil and in doing so you destroyed the lives of the people who loved you.'

I was stunned by my mother's words, and it was all I could do not to cry.

I hadn't realised that she too was struggling to cope with the guilt. It helped explain her behaviour towards me, especially after Leo died.

'I'm so sorry, Mum,' I said, because I couldn't think what else to say.

I felt my heart sink into my shoes and my throat catch. I started to rise from the chair, intent on giving my mum a cuddle, but just then Scar and Mark came back into the kitchen, and the moment was lost.

Scar sensed the tension in the air and gave me a look. But my brother was oblivious to it and started telling me about the flowers he'd planted in the garden and how well they were doing.

'That reminds me,' I said to my mother, in the hope of easing the tension. 'I would like to put some flowers on Leo's grave. Those roses that you left there were beautiful. Where did you get them?'

She had to compose herself before responding.

'They weren't from me,' she said.

'Oh? Then who . . .?'

My mother shrugged. 'I don't know who she is, but some woman has been putting flowers on the grave every week for the past eleven months or so. It started soon after Leo died.'

'Have you asked her who she is?'

'I haven't actually seen her. I only know it's a woman because I asked the cemetery manager and he told me.'

'Did he describe this woman?'

'She's middle-aged apparently and blonde. That's all he could say because he's only seen her a couple of times and from a distance.'

'So when does she put them there?'

'Usually on a Saturday morning, he said. I go to the grave during the week so I've never bumped into her. I did pop along one Saturday in the hope of seeing her, but she didn't turn up.'

The woman's identity was a mystery to me. I didn't know any middle-aged blonde women. There were no relatives who fitted that description, and if my mother suspected who she was I was pretty sure she would have said.

'Maybe she's just someone who visits the graves of strangers,' Scar said. 'I've read about people who do that. It's more common than you think.'

It was an explanation, I supposed, but I wasn't convinced. I couldn't believe that anyone would visit the grave of someone they hadn't known, every week for almost a year. Surely there had to be a more valid reason.

Various scenarios spun around inside my mind until one of them stood out.

I was suddenly convinced that Leo's grave hadn't been chosen at random by the woman. She was leaving the flowers there because she felt compelled to. Not because she had read about him dying. Or because she'd been moved by the words on his headstone.

No, it was more likely out of a sense of guilt.

It seemed to me that this was the most plausible explanation. And if so then it raised two very interesting questions.

Who the hell was this woman?

And why did she feel guilty?

We stayed at my mother's longer than I'd intended because Mark invited us to dinner.

My mother clearly wasn't happy about it. She rolled her eyes and heaved a sigh. But she didn't voice an objection, probably because her son looked so happy and she didn't want to upset him.

I had a feeling that she was also curious about Scar and did not want to pass up the opportunity to find out more about her – and the relationship she had with me.

It was a bit awkward to begin with, and Mark was the only one doing the talking as my mother set about preparing four portions of cheese on toast.

The scene brought a lump to my throat. It was years since my mother had cooked a meal for me, and I was reminded of my childhood and the happy years before things started to go wrong.

It was hard to believe that not all my memories were bad ones. But most of them were. Fate had been unkind to my family, and at the same time I'd brought pain upon myself.

Oh, how I bitterly regretted turning into an obnoxious, rebellious teenager from the age of fifteen, driven by the sheer arrogance of youth.

My mother had described me as a bad seed and told me more than once that I had made too many wrong choices. And she'd been right. My only achievement in life had been giving birth to a beautiful boy. A boy whose unconditional love I'd had and then lost.

As we sat around my mother's table, I was only half-listening to the rather stilted conversation between her and Scar and my brother's often incoherent babble.

My mind was focused instead on the disturbing thought that by pursuing the truth behind Benedict's murder I might well be unleashing another torrent of pain and misery on myself and my family.

10

The evening was drawing in by the time we left my mother's house and dark clouds had formed overhead. I came away heartened by the fact that we hadn't argued.

In fact it had been a rather pleasant couple of hours, and my mother seemed quite taken with Scar. Turned out they had a few things in common. They were both big fans of *Coronation Street*. George Clooney was their all-time favourite actor. And they were both Cancerians.

My mother did not enquire directly as to the nature of our relationship. But she didn't have to because Scar dropped so many hints that even my brother must have realised we were lovers.

Thankfully it didn't become an issue, although I could tell from the way my mother looked at me that she was confused and maybe disappointed.

'I like your mum,' Scar said, when we were in the car. 'She was friendlier than I thought she would be.'

'That took me by surprise too,' I said. 'She probably didn't want to kick off in front of you. Besides, it was obvious you made a good impression. On my brother as well.'

Scar grinned. 'I hope so. Mark is adorable.'

I told her what my mother had said about feeling guilty over Leo's death. This steered the conversation towards my son's grave, and the lady who'd been leaving flowers there for almost a year.

'It's kind of freaky,' Scar said. 'Why would she do that?'

'It must be because she feels guilty,' I said. 'I can't think of any other plausible explanation. I don't know any middle-aged blonde women and neither does my mother.'

'So if she didn't know Leo and doesn't know you then what would she have to feel guilty about?'

'That's the million-dollar question.'

'Could she be the GP who misdiagnosed Leo's condition?' Scar said. 'This is her way of assuaging her guilt?'

'The doctor is a man,' I said. 'His name's Patel, and according to my mum he moved back to India six months ago.'

'Then maybe she *is* just some kind-hearted stranger.'

I shook my head. 'I don't buy that. I'm sure there must be more to it. I need to find out what it is and who *she* is.'

Scar took her eyes off the road to look at me.

'Are you thinking what I think you're thinking, Lizzie? That this woman knows something about Benedict's murder?'

I shrugged. 'It has to be a possibility. If she knows I didn't kill Benedict then putting flowers on Leo's grave might be her way of dealing with her conscience.'

Scar gave a low whistle. 'Now that's what I call clutching at straws.'

'Not at all. If I was a real detective I'd call it a possible lead. That's why I intend to follow it up.'

111

'Really?'

'Too right I am. First thing tomorrow I'm going to the cemetery. According to my mum that's when she usually visits. So if I'm to find out who this woman is then that's the obvious place to start.'

We didn't go straight back to the flat. On the way Scar took a call from her ex-husband, Craig Decker – or Tiny as she preferred to call him – and he suggested meeting up at a city centre pub.

I'd actually forgotten that he was coming to Southampton to see me, but in view of what had happened in the alley I was glad. I couldn't rely on the police to keep an eye on my mother and Mark. It was therefore down to me to take steps to keep them safe.

The King's Tavern was a short walk from the main shopping street, and it overlooked a small leafy park. We left the car on a meter outside and went in.

It was still fairly early so the place was almost empty, save for a couple of diehard drinkers at the bar. But even if it had been packed to the rafters, Tiny would have stood out.

Scar hadn't exaggerated when she'd told me that he was built like a brick shithouse. He was well over six feet tall and almost as wide across the chest. But he wasn't fat. He was lean and solid and it was obvious that he took good care of himself.

There was a touch of vanity about his appearance. His dark, shoulder-length hair was slicked back with gel, and the top three buttons of his white shirt were undone, revealing a mat of curly hairs on his chest.

'I'm impressed,' I said quietly to Scar as we walked towards him. 'Seems you had good taste in men before you decided to give up on them.'

Her eyes swivelled towards me and she flashed a smile that told me she considered it a compliment.

Up close, Tiny was ruggedly handsome with a strong, square jaw and skin drawn tightly over his cheekbones. His eyes were dark brown, almost black, and he sported a faint designer stubble.

He and Scar clearly still had a soft spot for each other. As we approached, he held his arms out, and she stepped eagerly into his embrace. It was a tender moment, and in my mind's eye I had a fleeting image of them making love. And making a baby. It was weird, but touching.

She then introduced him to me. He gave my hand a firm shake and said, 'You're a lucky lady, Lizzie. Donna is a wonderful woman.'

The man was indeed a charmer, and I took to him instantly.

'I have no idea how much she's told you about me,' he said. 'But you should know that I still consider her a close friend. So when she asked me if I'd help you out, I didn't hesitate to say yes. And it's not just because I'm hard up financially.'

I smiled. 'I think I know that.'

'Good. You should also know that she hasn't given me the full story. I know why you went to prison. And I know you've only just been released. I also know that you've always claimed you were innocent, even though you pleaded guilty to manslaughter.'

'So what else do you know?' I asked.

He shrugged. 'Only that you want someone to watch out for your family because threats have been made against them.'

'That's right,' I said. 'But I think you should be aware of what you're letting yourself in for.'

'Then why don't you fill me in over a drink?' he said. 'What can I get you both?'

We sat in a booth with leather seats and shared a bottle of

white wine. I told Tiny everything, beginning with Benedict's murder and how I had come to be in that hotel room.

He listened intently and I had his full attention, his gaze unblinking. Only twice did he throw a glance at Scar – when I mentioned Leo's death and when I said my goal was to track down the bastards who had framed me because I didn't want them to get away with it.

He was shocked to learn that both my brother and I had been attacked. Scar hadn't conveyed to him the seriousness of the situation because I'd told her I wanted to tell him myself. That was so I could gauge his reaction and determine whether or not to enlist his help.

After I'd put him in the picture, he sat back and blew out a breath between pursed lips.

'This is heavy shit,' he said. 'I can see why you're so concerned about your mother and brother.'

'So are you having second thoughts about helping us out?' I asked him.

He picked up his glass and drank some wine. Then he licked his lips. 'If you knew me you wouldn't be asking that question, Lizzie. I don't scare easily and shitbags who threaten and intimidate vulnerable people really piss me off.'

'So you're not concerned that watching out for my family might place you in danger?' I said.

He grinned. 'Of course I'm concerned. But it's part of the job. And since this now sounds like an interview you ought to know that I've got experience in this area.'

'Donna told me you're a bouncer.'

'Until recently I was,' he said. 'I worked off and on as a doorman outside clubs in Portsmouth and Southampton. Then about six months ago I realised it was a mug's game and packed it in. And for your information the guy I worked for was none other than Joe Strickland.'

'Well I didn't expect that one,' Scar said. 'But then you always did mix with a bad crowd.'

Tiny smiled and shrugged. 'I'm also familiar with the two coppers who arrested you four years ago, Lizzie. Martin Ash and Neil Ferris. And I'm pretty sure that one or both of them were on Strickland's payroll as well.'

Tiny's revelation shocked me into silence. I felt my chest inflate and my throat narrow. The air in the bar suddenly felt like it was charged with static.

If what Tiny had said was true then it was no wonder the police had cleared Joe Strickland of any involvement in Benedict's murder, despite the fact that he had made threats against the reporter.

'Strickland owns two nightclubs in Portsmouth,' Tiny said. 'Plus the upmarket Centurion Bar and Restaurant in Southampton. He also owns a company that supplies doormen to clubs and pubs all over Hampshire. That's how I came to work for him. I applied for a job and he gave me an interview. Took me on there and then and I did stints at all three of his establishments.'

'I gather he's got a bunch of other businesses,' I said.

Tiny nodded. 'He's into property big time all along the south coast. I actually live in a block of flats that his company built.'

'According to my lawyer his property portfolio was one of the things that Benedict was looking into,' I said.

'That's what I heard too. Allegations of corruption were flying all over the place apparently. But that's no great surprise in an industry where bribes and backhanders are commonplace.'

'I suppose not.'

'Mind you, whatever dubious business practices he employed

when doing property deals would be nothing compared to what else he's supposed to be getting up to.'

'What do you mean?'

He shrugged. 'Well the rumours have been rife for years that he's heavily involved in drugs and prostitution. It's where the big money apparently comes from. But you'd struggle to prove it, especially since he's had bent coppers looking out for him.'

'You mean Ash and Ferris?'

'Among others. Those two names came up time and again because they were pretty high profile. Both of them were frequent visitors to the Centurion when I was working the door there. That's how I met them.'

'But you can't be sure they were on the take?'

'Of course not, but I do know Strickland was on first-name terms with them. And I suspect that's why he's never had any hassle from the drug squad and vice.'

'So you were working for Strickland at the time of the murder.'

'Yeah. I heard he was interviewed by Ash and Ferris because Benedict had claimed Strickland had threatened to have him beaten up if he didn't stop snooping around. But nothing came of it and then shortly after that the news broke about your arrest.'

I sucked in a breath, let it go. I could feel my heart drumming in my chest. For me this was a breakthrough. A stroke of pure luck. Here was a man who had met Joe Strickland and had some knowledge of his nefarious activities. On top of that he'd been able to confirm my suspicions that the police were more than likely protecting him.

I could barely contain my excitement. My head was filling up with questions and my palms were starting to prickle with sweat.

116

It didn't help that two glasses of wine had already gone to my head. I wasn't used to drinking and I could feel it teasing my senses.

'The bottle's empty,' Scar said. 'Shall I get another?'

My eyes slid to her face and I raised a quick smile.

'Yes, please, babe,' I said. Then, on impulse, I leaned over and kissed her on the lips.

'What was that for?' she said.

'For bringing this man to my attention,' I told her. 'At least now I don't have to rely on the police to give me information. And I feel less worried about my mum and brother.'

'Does that mean he's got the job?' Scar said.

I turned back to Tiny and raised my glass towards him.

'Of course it does,' I said. 'So how about we all drink to it?'

After we clinked our glasses, it was back to business, with me pumping Tiny for more information. He told me what I already suspected – that Joe Strickland was a ruthless individual.

'He comes across as open and friendly,' Tiny said. 'When he interviewed me he was softly spoken, polite. But I soon discovered that he has an ugly, vicious streak. I was on duty once when he got two of his bodyguards to hold a punter up against a wall while he kicked him repeatedly in the bollocks. I was then ordered to cart the poor sod outside.'

'What had he done?' I asked.

'Believe it or not, all he did was smile at Strickland's wife who was in the place with him at the time.'

'Jesus,' Scar said. 'He sounds like a right nut job.'

'He is,' Tiny said. 'During my time working for him I heard a lot of stories that convinced me he lives up to his reputation as a hard, vindictive thug.'

Scar nudged me with her elbow. 'In other words someone you

should be steering clear of, Lizzie. Not the kind of dude you want to go up against.'

I rolled my eyes. 'So what about those two bodyguards, Tiny? Did either of them have a tattoo on his chest depicting a growling pit bull?'

He creased up his brow. 'Not that I know of. But then I don't think I ever saw their chests.'

I asked him to describe the men. He said they were both English and about his size and build, with cropped hair and bad attitudes. I then described the two men who had attacked me in the alley.

'Leaving the tattoo aside,' he said. 'Those descriptions match about half the heavies on the south coast. I haven't a clue if the pair who attacked you and your brother are on Strickland's books. He's got quite a few blokes working for him.'

I then asked Tiny if he knew for sure whether Strickland was involved in prostitution.

He shook his head. 'It's only what I've heard.'

'Would you be able to find out for me? I'd really like to know if he's ever been involved with Ruby Gillespie's agency.'

'I could ask around, I suppose.'

'Thanks. I'd really appreciate it. If he is then it's probably him who Ruby is scared of.'

'But surely the police can tell you that,' Scar said. 'Why don't you ask them?'

'Given what Tiny has told us about the cops, I doubt I'd get an honest answer,' I said.

'What about Detective McGrath? You said you were going to try to win him over. Get his support.'

'I will if I can,' I replied. Then I asked Tiny if he had ever come across DS McGrath.

'No, I haven't,' Tiny said. 'But I've heard the name mentioned. As far as I know he doesn't have a bad rep.'

'Has it ever been determined why Ferris threw himself under a train?' I asked.

Tiny shrugged. 'I don't think so. It was hot gossip for a while, and there was a lot of speculation, but it soon died down and I haven't heard his name mentioned in ages.'

Ferris's suicide had come as a shock when I read about it just a week after Leo's funeral. I hadn't known Ferris well, but he'd spent many hours interviewing me, and I would never have considered him the type to kill himself. He'd seemed too smart and well adjusted.

'I think it's time we called a halt to the drinking,' Scar said. 'We've gone through two bottles of wine, and if I have another glass I'll be over the limit.'

She was right. I was already feeling slightly drunk. I asked Tiny when he could start keeping an eye on my mother's house.

'I came prepared to start this evening,' he said. 'I've got a flask of coffee and some sandwiches in the car. You just need to tell me where it is.'

We agreed that he would watch the house during the evening up to midnight – the period when I thought Mum and Mark would be most vulnerable. If one of them left the house he would follow on foot to make sure they came to no harm. He said that £50 a day was fine and that I could pay him when the job was finished.

We shook on it and I told him to follow us to my mother's house. Before setting off he asked me if I intended talking to Joe Strickland.

'I have to,' I said. 'The more I think about it, the more sure I am that he was somehow involved in Benedict's murder.'

'Then you need to be careful, Lizzie. He won't take kindly to you asking questions. If he is the person who's been warning you off then he might decide to take it to another level.'

'He doesn't scare me,' I said.

Tiny tutted. 'Well, he ought to. The man's dangerous, and he won't baulk at hurting you.'

'You let me worry about that, Tiny.'

'So when are you going to see him?'

I looked at my watch. Nine o'clock.

'I had been toying with the idea of going to his house this evening, but maybe it's too late now.'

'He won't be there anyway,' Tiny said. 'Most nights he's at the Centurion until about eleven.'

I felt my brow shoot up involuntarily.

'Oh shit,' Scar said. 'I'm not sure you should have told her that.'

11

The Centurion was a relatively new venue in the Oxford Street area of the city. It had opened shortly after I went to prison, and according to Tiny it was popular with a more mature crowd.

Scar tried to talk me out of going there, but it seemed like too good an opportunity to miss. I declined Tiny's offer to accompany us as I felt that was a sure way to antagonise Strickland. So instead he followed us to my mother's street and I watched him park his Renault on the kerb directly across the road from her house. When I knew he had his bearings and was settled we went back to the flat and changed.

I put on my new black skirt that was short and clingy and a yellow blouse that showed off some flesh. The shoes felt less comfortable because it was so long since I'd worn high heels.

I stood in front of the hall mirror and thought that I didn't look too bad for a bird who had spent the best part of four years in jail. There was plenty of room for improvement, though. My skin was too pale from lack of sunshine. I needed to put on a bit of weight, to bring back some curves, and get rid of the shadows beneath my eyes. But that would come. I was sure of it.

Scar, on the other hand, looked absolutely ravishing in a pair of tight beige trousers and a white sleeveless top. She'd applied enough make-up to almost cover the scar and her dark hair was sprinkled with glitter.

My jaw dropped as I stared at her, and I realised just how much I'd changed. Four years ago I would not have been turned on by the woman who stood before me. But I was now. In fact I had to resist the urge to drag her into the bedroom and make mad, passionate love to her.

'Are you sure you want to do this?' she asked me. 'I really don't think it's a good idea.'

I picked up my purse from the table. 'Look, Strickland might not even be there. If he isn't we can go somewhere else. A bar crawl maybe.'

'But if he *is* there what do you think is going to happen?'

'I don't know. It depends how he reacts when I confront him.'

'That's what I'm worried about, Lizzie. His bloody reaction.'

'Then don't come,' I said. 'I really won't mind. I can go by myself and meet you afterwards.'

'Yeah, like I'm going to let you do that.'

Just then a car's horn blared outside. The taxi we had ordered. As we walked out of the flat I registered a knot of tension in my stomach. I knew that what I was about to do was risky and perhaps extremely stupid. But I was going to do it nonetheless, regardless of the consequences.

It said a lot about my state of mind after so long in prison.

And about the burning sense of righteous indignation that was no doubt clouding my judgement.

It was Friday night so town was busy. Southampton is a university city so it's always full of students. They were out in force as usual, mostly in raucous groups. A couple of cruise ships were in, adding to the number of revellers.

It was only my second night of freedom, and yet I already felt like I'd been out for a lot longer. So much had happened in such a short space of time. My mind was buzzing and my body felt electrified.

I was like an animal that had been let out of a cage. Restless. Determined. Eager to release all the pent-up energy – and desperate to find out why I had lost so many years of my life.

The Centurion didn't look much from the outside. It was sandwiched between two restaurants that had tables spilling out on the pavement. There was a doorman at the entrance dressed in a black suit and looking like a gorilla on steroids.

His eyes were on us as we climbed out of the cab, and he smiled a greeting as we walked past him into the bar. I thought about asking him if he knew Tiny, but decided not to.

The interior was upmarket, classy. There was a drinking area with a long, well-lit bar, a few leather sofas and about a dozen glass-topped tables, most of which were occupied by couples and groups. The average age was about forty.

Scar and I drew looks from some of the guys as we stepped up to the bar. I'd forgotten what it was like to attract attention and I was flattered. I wondered if any of the guys suspected we were lovers. Or did most of them assume we were out on the pull? I prayed silently to myself that none of them had paid me for sex while I was an escort.

'So what's it to be?' Scar said when we hit the bar. 'Wine or a spirit?'

'I fancy a vodka tonic,' I said.

We'd talked about how to approach things on the way over. The plan was to just act like a couple of women on a night out. If Joe Strickland was here I'd simply introduce myself to him and try to engage him in a conversation. I'd had to promise Scar that I wouldn't lose my cool and get us thrown out.

I didn't know what he looked like, but Scar did. She'd made it her business during the past few weeks to find out. His picture had apparently appeared several times in the business section of *The Post*.

I looked around as Scar ordered the drinks from a young Eastern European barmaid. We weren't the only women without male companions. There were four other pairs and two groups of three. All of them, like us, dolled up to the nines. But, unlike us, they were here to have a good time – not stir up trouble.

Scar handed me a large vodka and the first mouthful burned a warm glow down the middle of my chest. I was reminded of all those nights lying on the bunk in my cell when I would have sold an organ for a drink.

Scar cast her eyes around the room while sipping at a glass of white wine. Lipstick smudged its rim.

'I don't see him,' she said, sounding relieved.

Half an hour and two more drinks later he still hadn't appeared.

'With any luck he might have decided to have a quiet night in with the missus,' Scar said.

She pressed out a smile, but behind it I could tell she was nervous. It made me feel guilty. I should have insisted on coming here alone. And perhaps I would have if not for the amount of wine I'd consumed in the pub earlier. Four glasses had made me act on impulse without really thinking it through. It was yet another example of the reckless behaviour that had blighted my life.

I was about to ask Scar to forgive me, and tell her that we should go somewhere else, when her eyes suddenly flared and she almost choked on a mouthful of wine.

'Bloody hell,' I said, gripping her elbow. 'Are you all right?'

She coughed and sucked in a sharp breath.

'Not really,' she said, keeping her voice low and her eyes on the floor. 'Strickland just walked out of the restaurant. He's right behind you.'

I spun round. There were two middle-aged couples standing not six feet away. One of the men was suited up, the other in shirt sleeves and chinos.

Both women wore summer dresses and had fake tans. One had shoulder-length blonde hair with dark roots and the other was a hard-faced brunette.

'Strickland is the one in the suit,' Scar said, lifting her eyes to look.

Strickland was asking the others what they wanted to drink. His husky smoker's voice carried above the general din of conversation in the bar.

He was stockily built, about five eight, and not bad looking. Prominent cheekbones, strong rugged chin, neat grey hair.

I felt a tightness in my chest as I eyeballed him and my fingers rolled into fists.

Having taken the drinks order, he gestured towards an empty table, and as the others went to sit down Strickland stepped up to the bar.

Scar had her back to him. She tilted her head towards me and whispered, 'Not here, Lizzie. You're a bit drunk and it's too public. Let's leave it.'

125

But that wasn't going to happen, not while the drink was instilling me with Dutch courage.

Strickland was one of the people I'd obsessed about in prison and I couldn't pass up the chance to finally confront him. No matter how many people were around.

I waited until he gave the barmaid his order and then eased Scar out of the way and sidled up to him like a hooker pouncing on a prospective punter.

'Hi, Joe,' I said breezily. 'You and I need to have a chat.'

He turned to me, slightly startled. 'I beg your pardon?'

'You heard me,' I said, raising my voice an octave. 'We need to have a chat. Right here. Right now.'

I tried hard not to slur my words and just about managed it.

'Am I supposed to know you?' he said, frowning.

'I'm Lizzie Wells. I'm sure you recognise the name. And you'll know that I spent four fucking years in prison for killing a reporter named Rufus Benedict.'

It dawned on him then and his face froze. But only for a couple of beats. He recovered quickly and dredged up a smile.

'Lizzie Wells. Of course. I had no idea they'd let you out.'

He was a smooth bastard, I thought. And a bare-faced liar. I could tell from his expression that he had probably been expecting me to turn up sooner or later.

He rubbed a knuckle under his nose and said, 'So why are you here and why do we need to have a chat?'

I gave him a hard, uncompromising stare.

'Because I didn't kill Benedict,' I said. 'I was stitched up. Now I want to find out what you know about that.'

He tossed a look at Scar like he expected her to say something. When she didn't, he snapped his eyes back to me.

'I don't understand,' he said. 'Why would I know about it? I didn't really know Benedict and I don't know you.'

I exhaled a breath, willing my body to relax.

'Benedict was investigating your business affairs at the time,' I said. 'He was going to expose you as a corrupt scumbag. And you threatened him. That's why I'm convinced you had something to do with his murder.'

I expected him to explode at this point. Instead, he curled his mouth into a wry smile and said, 'That's an outrageous allegation to make, Miss Wells. Did your spell in prison turn you into a raving lunatic?'

'I'm glad you think it's funny,' I shot back at him. 'But we both know it's true. Which is why you've been trying to stop me from asking questions.'

'I don't know what you're talking about.'

'Really? So you didn't get two of your heavies to beat me up in an alley after I left Ruby Gillespie's house?'

'Are you insane? And who the hell is Ruby Gillespie?'

'She's the woman – or should I say the madam – who lied about me in court. And I reckon it was because you told her to.'

He shook his head. 'This is ridiculous. You're obviously spouting nonsense because you've had too much to drink. So I want you to leave the premises before I lose my temper. I'm here to enjoy an evening out with my wife and our friends, and that's what I intend to do.'

'Why should I leave?' I said.

'Because I own this bar as I'm sure you know. And because you're clearly here to cause trouble.'

'But we haven't had a proper chat yet. I've got more questions to ask you and I'm determined to bloody well ask them. If not now, then I can always drop in on you and your wife at home.'

The barmaid placed his drinks on the bar and said something, but he ignored her and kept his eyes on me.

I could tell he wasn't sure how best to handle the situation. He obviously wanted to avoid an ugly scene, but at the same time he was probably curious about what I had to say.

After giving it some thought, he said, 'Very well. You've got ten minutes.' He pointed to an empty table by the wall. 'But just you and me. Your friend stays here.'

I looked at Scar and she shrugged.

'Okay,' I said.

'Then go and sit down while I take these drinks over to my party,' he said.

I watched him carry the drinks over to the table where he bent down and said something to his friend in the shirt. He then gave the blonde woman a quick kiss, and she shot me a disgruntled look.

'Are you going to be all right here for a few minutes?' I asked Scar.

'I'll be fine,' she said. 'It's you I'm worried about.'

'Well, don't be.'

'Promise me you won't lose your cool, Lizzie.'

'I promise. I just need to suss him out and maybe get him to incriminate himself.'

'Fat chance of that. The guy's not stupid. He won't tell you anything he doesn't want you to know.'

'Well I have to try,' I said. 'I'm guessing this is the only chance I'll get to put him on the spot.'

I sat at the table with my back to the wall, wishing I hadn't drunk so much.

I hadn't really worked out in my head all the questions I wanted to ask him and the booze would only make it more difficult for me to make sense of his responses.

But then why should I have expected any more of myself? I was a twenty-something former prostitute and all round bad girl. Not an experienced detective or hard-bitten private eye. Ash had been spot on when he'd told me that I was way out of my depth.

Joe Strickland walked towards me with an exaggerated swagger. If I hadn't known better I would have taken him for a flashy car salesman or estate agent.

As he sat down opposite me, I tried to play it cool by rattling the ice that was melting in my glass.

'Okay, Lizzie Wells,' he said. 'You have my attention for the next ten minutes. That's about how long it will take the police to get here.'

'What are you on about?'

He leaned across the table towards me, a menacing glare in his dark eyes. 'I just asked my companion to phone them to say you're here causing trouble. You didn't seriously think I'd let you get away with talking to me the way you just did? As far as I'm concerned you're a filthy little whore who should still be in jail. You're also barking mad if you think you're going to get me or anyone else to admit to being involved in a crime that happened years ago.'

I felt like I'd been slapped around the face. The bastard had played me. I was now on the back foot, conscious that the police were on their way. He had also managed to separate me from Scar, so there was no one to hear him if he threatened me or confessed to something.

'So come on,' he said. 'Get it off that near-flat chest of yours before the Old Bill cart you away and put you back where you belong.'

I sucked in air between my teeth and tried to ignore the acidic rise of heartburn.

'You must have something to hide if you feel the need to call the police,' I said.

'Is that what you think?'

'It's obvious. Why else would you panic because I've turned up here?'

He made a show of looking at his watch.

'I reckon you've got seven minutes at the most before the uniforms come crashing through the door. So I suggest you get on with it.'

I read his eyes. Saw that he was now enjoying himself, having seized control of the situation.

'I'm not scared of you,' I said.

He shrugged. 'There's no reason why you should be. If you keep your nose out of my business and stop stirring up shit, I won't have a problem, and you can get on with the rest of your life.'

'So you are behind what's happened to me.'

'I didn't say that.'

'You didn't have to.'

He sat back in his chair and passed his tongue over his upper lip.

'Look, you're living in fantasyland if you seriously believe that this crazy quest of yours will achieve anything,' he said. 'Even if I had been involved in Benedict's murder there's no way you would ever prove it.'

'Then what are you worried about?'

'I'm not worried. I'm annoyed because some stupid bitch is trying to blacken my name and ruin my reputation.'

'What reputation? Everyone in this town knows you're a crook. Isn't that why Benedict was trying to expose you?'

His mouth tightened, and I could sense his anger mounting.

'So how did it work?' I said. 'Did Ruby Gillespie tip you off that Benedict was in the hotel room with me that night? And then your people came to kill him? Afterwards they made it look like it was me who stabbed him so that you, as the obvious suspect, would be in the clear?'

'The police know I had nothing to do with it. Ask them yourself.'

'Oh, I have. And they told me that you had an alibi for that night and that there's no evidence linking you to any of it.'

'So why isn't that good enough for you?'

'Because I know it's a pile of crap. You've got them in your pocket.'

'You must be confusing me with someone else,' he said. 'I'm a respectable businessman.'

'Who also happens to be into drugs and prostitution and God knows what else.'

'You shouldn't believe everything you hear.'

'I don't, but I do believe that you were involved. It stands to reason. You had the motive and the resources to see it through.'

He started to respond, but at that moment the bar door was pushed open, and it seized my attention. I stared over his shoulder, fearing the police would appear.

But it wasn't the police who came through the door. It was a guy in a leather jacket and jeans.

As I watched him walk up to the bar, I felt the blood turn to ice in my veins.

The man was instantly recognisable to me.

He was the tattooed prick who had attacked me in the alley.

I had a fleeting glimpse of Strickland's shocked expression as I dropped my glass on the table and sprang to my feet.

I pushed the table aside and brushed against him as I threw myself towards the bar.

I was halfway there before the tattooed creep turned and saw me approaching him.

'You're the bastard who attacked me,' I yelled out in order to draw him to the attention of everyone in the bar.

His face registered alarm and he seemed confused as to how to react. Before he could I went charging into him with all the force I could muster.

We both crashed against the bar a few feet from where Scar was standing. I heard her scream as I grabbed the man's T-shirt and pulled him down with me.

We hit the floor together, with him on his back and me on my left side. It gave me a slight advantage, which I was quick to seize.

I rolled towards him and lashed out with my right fist, striking a savage blow against his jaw. As he cried out, I grabbed him by the throat, and dug my nails into his windpipe.

He reacted instantly by seizing my wrist in a vice-like grip. But I was so fired up with hate and adrenaline that I managed to hold firm as he tried to prise my hand away. At the same time I kept screaming: 'You bastard . . . you bastard . . . you bastard.'

I would probably have choked him to death if I hadn't been dragged off him. I felt hands grab me. I heard people yelling. But I was in such a state that it was a good twenty seconds before I loosened my grip on his throat.

And I didn't stop screaming until they had me up against the bar, and voices were telling me to calm down. Scar's was among them, and it was *her* face I saw when I opened my eyes.

'It's okay, babe,' she was saying. 'I've got you. Just relax.'

'He's one of the men who attacked me in the alley,' I shouted. 'Don't let him run away.'

The tattooed man was being helped to his feet by the other customers. He was holding his throat and struggling to breathe.

I felt myself being pulled away from him. For a brief moment we locked eyes on each other. His were out on stalks and filled with a dark rage.

'He beat me up,' I yelled. 'Get the police.'

He pulled his hand away from his throat and stabbed the air with his finger.

'Keep that crazy bitch away from me,' he shrieked. 'I've never seen her before in my life.'

I tried to break free so that I could have another go at him, but I was restrained and pulled unceremoniously towards the far end of the bar.

My heart was pounding in my chest, and I was panicked into thinking that he would be allowed to walk away.

But I wasn't so far gone not to realise that my outburst had created a degree of chaos and confusion. Some of the onlookers were probably alarmed by my claim that the guy had attacked me earlier. Others might have already jumped to the conclusion that I was a drunk who had attacked *him* for no apparent reason.

'Don't worry, Lizzie. The police are here.'

It was Scar's soothing voice, and she was standing in front of me as two men pushed me into a chair.

'Everything's all right, babe,' she said. 'That man isn't going anywhere.'

My lungs were struggling for oxygen as I focused on her face, which was now as grey as a tombstone. I could see the anxiety in her eyes.

'It's him,' I said again. 'He was one of them.'

She placed a hand against me cheek. 'I believe you, Lizzie.'

They let go of my arms, but I could still feel pressure on my shoulders, so I just sat there, gulping air to try to fill my lungs.

I stared at the throng of people in front of me, desperate to work out what was going on. But it was difficult because my vision was clouded with tears.

After what seemed an eternity, two cops in uniform appeared and stepped up to me. They were accompanied by Joe Strickland who had a manic gleam in his eyes.

'That's her,' he said accusingly. 'Everyone here was a witness to what she did. It was a totally unprovoked attack on an innocent man.'

I realised then that I was in trouble. I tried to speak, but my jaw didn't work. I watched as Scar stepped in front of me and started to remonstrate with the officers. But I was only vaguely aware of what she was saying.

My brain had been scrambled by booze and adrenaline. I closed my eyes to try to stop my thoughts spinning out of control. But instead it made me feel dizzy and sick.

And it triggered a fierce tide of emotion that caused my body to slump forward, and my face to collapse under a weighty flood of tears.

12

The coppers led me outside onto the pavement and asked me to give them my version of events. Scar stood close by, and I was glad to see that she'd retrieved my purse which I'd forgotten about.

They told me that the man I'd attacked was being interviewed in the bar manager's office and was claiming he had no idea who I was.

'That's bullshit,' I snapped. 'I recognised him straight away as one of the two men who beat me up earlier.'

I told them to contact DS McGrath or DCI Ash, but they said that would have to wait until I was at the station. I said I wanted Scar to go with me, but they said that was out of the question.

'Don't worry, Lizzie,' Scar said. 'I'll go home and wait for you to call me. And please don't make things worse for yourself.'

I had no intention of kicking up a fuss. I didn't want the plods to think I was just another dopey bird who became violent after having too much to drink.

Two patrol cars were parked at the kerb in front of the bar, and I was told to get in the back of one of them.

'Don't let that bastard talk his way out of it,' I told the officers who got in the front. 'He's as guilty as sin.'

'We'll bring him in as well if necessary,' one of them said. 'And for your information we'll also get witness statements from customers and staff.'

It wasn't until we set off that I realised it had started to rain. At first it was just a light drizzle smudging the windscreen, but by the time we got to the central police station it was beating a rough percussion on the patrol car's roof.

The station was busy, just as I'd expected it to be. Southampton, in common with most other British towns and cities, is a hotbed of violence and drunkenness on Friday and Saturday nights. Gobby, aggressive behaviour that puts an enormous strain on the emergency services.

During my own late teens I got into trouble a few times. Twice I collapsed after binge drinking myself into oblivion and had to be taken to hospital. And once I got mixed up in a fight and ended up in a cell until the following morning.

I wasn't proud of that period of my life. I was wild and irresponsible, and the strain it put on my mother must have been intolerable.

This time I wasn't put in a holding cell while they decided what to do with me. The custody sergeant said I was to be taken up to an interview room where I'd have to await the arrival of DS McGrath. I was relieved, and I hoped it meant they were taking my allegation seriously.

While I waited for McGrath to arrive I was watched over by a uniformed officer who wouldn't let me use my phone, so I couldn't call Scar. In the jungle heat of the room I was beset by feelings of dread and foreboding.

What if no one believed me? After all, it would be my word against the tattooed thug. I had no proof that he had attacked me.

Joe Strickland's voice rang in my ears: '*Everyone here was a witness to what she did. It was a totally unprovoked attack on an innocent man.*'

Sweet Jesus.

I rested my elbows on the table and buried my head in my hands. As I gradually sobered up I became more conscious of the headache that was hammering away at the base of my skull.

It was glaringly obvious to me now that I should have taken a more measured approach. I could have drawn everyone's attention to the creep without getting physical. But if I'd done that then he would probably have fled as soon as he saw me.

The upside was that at least now the police got to question him, and his presence in the bar was proof – at least for me – that he was known to Joe Strickland.

But there was a downside too. What I'd done could result in an assault charge and get me sent straight back to prison.

I resigned myself to having a long wait, and since I had nothing better to do I closed my eyes and let the memories accost me.

I was carried back to the day I was told that Leo had died. Even after all this time the governor's words still resonated inside my head and kept we awake at night.

'*I've got some bad news for you, Lizzie . . . Leo passed away.*'

It took days for me to get over that initial shock. If it hadn't been for Scar's support I might well have topped myself.

Fortunately it took Sofi Crane a lot longer to recover from the injuries I inflicted. The bitch was laid up for a week with a broken nose and fractured rib.

I lost some privileges but I got off reasonably lightly because of my state of mind at the time, and because I'd been goaded into attacking her.

When Sofi was back on her feet I made a point of going to her cell and warning her to steer clear of me.

'If you ever try to wind me up again I'll break every bone in your body,' I said.

She gave me a look of sneering contempt, but that was to save face. It was clear she got the message and after that she avoided me like the plague. As did all the other wind-up merchants who decided I was too dangerous and unpredictable to mess with.

And that was good because it meant that I was able to stay out of trouble during those last months inside. I didn't lose my temper or have cause to resort to violence.

I wondered now if I'd just been saving it up until I got out.

I was kept waiting for almost two hours. When DS McGrath finally turned up, he looked none too happy to see me. He was wearing jeans and a plaid shirt so I guessed he'd been off duty.

'You took your time getting here,' I said.

He sat down, gave me a disapproving look.

'I've been at the Centurion, talking to people who said they saw you flip.'

'Have you also talked to the bloke with the tattoo?'

'I've actually just finished interviewing him in another room. I'm sure it will come as no surprise that he's denying he attacked you. He says he's never seen you before.'

'Well, he's lying. How else would I have known about the tattoo?'

'Lots of people have tattoos, Lizzie.'

'You're joking, right? Have you even checked to see that he's got one?'

He nodded. 'He has and it's like the one you described. But I'm afraid that's not enough for us to bring a charge against him. For one thing the tattoo is high up on his chest and visible through the open shirt he's wearing. So you could have seen it when he walked in. He also says he was nowhere near Bevois Valley around the time the assault on you took place.'

'Well, I'm not mistaken. I know it was him. You only have to look at the photofit. He's the bloke I described.'

'That's not enough, Lizzie.'

'Then find out where he was when I was attacked.'

'We already know. The guy works for Joe Strickland and Strickland says he was with him at the time you were attacked. They were driving around together in Strickland's car. It's a water-tight alibi.'

'Well, does he also have an alibi for Thursday night when Mark was beaten up?'

'He does. He was at home in bed apparently, and he's given us the name of a woman who he says will confirm that. We're checking it out.'

'So who is he?'

'You know I can't tell you that.'

'I don't see why not.'

He sighed. 'If I gave you his name you'd only use it to dig yourself a deeper hole.'

I tried to ignore the panic that flared inside me, but it wasn't easy. I'd made a bad situation a whole lot worse.

'I think you should go home, Lizzie,' McGrath said. 'You're in no condition to make a formal statement. We can do that tomorrow.'

'So is that it?' I said, surprised. 'You're letting me go?'

'Well, I don't see the point in keeping you here overnight. I don't think there's a risk of you fleeing the country. We'll decide in the morning what action, if any, to take. By then we'll be in possession of all the facts, and we'll know if the guy wants to press charges.'

'It's me who should be pressing charges,' I said. 'That man is a violent thug.'

'That's what he's saying about you.'

I felt the anger swell up inside me. 'This is like a bad dream.'

'You only have yourself to blame, Lizzie. You shouldn't have tried to take the law into your own hands.'

'So what was I supposed to have done? I saw the man who gave me a hiding, and I tried to stop him doing a runner.'

'You knew the police were about to arrive because Strickland told you. Why didn't you just keep your head down and wait for them?'

'I don't know. I didn't think.'

'And that's your problem. You're not thinking straight. You came out of prison intent on creating merry hell, without fully considering the consequences. You're saying you were framed and you're making wild accusations that are bound to get you into trouble again.'

'They're not wild accusations. Everything I've said is true.'

'Well, don't expect others to believe it. It's a matter of record that you killed Rufus Benedict.'

'But I didn't.'

'Even though you as good as admitted it in court with a plea of manslaughter?'

'You know I didn't really have a choice back then. I was told that I didn't have a hope in hell of getting off if I pleaded not guilty to murder.'

140

I wasn't telling him anything he didn't already know. I was singing the same old tune, and he knew it. But I sensed from the softening of his expression that he at least had some sympathy for me.

'If what you say is actually true then my heart goes out to you, Lizzie,' he said. 'It must have been awful. But shit happens. So I'll repeat what I said before. You should put it behind you and move on.'

'That's easy for you to say, detective. You didn't lose years of your life and your only son didn't die while you were in prison.'

He chose not to respond to that, and I didn't know what else to say. I felt utterly deflated. I just sat there in swirls of dark thought as McGrath assessed me with a steady gaze.

After a while, he said, 'Come on, Lizzie. Let's get you out of here. I'll give you a lift home.'

I sat in the passenger seat of McGrath's Range Rover. The rain was lashing the windscreen, sharp and unforgiving. Outside, the street lights cast orange puddles of wet light.

I felt awful. My head was pounding, and my body felt like it was running on empty. I couldn't wait to get into bed.

'Thanks for the lift,' I said. 'I appreciate it.'

And I did. He didn't have to take me home. He could have sent me in a patrol car or called me a cab. I saw it as a sign that he still had some sympathy for me despite what I'd done.

'Am I right in assuming you were off duty tonight?' I asked.

He nodded without taking his eyes off the road. 'I was enjoying a quiet night in watching the box. The wife wasn't too happy when I left midway through a movie.'

'So why did you? Surely what happened could have been dealt with by uniform.'

'DCI Ash called and told me to go to the Centurion. He was concerned because you were involved. You're lucky he was too busy to go himself. If he had I'm sure you would have been given a much harder time of it.'

'Is that because Strickland and him are mates?'

He snapped his head towards me. 'What makes you say that?'

I shrugged. 'There are rumours doing the rounds that Ash is bent and on Strickland's payroll.'

'That's rubbish.'

'Is it?'

'Yes. I've known the governor for years and he's as straight as they come.'

'And I suppose Neil Ferris was too.'

We came to a set of traffic lights, and he applied the brakes so hard we were both thrown forward.

'For fuck's sake, Lizzie. Are you deliberately trying to wind me up? Neil Ferris was a good, honest copper.'

'I heard he was bent.'

'So where did you hear that?'

'A little birdy told me. The same little birdy who told me that Ash and Ferris were bum chums with Joe Strickland four years ago when I was stitched up.'

'So who is this little birdy?'

'I'll give you his name if you give me the name of the man with the tattoo.'

'Grow up, Lizzie. You're acting like this is a big game. It's anything but that.'

'Sounds like I've touched a nerve,' I said. 'Must mean there's some truth to the rumours.'

The lights changed to green, and we lurched forward. I studied

McGrath as he drove. His features adopted a sullen expression, and he tightened his grip on the wheel.

'So why did your friend Ferris kill himself?' I said. 'He didn't seem the type to me.'

'You didn't know him.'

'I spent a fair amount of time with him in the interview room. He came across as a decent bloke. Unlike Ash.'

'He was decent, and honest. What happened was a tragedy.'

'Did it have anything to do with him being corrupt? Is that it?'

McGrath cleared his throat. 'Just drop it, will you? You're out of order and I don't want to hear it.'

'Ferris wouldn't be the first copper to top himself after being exposed.'

McGrath puffed out his cheeks. 'Jesus, Lizzie. You can be so bloody annoying. I can see now why the governor reckons you're dangerous. He said you were on a mission to stir up trouble.'

'And he was right,' I said. 'How else will I get to the truth? I can't flash a warrant card and make people talk to me. And I don't have access to police files. All I can do is chip away at a brick wall until a crack appears.'

He wheezed out a sigh. 'And you really believe that's going to happen?'

'I don't believe it,' I said. 'I know it. The fact that I've already got people in a panic suggests to me that the wall has started to crumble.'

McGrath remained silent during the rest of the drive to the flat. I reckoned it was because I'd given him a lot to think about.

I couldn't tell from his reaction if he was genuinely shocked to hear that his boss and his former colleague were the subject of unsettling rumours. Or even if he was being honest when he said that there was no truth in them.

'I'll call you tomorrow,' he said when we pulled up outside the house just before midnight. 'You'll probably have to come back to the station to make a statement. But for what it's worth I'll do what I can to play this down.'

'And why would you do that?'

He shrugged. 'Well, don't tell anyone I told you this, but Mr Tattoo man came across as an arrogant tosser. He probably deserved a slap.'

I grinned. 'So what's happening to him?'

'He's also on his way home. I'll talk to him tomorrow as well.'

Questions had been piling up inside my head like dirty dishes, but it was too late to see if McGrath would answer them. So I thanked him for the lift and said, 'It might not be too late to go home and finish the movie.'

Then I got out of the car and made a dash for the front door. Scar had it open before I reached it.

'I've been waiting for you to call,' she said. 'Are you okay?'

'I need a cup of hot tea,' I said.

I stepped over the threshold and into her arms. The hallway light was on and my eyeballs retreated from the glare.

'I've been so worried about you,' Scar said.

We clung to each other for about half a minute and then she took my hand and led me up the stairs to the flat.

Tiny was there, having come straight from his vigil outside my mother's house. No one had turned up there, thank God, and he said all the lights were off inside when he left.

As Scar made the tea, I told them what McGrath had said.

'So the guy does work for Joe Strickland,' Scar said.

I nodded. 'And Strickland has given him an alibi for when I was attacked.'

'Did McGrath tell you who this bloke is and whether he's going to press charges?'

The injustice of it was so bloody galling. The tattooed beast had carried out assaults on my brother and me and yet he was the one being labelled the victim.

'He wouldn't give me his name,' I said. 'And we won't know until tomorrow whether or not he wants to take it further.'

'It'll be an outrage if he does,' Scar said. 'It's not as though he was hurt. He didn't have a scratch on him.'

I turned to Tiny. 'Any chance you can find out the bloke's name now we know he's on Strickland's books?'

'I'll try,' he said. 'I can make some calls.'

'Thank you.'

'I've already got something for you,' he added. 'Confirmation that Ruby Gillespie's agency is part of Strickland's illicit empire. Has been for four or five years apparently.'

As far as I was concerned the evidence was piling up. There was no doubt in my mind that Joe Strickland was complicit in Rufus Benedict's murder and with what subsequently happened to me.

Despite that, Scar tried to persuade me to draw a line under the whole thing.

'It's not worth it, Lizzie,' she said. 'Even if you don't face a charge after last night you'll end up inside if you keep pushing this.'

Tiny was quick to agree with his ex-wife, which made me wonder if they had been discussing it before I got here.

'Donna has a point,' he said. 'Strickland is ruthless and resourceful. If he feels threatened by you, then I hate to think what he might do.'

Their concerns were justified. I knew that. But what had happened over the past two days had sparked in me an anger I was finding hard to control. I wanted desperately to uncover the truth. For myself. For Leo. And for the man who had died in that hotel room four years ago.

Before we called it a day I told them I wanted to dig a little deeper.

'Just another day or two,' I said. 'Provided I'm not hauled back to Holloway, that is.'

They listened resignedly as I explained what our next move would be.

'I'm going to the cemetery tomorrow,' I said. 'If I'm lucky I'll catch sight of the mystery woman who's been putting flowers on Leo's grave. Maybe she's involved somehow, and if so can shed some light. Mum said she goes there on Saturday mornings.'

I then asked Scar if she would try to find out more about the Polish prostitute who Benedict had apparently been obsessed with.

'Her name is Karina Gorski and according to Ruby she suddenly stopped contacting the agency,' I said. 'That's how come I ended up being sent to The Court Hotel that night. Karina used to live in Derby Road apparently, so maybe that's where you should start. She may even still live there.'

Tiny said he would park up outside my mother's house as agreed. He then bid us goodnight and left.

Scar fell silent after he'd gone and I sensed she was anxious and perhaps a little annoyed with me. But I could hardly blame her. I'd embarked on a mission that was fraught with risk and danger.

And I wouldn't be the only one to suffer if it all went belly up.

13

When I woke up the next morning my headache was still there. I'd had a restless sleep. I'd dreamt about what happened that night in The Court Hotel. It's a recurring dream and it's always horribly vivid.

I see Rufus Benedict on the bed, the blood-soaked sheets, the knife that was used to kill him. And I hear myself screaming, a sound that doesn't seem human.

And as always the dream left me yearning for answers to a ton of questions. Who came to our room that night? Who delivered the drugged champagne? How did the killers bypass the security cameras?

For nearly four years those questions had dominated my thoughts. But now I had something else to think about – and that was the prospect of going back to prison. It filled me with dread. But so too did the possibility that I might be forced to accept defeat and never get to the bottom of what had happened and why.

In prison my obsession with finding out the truth had kept

me going. It had given me something to believe in; a goal to aim for. And, as a result, my optimism had remained improbably intact.

But now I was scared and confused – and increasingly conscious of the fact that my abilities were limited.

The goal I had set myself seemed suddenly beyond reach. Sure, I'd already stirred up a hornet's nest, and certain people were in a panic. But I'd also ramped up the threat level against myself and my family.

I certainly hadn't expected things to move at such a rate of knots. It was only two days since I walked out of Holloway, and in that time my brother and I had been attacked and I'd assaulted a man in a bar. Plus, I was now in trouble with the law and facing threats against my life.

A voice in my head was urging me to listen to Scar and the others and give up before more serious damage was done.

But it was being drowned out by a louder voice that was telling me to carry on because if I didn't, I'd regret it for the rest of my life.

Scar and I had breakfast together. She made the coffee, and I made the toast. To her credit she didn't bang on about how stupid or stubborn I was. But she was clearly worried that I might end up back in jail.

We discussed the day ahead. How I'd spend it would depend on whether I was ordered to report back to the police station.

'In the meantime, I'm going to the cemetery,' I said. 'I'll get there early and wait around as long as I can to see if the blonde woman turns up.'

'And if she does?'

'Then I'll confront her and ask her what the hell is going on.'

Scar said she would see what she could find out about the

Polish prostitute who Rufus Benedict had had a thing for. Since she used to live in Derby Road – which was within walking distance of the flat – we agreed that I would take the car.

I hadn't been behind a wheel in over four years, but it came back to me as soon as I fired up the engine. On the way to the cemetery I only stalled it once and managed to avoid colliding with another vehicle.

It had stopped raining hours ago, but the sky was still a bruised mass, pulsing like something alive. It made the cemetery grey and gloomy. Dew glistened on the grass between the brooding head-stones and the air had a damp chill to it.

I parked up on the main road and walked towards where Leo was buried. But I didn't approach his grave. Instead I stopped some distance away and sat on a bench. From there I'd be able to see anyone walking up to it.

It was nine o'clock and people were starting to appear, most of them carrying flowers and watering cans. I sparked up my first cigarette of the day and waited.

I found it hard to shift my gaze away from my son's headstone. As I stared at it, I felt a hot stab of tears in my eyes. Before long I was holding my face in my hands and sobbing.

The memory of the funeral was stark and raw. In my head I pictured the scene at the graveside. A surprising number of people turned up, including a couple of the girls who had worked as escorts for Ruby.

Mark and my mother stood either side of me as the priest spoke. The two guards who had escorted me from Holloway stood a discreet distance away, alongside Detective Neil Ferris. I hadn't expected him to be there and I didn't bother to acknowl-edge him. Why would I? He was one of the people who had put me away.

My mother didn't speak to me once throughout the service, except to deliver her damning indictment that if it hadn't been for me Leo would have still been alive.

Even after all this time it was hard for me to accept that my boy was dead. My beautiful child was rotting in the ground while a rodent like Joe Strickland enjoyed the high life on his illicit gains. It was sickeningly unfair and it made my blood curdle.

An hour passed and the sky got darker. But the rain held off, and the temperature rose. The peace and tranquillity of the cemetery meant that sitting there wasn't an altogether unpleasant experience. I felt close to Leo and I felt relaxed for the first time since walking out of Holloway.

I watched the people tending the graves of their loved ones and I dared to let myself think about the future. It was a future I could no longer imagine Scar not being a part of.

I felt closer to her than ever. The doubts I'd harboured for so long were being replaced by the growing conviction that she was the one who was going to make me happy. It no longer mattered that it was not a heterosexual relationship. The last forty-eight hours had shown me that Scar was able to satisfy my physical and emotional needs. I was growing fonder of her by the day, and if I wasn't already in love with her then I would be soon.

I felt a sudden urge to call her just to let her know that I was thinking about her. But as I reached for my phone, it started to ring.

'Hello,' I said.

'Is that you, Lizzie?'

I recognised McGrath's voice. It still sounded strange to hear him use my first name.

'Yeah, it's me.'

'I'm with DCI Ash,' he said. 'We'd like you to come to the station right away.'

I experienced a shiver of trepidation.

'Does that mean I'm in the shit? Are you going to charge me?'

'You'll know when you get here,' he said. 'Do you want me to send a car to pick you up?'

'No. I can get there under my own steam.'

'Good. We'll be waiting.'

He hung up abruptly, and I was left holding the phone to my ear as my heart started beating furiously against my chest.

I had a feeling they were going to charge me with assault and send me back to prison. And it was my own bloody fault.

But before I could work myself up into a state, I was distracted by the sight of a woman walking along the road towards Leo's grave.

I screwed up my eyes and stared at her. She was wearing jeans and a short red jacket. And she was tall, maybe five ten allowing for the heels.

She was carrying a bunch of flowers in one hand and a bag in the other.

And she had dishwater blonde hair.

My jaw was clenched tight as I watched her walk up to Leo's grave. She gave a furtive look around, but didn't seem to notice me.

She stood looking at the headstone for about fifteen seconds before kneeling down and replacing the old flowers with the new ones.

My body grew rigid, and every nerve ending tingled. I was rooted to the spot as the woman stood up again and dropped her chin onto her chest, as though praying. She was in her forties, but I was too far away to be certain that I didn't know her. So I started moving slowly towards her, trying to work out in my head what I was going to say.

She heard me approach when I was about ten yards away and looked up.

'Hello,' I said.

She pushed her hair from her eyes and frowned at me. There was no hint of recognition in her expression, but she did appear taken aback.

'Do I know you?' she asked, her voice thin and wheezy.

I got to within a few feet of her and stopped. I saw then that her face, though not unattractive, was pale and drawn. She had full, pouty lips and a button nose. But her eyes were moist and set in dark shadows.

'I'm not sure,' I said. 'But I'm really curious to know who you are.'

She wrapped her arms around her chest and tilted her head to one side.

'Why? What is it to you?'

I gestured towards the headstone.

'Leo Wells was my son. I'd like to know why you've been putting flowers on his grave since shortly after he died.'

Her face creased in disbelief. 'Oh my God. I thought you—'

'You thought I was in prison,' I cut in. 'Well, I was until a few days ago. Now I'm out and I'd like an explanation.'

Panic seized her features, and for several seconds she didn't move, just stared at me with dilated pupils.

'Look, I'm not ungrateful for what you've been doing,' I said. 'But you didn't know my son and you don't know me. So what's with the flowers?'

She shook her head and struggled to get the words out.

'That's my business,' she said. 'I don't have to tell you anything.'

'But why would you keep it a secret?'

152

She unwrapped her arms, turned on her heels. Our shoulders touched as she shuffled past me and headed across the grass towards the path.

'For Christ's sake talk to me,' I yelled as I followed her. 'What the fuck have you got to hide?'

'Just leave me alone.'

'Not until you tell me what your connection is to my son.'

She strode forward, picking up pace as she hurried in the direction of the cemetery gates. I reached out and grabbed her arm, forcing her to stop. She spun round and jerked herself free.

'If you touch me again I'll scream,' she shouted. 'And then I'll call the police and tell them you're harassing me.'

'But this is ridiculous,' I said. 'Just tell me what's going on. Why have you been coming here every week if you didn't know Leo?'

But she ignored me and carried on walking. Then, as I pursued her, she broke into a run.

'Do you feel guilty about something?' I yelled after her as I tried to keep up. 'Is that it?'

She didn't respond, just kept running. As she passed through the open gates I caught up and stuck out my arm to slow her down. But this time she reacted by lashing out with her fist, catching me full in the face.

I cried out and lost my balance, falling with a painful thump onto the gravel.

The woman surged ahead. As I struggled to get back on my feet, I saw her stop next to a black VW Beetle about fifteen yards away. She quickly inserted the key in the driver's door, wrenched it open.

I reached the car just as she slammed the door shut behind her and pressed the central locking switch.

'Please don't go,' I screamed at her through the side window. 'I need to know who you are and why you're here.'

The engine spluttered to life. I banged on the window with both fists, but the woman didn't turn to look at me as she engaged first gear and slammed her foot down on the accelerator.

There were no cars in front, so the VW lurched forward with a screech of rubber.

As I watched it roll away from me my eyes were drawn to a bright blue rectangular sticker on the inside of the rear window. The white lettering was bold enough to register even though the words were visible for barely two seconds.

Arnold Royce Estate Agents, Southampton.

I stood there gasping for air as the car sped along the road away from me and the cemetery. I thought about trying to follow in Scar's car, but realised it'd be a waste of time. The bitch had too much of a head start.

I dragged a hand through my hair and tried to think through what had just happened. But it didn't make sense. The mystery blonde remained a mystery.

I just didn't get it. Why had she panicked when I asked her who she was? What secret was she desperate to keep?

I was certain now that I had never met the woman. She was unfamiliar to me. If our paths had ever crossed, even fleetingly, I was certain I would have remembered.

Surely if there was an innocent explanation for what she'd been doing she would have revealed it to me. But she had chosen to flee instead like some common criminal caught in the act.

I obviously couldn't leave it at that. I had to find out why she felt compelled week after week to put flowers on my son's grave.

I reached for my mobile phone as I walked back to the car. It took me a few moments to work out how to get online. On the

154

Google search page I tapped in the words *Arnold Royce Estate Agents, Southampton.*

The business came straight up along with a phone number and an address in the centre of town.

Seconds later I was through to them. I told the girl who answered the phone that I was with Hampshire police and that we were trying to trace the owner of a black VW Beetle that had been involved in a minor accident.

'It had one of your company promotional stickers in the rear window,' I said.

There was a brief pause on the other end of the line, and I thought she was going to tell me that she couldn't give out such information over the phone. But instead she said, 'As a matter of fact one of our staff members does own a black VW. Is she okay?'

'We think so,' I said. 'There's no one actually with the vehicle, which is why we're checking out the registration to find out who the owner is. But I thought I'd call you as well.'

'I see. Well Pamela who works here has a black Beetle and she's off today.'

'And what's Pamela's full name?'

'Ferris. Pamela Ferris.'

I felt my pulse surge.

'Did you say Ferris?' I said.

'That's right. In fact you might even have known her late husband, Neil. He was a detective with Southampton police and died about a year ago.'

I hesitated, lowered my tone. 'Of course I remember him. Can you give me her address?'

'I don't have it, I'm afraid. The manager does, but he's not here at the moment. I can call him if you—'

I hung up before she could finish the sentence.

155

14

Questions tormented me as I drove across town to the central police station. Why would the widow of the copper who had arrested me put flowers on my son's grave? And was it a coincidence that her husband had committed suicide just a week or so after attending Leo's funeral?

It was impossible to imagine that there wasn't a connection. But the nature of it eluded me. I kept coming back to what seemed to be the most plausible explanation – that the flowers were a way of appeasing a guilty conscience. But why did she feel guilty? And why did she want to keep it a secret?

To find out I would need to confront Pamela Ferris again and put her under a good deal more pressure. But I was well aware that the opportunity might not arise if I finished up back behind bars.

So as I approached the central police station I could feel the unease working its way through every part of my body. My breathing became shallow and erratic, and I had to force back a rush of nausea.

But when I walked into DCI Ash's office ten minutes later, I held my head up high and put on a brave face.

I didn't want him to see how scared I really was.

To my surprise, Ash was alone behind his desk. There was no sign of DS McGrath.

When my uniformed escort closed the door behind me, Ash gestured for me to sit opposite him. As I did so he gave me a scathing stare, and his eyes were filled with an unnerving coldness. I steeled myself for bad news and felt a sudden rush of needles across my lower back.

'What you did last night was unacceptable,' he said, without preamble. 'I've given my officers a bollocking for not holding you in custody overnight. They were too fucking lenient.'

He spoke quietly, but the menace in his voice came through clearly.

'I gave you a warning, Wells. I told you I didn't want you stirring up trouble. But you ignored me. First you upset Ruby Gillespie. Then Joe Strickland. And then a man who happened to walk into a bar while you were there making mischief.'

'He was one of the men who attacked me earlier in the day,' I said.

His eyes flashed with fury. 'For your information I don't even believe that attack took place. We've found no evidence to back up your claim. I think you made it up to get attention. And that's also why you assaulted one of Mr Strickland's employees.'

'That's ridiculous,' I said.

'Not to me it isn't. You're behaving as though you've completely lost the plot. You're harassing people and making false and slanderous allegations against them. And all because you've got into your head the crazy notion that you were stitched up.'

'I was.'

'No you weren't. You killed a man and you admitted it in court.'

'But you know why I pleaded guilty.'

'Of course. Your lawyer told you it was the surest way of avoiding a life sentence for murder. And you got a result considering what happened in that hotel room. Just four measly years. But now you're out and intent on making trouble for no good reason.'

'I want to find out who really murdered Benedict and why.'

'But it's a futile exercise and in your heart you must know it.'

'It's all I've been thinking about for four years.'

His eyes narrowed dangerously. 'Listen to me, Wells. I'm going to give you one final warning. Let this thing go. Just forget all about it. If you don't then you really will go back inside. Do I make myself clear?'

I ignored the question and said, 'So you're not charging me?'

He pursed his lips and shook his head. 'I've talked to the man you clobbered and he's gone against my advice and decided not to press charges.'

'Why?'

'Because both he and Mr Strickland want to avoid the publicity. So you're one lucky bitch, Wells.'

And I felt it too. I exhaled a long breath as the tension eased out of me.

'What about Ruby Gillespie?' I said.

'I haven't heard from her, so I'm assuming she doesn't want the hassle of making a formal complaint.'

'That's good to know.'

'But there'll be no more chances, Wells. You need to understand that. If you harass anybody else then you've had it.'

'I get the message.'

'And what exactly does that mean?'

'It means I'll think about how to react to your threat.'

What he did next took me completely by surprise. He laughed. But it was a harsh, crude laugh.

'I'll say one thing for you, Wells. You've got balls for someone in your position. Seems to me that your time inside didn't change you much. You're still a stroppy, over-confident little gobshite.'

'And you're still a bent copper with a serious attitude problem,' I said.

He raised his eyes to the ceiling. 'So now it's my turn to be on the receiving end of your unfounded allegations.'

'We both know you're not straight,' I said. 'I've been told that you take backhanders from Strickland. And so did your man Neil Ferris before he topped himself. No wonder Strickland was never in the frame for Benedict's murder. He had the two of you looking out for him.'

I thought for a moment that Ash was going to blow a fuse. His eyes spread wide and his nostrils flared alarmingly. But when he spoke, his voice was seamless and flat, devoid of emotion.

'You have a way of winding people up, Wells. But I'm not going to rise to it. I'll tell you this, though. You're wrong on both counts. I'm not bent and I did not stitch you up. I didn't have to. The evidence against you was overwhelming.'

'Of course it was. That was how it was meant to be.'

He shook his head. 'You can say and think what you like, but my conscience is clear. We conducted a fair and thorough investigation.'

'So why did Ferris kill himself?'

He seemed genuinely shocked. 'What's that got to do with it?'

I shrugged. 'You tell me. Your detective threw himself off a railway bridge a week after my son died of meningitis. And ever since then his widow has been putting flowers on Leo's grave. Could it be that *her* conscience isn't as clear?'

He sat bolt upright and stuck his chin out. 'Please don't tell me you've been harassing Pamela Ferris. If you have then so help me I'll—'

'I bumped into her at the cemetery this morning,' I said. 'She was placing fresh flowers on the grave.'

He said nothing, but his eyes seemed to go out of focus, and he appeared confused.

'You didn't know about that, did you?' I said.

'What Pamela does is none of my business,' he replied sharply.

'Well, she's made it my business by visiting my son's grave. I want to know why, since she's not a friend or a relative.'

'Did you ask her?'

'Sure I did. But she refused to answer and ran away. Now don't you think that's bloody suspicious?'

He continued to aim unblinking eyes at me, but seemed lost for words.

'It's another part of the puzzle,' I said. 'And surely as a detective you can appreciate why I want to solve it.' I held up my right hand and started counting off the fingers as I spoke. 'As soon as I was released from prison I got a note threatening me, then my brother was beaten up, then Ruby Gillespie admitted that she'd lied in court, then I was attacked, then I found out that Joe Strickland is the moneyman behind Ruby's escort agency. And on top of all that I've discovered that the widow of one of the officers who arrested me has been mourning the death of my son.'

He sat there in sullen silence, as though trying to wrap his thoughts around what I'd told him.

'When you put all that together it sounds really dodgy, doesn't it?' I said. 'And that's why I'm reluctant to walk away just so that you and whoever else is involved can keep a lid on it.'

I knew I was pushing my luck, but I reasoned with myself that it was probably worth it. If DCI Ash was telling the truth – and he was not involved in a murderous conspiracy – then he might be inclined to start taking me seriously. If, on the other hand, he was a lying toerag, then I'd given him even more reason to put me out of harm's way.

We sat there staring at each other for perhaps half a minute, and I would have paid a King's ransom to have known what he was thinking. I did detect a trace of uncertainty in his expression, though. It looked out of place on a face that always reflected such unbridled arrogance and self-assurance.

Eventually he broke eye contact and checked his watch.

'I've heard enough of this paranoid drivel,' he said. 'I want you to get out of my sight. If you continue making a nuisance of yourself I'll have you banged up again.'

His delivery was slow and threatening, and it made me realise that no matter how much evidence there was to back up my case, this bastard would make sure it was buried for ever.

DS McGrath was waiting for me outside Ash's office.

'The governor asked me to show you out,' he said. 'I gather he's told you that you won't be facing charges.'

'That's right,' I said. 'But he also accused me of lying about the attack in the alley. He said he doesn't believe it happened.'

'That's because we only have your word for it, Lizzie. There were no witnesses, and one of the guys you say jumped you has a firm alibi.'

'So what's the point investigating it?'

'Because although he's not convinced you were attacked, I am,'

161

he said. 'It could be you've identified the wrong man. Maybe there are two thugs in this town with the same tattoo.'

'I'm not stupid,' I said. 'The guy in the alley and the guy in the bar are one and the same.'

'Victims of violence are often confused about the details, Lizzie.'

'Well, I'm not. I'm a hundred and ten per cent certain.'

Going down in the lift, he asked me what I had said to Ash.

'I told him I knew he was bent,' I said. 'He denied it, naturally.'

'That's because he's an honest copper.'

'Yeah, right. And I'm a sweet little virgin.'

When the lift doors opened on the ground floor, we stepped out into the reception area.

'I'll let you know if there are any developments,' he said.

As soon as I exited the building, I phoned Scar to tell her that I hadn't been charged.

She shrieked with relief and told me she'd been waiting anxiously for my call. I gave her an edited version of what Ash had said and told her I'd flesh it out later.

'Meanwhile, have you had any luck with Karina Gorski?' I said.

'Actually I have,' she replied. 'I've been knocking on doors in and around Derby Road. Quite a few people remember her, but she hasn't been seen for some years. Apparently she lived with her brother in one of the terraced houses. I've called there, but nobody's at home so I'm going to check the local pubs.'

'Let me know if you manage to track her down.'

'I will. What are you going to do?'

'I'm hoping to see the editor of the local newspaper,' I said. 'He was Benedict's boss and he's been trying to get hold of me. I'm guessing he wants an interview.'

'Aren't you worried how Ash will react if they carry a story?'

I laughed. 'Oh, I know how he'll react, and I only wish I could be there to see it.'

The Post was the city's only evening newspaper. It was headquartered on an industrial estate about three miles from the central police station.

I took out the piece of paper my mother had given me and called Dewar's number in the hope that he was in on a Saturday. It so happened that he was. I told him my mother had passed on his message and he said he was keen for one of his reporters to interview me. I said I was prepared to come and talk to him personally, but in return I wanted information on Rufus Benedict.

'I'll tell you what I can,' he said. 'So long as you give me a good story.'

Dewar was waiting for me when I walked into the paper's sprawling single-storey office building fifteen minutes later. He was a cube of a man in his fifties, with grey hair and a beer belly.

We shook hands and he took me to his office, which was small and cluttered, with a view of the car park out front.

'We got tipped off that you'd been released,' he said, when we were facing each other across his desk. 'As you probably know we gave extensive coverage to your trial. Now we'd like to hear what you have to say about that and about your time in prison.'

'And in return I want to know more about Benedict,' I said. 'I'll treat whatever you tell me in confidence. The more open you are with me the more forthcoming I'll be with you. Is that understood?'

'Of course, but may I ask why you want this information?'

'Because I didn't kill him, and I want to find out who did.' He looked perplexed, so I continued. 'I pleaded guilty to manslaughter rather than risk a life sentence for murder. But I was framed.'

'I've looked back at the cuttings,' he said. 'You testified that you were drunk or drugged and weren't fully aware of what was going on, except that you were attacked and that you must have used the knife to defend yourself.'

I nodded. 'That's about right. But it wasn't your lecherous reporter who attacked me.'

He gestured towards a digital recorder on his desk.

'Is it all right if I tape the interview? I want to make sure I get everything down.'

'No problem,' I said. 'But before I say any more I've got some questions for you.'

'Then fire away.'

I took a moment to collect my thoughts. My eyes felt heavy and dry and my pulse roared in my ears. I knew that when the story appeared, Ash would go ballistic. But I also knew that the publicity would probably work in my favour. Hampshire police would be forced to deny that I'd been threatened and intimidated by one of their senior officers. Ash would be thrust into the limelight and would have to be careful what he said and did. He'd hopefully be ordered by his superiors to steer clear of me.

'At the time he was killed, Benedict was working on a story for you about Joe Strickland,' I said. 'What exactly did he find out?'

Dewar stuck out his bottom lip. 'Nothing we could publish. I told that to the police and to your lawyer when he came to see me.'

'So how long did Benedict spend on the story?'

'A couple of months. As our investigative reporter, Rufus worked to his own timetable. He kept telling me he was gathering evidence that would prove Joe Strickland was involved in all kinds of illegal activities. But I never got to see any of it before he died.'

'What about his notes and computer files?'

'The police took it all away, but they said they couldn't find anything to do with the investigation.'

'Wasn't that strange?'

'Yes, but then Rufus always played things close to his chest. He probably kept all his research material in a safety deposit box or an online storage facility that nobody knew about.'

'But surely as his editor he would have spoken to you about what he was up to.'

'Of course he did. We had regular meetings. But the Strickland investigation was only one of the stories he was working on, and it wasn't one that I assigned him. He convinced me it was going to result in a big exclusive. So I let him get on with it. That was how Rufus liked to operate.'

'What about his contacts and the people he spoke to?'

'He interviewed a lot of people during the course of the investigation, and I gave their names to the police. Among them was the woman who was apparently his main source of information and the person who got him started on it in the first place.'

'Who was she?'

'Her name's Karina Gorski and she's Polish. Rufus claimed she had some sort of relationship with Joe Strickland and had information on his dodgy dealings.'

My heart slammed to a stop.

'Are you sure that was her name?' I said.

'Absolutely. I signed over three cash payments to her totalling four thousand pounds.'

My mind whirred. This had to be a significant lead. Karina had worked as an escort and according to Ruby Gillespie, Benedict had been one of her regular clients.

'*Benedict only ever wanted one girl*,' Ruby had told me. '*He was*

165

infatuated with her and when she suddenly disappeared from the scene he stopped calling.'

So where did Strickland fit into it? I wondered. And what kind of 'relationship' had he had with her? Did it involve more than taking a cut of her earnings?

'Do you know where I can find Karina Gorski?' I asked.

'That's the thing,' Dewar said. 'Nobody knows. She vanished four years ago. Benedict said he had no idea why, and he was very anxious about it. He didn't want to admit that she might have strung him along to get paid before doing a runner.'

'So what did Benedict actually tell you about her?'

'Nothing much. We didn't discover until after his death that she was a sex worker living in Southampton. We tried to find her ourselves but got nowhere.'

'Did the police manage to question her?'

'Apparently not. I've spoken a few times to the detective who was in charge of the case, and he reckons she probably went back to Poland.'

'You mean DCI Ash?'

'Correct. He told me that he suspects Rufus was actually visiting the woman as a client. But that didn't surprise me. It was common knowledge here at the paper that he went with escorts even before it all came out at the trial. He confided in a colleague once that he was hooked on sex with younger women despite the fact that he was married with a family.'

'But you're saying you didn't know that Karina was an escort until after Benedict died?'

'That's right. Rufus didn't tell me and neither did he specify the exact nature of her connection to Joe Strickland. He simply said she had a relationship with him. But Strickland told the police he'd never even heard of the woman, let alone met her.'

'So do you think he was telling the truth?'

Dewar gave a mirthless grin. 'Between you and me I think Strickland is a lying shit. He's a crook who pretends to be an honest businessman. We've been trying to get something on him for years, but without success. I'm convinced he knew Karina Gorski, but the police took his word for it that he didn't. They drew the same conclusion as I did – that she'd most likely fed Rufus some spurious information with a view to ripping the paper off.'

I thought about this and realised it had to be a distinct possibility. Like me, Karina had turned to prostitution because she'd been desperate for money. I'd only met her once when we shared a bottle of wine at Ruby's place. As well as being very pretty she had struck me as shrewd and hard-headed. I certainly wouldn't have put it past her to exploit a randy dickhead like Rufus Benedict.

'Are you aware that Strickland is involved in the agency that I used to work for?' I said.

Dewar shook his head. 'As a matter of fact I wasn't.'

'Well, that's what I've been told. I didn't know it at the time, and I never met the man before yesterday.'

'But am I right in assuming that you did know Karina?'

'I didn't know her,' I said. 'But I did meet her once.'

He drew a breath. 'Then I reckon it's now your turn to answer *my* questions, Miss Wells.'

I left Dewar's office after giving him an interview and allowing one of his photographers to take a couple of photos of me. He said he would carry it on the front page of Monday's edition of *The Post*, since they didn't publish on Sundays.

At first he'd asked me to describe what had happened in the hotel room four years ago, even though it was more or less a repeat of what I'd said in court. Then he questioned me about prison and how I'd coped after Leo's death. That was the hardest part, and it made my eyes water.

But for Dewar the most newsworthy element of the interview was when I told him what had happened since my release. He hadn't known about the threats and the attacks on my brother and me. Or about the episode in the Centurion bar.

Some of what I told him he obviously couldn't print, including my allegations against Strickland, Ruby and the police. But he said that my quest to get to what I believed to be the truth made for a cracking human interest story.

Of course, I wasn't sure how much of it he believed, but that didn't matter so long as he drew attention to what I was doing.

I kept some things back, including my relationship with Scar and my encounter with Pamela Ferris. And I insisted he shouldn't send reporters to harass my mother and brother.

All things considered, I was pleased with the way it had gone. Dewar struck me as an old school hack who would like nothing better than to stir up a shit-storm.

I was convinced that giving the interview was a good move. It was impossible to know if it would evoke much sympathy, but at least it would put paid to the idea that I could be muzzled. And I was hopeful it would encourage the police to continue investigating the attack on me, despite Ash's view that it didn't happen.

I was lost in thought as I walked out of the newspaper building and across the car park. So I wasn't aware that someone had fallen in step behind me until I heard a voice.

'Lizzie Wells.'

I stopped and turned. At first I couldn't put a name to the face. The woman was in her early fifties, slim and smartly dressed

168

in black trousers and white blouse. She peered at me through thick-rimmed glasses.

'I want to talk to you,' she said.

My stomach knotted with conflicting emotions when I realised who she was.

'Hello, Mrs Benedict,' I said.

Anne Benedict, the widow of the man I was jailed for killing, stood before me, her eyes small and unfriendly.

She'd lost weight since we'd stared at each other across the courtroom, and the last four years had not been kind to her. The black, shoulder-length hair was now grey and lifeless, and her face was hollow and pale.

'I was wondering if you would remember me,' she said.

'How did you know I was here?' I asked her.

She shrugged. 'My husband had many close friends at the paper. One of those who stayed in touch with me saw you arrive earlier and knew why you'd come. So she called to tell me, and I came over and waited.'

'I was going to contact you actually,' I said. 'I was wondering if I might ask you some questions about your husband.'

Her eyes narrowed inquisitively. 'Are you serious? Why on earth would you think I'd answer them? You're the whore who murdered him.'

I drew a careful breath and told her what I'd been telling everyone else: that I was not a murderer. But as she listened it was obvious she didn't believe me.

'So that's your game is it?' she said. 'Now that you're out of prison you're planning to cash in on your notoriety by saying you want to clear your name. You're a disgrace. How much is the paper paying for your story?'

'I'm not being paid and I'm not trying to cash in,' I said. 'I just want the truth to come out.'

She gave me a withering look. 'The truth is you stabbed my husband to death and wrecked my life. I've come here to ask you not to bring it all up again for my family's sake. My two sons are still grieving the loss of their father. I don't want your face splashed across the front pages again along with all the sordid details.'

My heart went out to the woman. She was another innocent victim of what had happened and like me she'd probably never fully recover from it.

'Have you no shame?' she said. 'Why can't you just go away, and let us carry on with our lives in peace?'

'It's not as easy as that,' I said.

'Well, it should be. You got off lightly considering what you did. It's a scandal that you're not still rotting in prison.'

There were tears in her eyes now, and her voice broke with emotion. Luckily there was no one else in the car park to hear her berating me. But that didn't make me feel any less uncomfortable. I realised there was nothing I could say to placate her – not unless I agreed to get the paper to drop the story. And that was out of the question.

She pointed at me accusingly. 'What you did was despicable. I know my husband wasn't perfect. He did some shameful and disgusting things. But he didn't deserve to die like that. And my boys don't deserve to suffer all over again because you want to exploit the situation.'

She took another step towards me and it made me flinch. I could tell she had already worked herself up into a frenzy that was borne out of frustration and a perceived injustice. It made her frighteningly unpredictable.

'Just go back in there and retract what you've told them,' she pleaded. 'The world doesn't need to hear your lies and excuses.'

'I can't do that,' I said.

Her face reddened, and she started to shake. 'You vile fucking whore. Have you any idea how much distress you're going to cause? Have you?'

'I can't help that,' I said, taking a step back. 'I just want to expose a wrongdoing.'

She shook her head. 'No, you don't. You want to inflict more pain because that's what people like you thrive on. You don't care how much damage you cause. That's why you sell your body and prey on weak and vulnerable men.'

I wanted to tell her that her husband had not been weak and vulnerable, that he was just a dirty sod who had enjoyed fucking young prostitutes. But I held my tongue because inside I understood how she felt and I sympathised.

'Rufus was a good man despite what he did,' she screamed at me. 'I won't let you drag his name through the mud again. It's not fair.'

A fierce rage shivered behind her eyes and just as I opened my mouth to respond, she lashed out at me. I failed to see it coming and her right hand struck my left cheek. The blow was loud and stinging, but it seemed to sap the woman's strength in an instant.

Her face crumbled, and her body appeared to collapse in on itself. She started to cry, and her shoulders heaved with every sob.

I reached out instinctively and touched her arm, but she pushed me away.

'Don't you dare lay a hand on me,' she shouted. 'Just go away and crawl under the nearest rock. That's where you belong.'

She was inconsolable, and the sight of her sent a great wave of sadness rolling over me.

I didn't want to leave her, but I knew I had no choice. If I stayed then things were likely to turn even uglier.

So I walked away from her, resisting the urge to say something. There was a sick feeling in the pit of my stomach and the guilt was tormenting me yet again.

I looked back when I reached the car and saw her standing there staring at me and looking utterly dejected and pathetic.

I wanted to go back and try to comfort her, to tell her I was sorry for all that had happened. But I knew it was a bad idea, so I pulled open the door, got in and drove away from there with a heavy heart.

15

I felt terrible. As I wrestled with my conscience, I couldn't clear my mind of the image of a tearful Anne Benedict.

It was bad enough that she knew her husband had paid me to have sex with him. But her pain and despair were magnified a hundred times over because she believed I'd also killed him.

How could I reconcile the fact that I was going to inflict more pain through my own desperate need to get at the truth? I was in a no-win situation.

I took out my phone and called Scar as I drove, but it went to voicemail. I was momentarily nonplussed. I didn't know what to do or where to go, but I realised I wanted to talk to someone. Anyone. If only to offload the guilt-inspired tension that was building up inside me.

Without giving it much thought I headed for my mother's house. Even if I got a frosty reception I reckoned it'd be better than going back to an empty flat.

I spotted Tiny's car as soon as I entered the street. It was parked about twenty yards back from the house so it couldn't be seen from the front windows. He was sitting behind the wheel and he gave me a wave as I pulled into the kerb in front of him.

I got out and walked back to his car. He wound down the window, and I asked him if everything was all right.

He smiled. 'Nobody has entered or left the house since I arrived a couple of hours ago. And I haven't seen anyone acting suspicious.'

'That's good. I'm just popping in to see them.'

'What's up, Lizzie? You look as though you've had a bad morning.'

'I have.'

'Well, get in the car and tell me about it.'

I got in the passenger side and was struck by the smell of coffee and cigarettes. Tiny offered me a smoke and I accepted. After lighting up, I told him about my morning, beginning with my encounter with Pamela Ferris at the cemetery. He listened in silence and raised his eyebrows a couple of times.

'It's all pretty odd,' he said. 'Especially that business with the Polish girl. If she was involved with Benedict and Strickland at the same time then maybe everything that happened revolved around her.'

'It would help if we could track her down,' I said.

'Is Donna getting anywhere with that?'

'I just called her, but it went to voicemail. She told me earlier she was trying to contact Karina's brother.'

'What about the police? Have you asked them about her? It could be she's officially listed as a missing person.'

'I haven't asked them yet, but I will. What about you? Did you manage to identify the guy with the tattoo?'

He nodded and took a small slip of paper from his pocket, which he consulted before speaking.

'His name is Sean Delaney and he's worked for Strickland for five years. I actually did come across him a few times but I didn't know about the tattoo. And it seems he's changed his appearance since I last saw him. He used to have long hair. He's a hard case who's done time for assault and for being in possession of a handgun. He has a reputation for being a brutal enforcer for Strickland and usually works with his cousin, a bloke named Ron Parks. He might have been his accomplice in the alley. Before moving to Southampton they both worked doors in London and were involved with a gang that operated south of the river.'

'Where did you learn all that?'

'From a mate who worked for Strickland until a few months ago. He described Delaney as a psycho and said no one messes with him.'

'Did you get an address for him?'

He laughed. 'No, and I'm glad I didn't. At least you won't be tempted to call on him. He's a dangerous dude, Lizzie. You need to stay away from him.'

His words sent a chill along my spine as I remembered what Delaney had done to me in the alley and what he'd done to my brother.

At least I knew his name now. That was progress even if I didn't have a clue what to do with it.

I thanked Tiny for his help and he assured me he would continue to keep an eye on my mother and brother.

It was Mark who answered the door to me. He beamed a wide smile and said he'd been hoping I would drop by.

'How are you feeling, bruv?' I asked him.

He gave me a hug and a kiss on the cheek. 'I'm good, sis. It's stopped hurting now.'

My mother was in the kitchen and had started to fill the kettle.

To my surprise she didn't seem unhappy to see me. At least that was the impression I got from her body language and insipient smile.

She turned away from the sink and asked me what I'd been up to. I didn't tell her what had happened in the bar or about my session with the police. But I did tell her that I had met the woman who'd been putting flowers on Leo's grave.

'She's the widow of one of the detectives who arrested me,' I said. 'The one who killed himself.'

Mum was puzzled, as was I, and she told me she'd never been in contact with Pamela Ferris.

'It makes no sense,' she said. 'Why would she do that?'

'Beats me, Mum. She ran away and wouldn't answer my questions. I know she works in town, though.'

'So where does she live?'

'I haven't a clue, but you've given me an idea.'

I got out my phone and went online. I typed in Neil Ferris's name on Google and was soon scrolling through stories about his suicide a year previously. One news item reported that he and his wife lived in Water Lane, Totton, on the outskirts of Southampton.

I told my mother and she said she didn't know the road or anyone who lived in Totton.

'I'll pay her a visit,' I said. 'Either at home or work. I want to know what's been going on.'

I then told her I'd given an interview to *The Post*.

'Oh, for heaven's sake, that was a stupid thing to do,' she snapped. 'Everyone will be talking about it again.'

'That's just the point,' I said.

'Well, I'm not happy about it, and I don't for the life of me see what good can come of it.'

'The publicity might encourage someone to open up and tell the truth,' I said.

She snorted. 'It's a mistake. Mark my words.'

'Well, it's done now so we'll see.'

My mother shook her head. 'You've always been headstrong, Lizzie. And you've never been prepared to listen to sensible advice. That's why you've made such a mess of your life.'

Her reaction stopped me from mentioning my encounter with Anne Benedict in the car park. And I sensed that she was about to launch into a major lecture that would inevitably lead to a full-blown argument.

So it came as a relief when my phone rang at that moment. I held up my hand to silence her and whipped it out.

'It's me,' Scar said. 'I've found Karina Gorski's brother. He's with me now and I think you should hear what he's got to say about his sister.'

'Where are you?'

'The Fountain pub, just off Derby Road.'

'I'm on my way,' I said.

The Fountain had seen better days. Everything about it was faded, from the scuffed leather sofas to the threadbare carpets.

Scar and her male companion were the only people in the bar. On the table between them stood three wine glasses.

'I got you the house Chardonnay,' Scar said as I stepped up to them. 'It's quite nice.'

I thanked her with a smile and turned my attention to Karina Gorski's brother. He was in his thirties, thin, with a dark beard that swallowed the lower half of his face.

Scar introduced us, and I sat between them. His name was Jakub and he lived close by and was unemployed. This pub was where he spent much of his time along with his benefits money. He had a thick Polish accent, but a decent command of English.

'I've told Mr Gorski who you are and why you're enquiring about his sister,' Scar said.

I began by telling him that I had actually met Karina and that I'd been struck by her good looks and charm.

'We shared a bottle of wine,' I said. 'Unfortunately it was the one and only time our paths crossed. I'm only sorry I didn't get to know her.'

'She's a kind and generous person,' Jakub said. 'But she started mixing with the wrong people soon after moving to this country, and they led her astray.'

His voice shrank to a whisper as he told me he had moved to England from a village just outside Krakow seven years ago in search of a better life. His sister had followed two years later and they'd rented the house in Derby Road, along with several other Polish immigrants.

But Karina had struggled to find work and had got involved with a group of people who were into heavy drinking and drug taking. She turned to prostitution as a way of financing her increasingly expensive lifestyle.

'She went to work for that Gillespie woman because she thought it would be safer than standing on street corners,' he said. 'And things went well for a time. The money rolled in and she even opened a savings account.'

'Did she ever mention any of her clients by name?' I asked.

While speaking he had been staring into the middle distance. Now he turned to face me and I saw that his strikingly blue eyes had a profound intensity to them.

'She mentioned Rufus Benedict a couple of times,' he said. 'She told me he was a reporter and as well as paying her for sex he was giving her money to help her with a story he was working on.'

'Did you know what it was about?'

'I didn't then but I've since heard that he was investigating Joe Strickland, who I'm sure you know. At the time Karina wouldn't tell me. She said it was best I didn't know. I asked Benedict, but he wouldn't tell me either.'

'So you met Benedict?'

He nodded. 'He came to see me after Karina disappeared. He was really worried. He wanted to know if I knew where she was. But I didn't then and I still don't.'

'Did you tell this to the police?'

'Of course, but I don't think any of it came as a surprise to them.'

'What do you mean?'

He shrugged. 'Well on the day she disappeared the police came to the house to talk to her. They refused to say what it was about, but I assumed it was in connection with her sex work. Anyway, she wasn't in and I didn't know where she was. After they left I tried to phone Karina, but she didn't pick up. I reported her missing to the police the following evening. The same two detectives came to see me and said they hadn't been able to find her the previous day. Then they searched her room and took some of her belongings away.'

'And you haven't seen her since?'

'No I haven't and I fear that something bad must have happened to her. Otherwise she would have contacted me.'

'Had she ever gone missing before?'

'Not since coming to England. She did go away occasionally at weekends, but she would always call me to let me know.'

'The police think that Karina went back to Poland,' I said.

'Well, that's only because they can't be bothered to carry on looking for her,' he said. 'But she hasn't turned up at the family home, and no one there has seen her.'

'Tell me about the detectives who came to ask you questions,' I said. 'Can you remember their names?'

'I'm afraid not. It was over four years ago and since then I've spoken to a lot of police officers.'

I mulled it over for a few beats and said, 'So do you know how your sister was able to help Benedict with his investigation into Joe Strickland? Was he one of her clients?'

'I'm not sure. She did have a regular client who she said had a lot of money and I suppose it could have been him. She often stayed overnight at this guy's flat in the city centre. When she turned up here the next morning she always had a pile of cash.'

By now Jakub's eyes were filled with unshed tears. He was clearly still upset by his sister's disappearance. He told us he had looked everywhere for her and had been in constant touch with the police, both in Hampshire and in Poland. But no one had heard anything from her and there hadn't been any sightings.

I could see why he had come to the conclusion that she had probably been harmed in some way.

By the time we left the pub I myself was convinced that if Karina Gorski ever did turn up it would be in a shallow grave somewhere.

16

It was a relief to get back to the flat. I was tired, and my head was in a constant spin.

The first thing we did when we closed the door behind us was to give each other a hug. The heat from Scar's body filled the cold space inside me. It made me feel so much better.

'Methinks you need to relax, babe,' she said. 'Why don't you have a shower while I fix us some dinner?'

'I'd rather have something to drink,' I said. 'It'll help me wind down.'

'Well, there's more wine in the fridge. I'll open a bottle while you go and freshen up. We can settle down to a cosy evening, and you can tell me all about your day.'

I stripped off and stepped in the shower. I endured the jagged needles of hot water while reliving the events of the day in my head. I tried to put all the fragments of information I'd gathered into something that made sense. And the more I thought about it, the more convinced I became that it was all connected.

Benedict's murder.

Karina Gorski's disappearance.

The Ferris woman's visits to my son's grave.

There'd been a cover-up that extended beyond the murder and involved Joe Strickland and the police. I was absolutely sure of it. But my reappearance on the scene was now a threat to them – hence the intimidation against me and my family.

I was like a dog with a bone, though. And they must have realised by now that I wasn't going to throw in the towel. It made what I was doing all the more dangerous.

Scar and I trashed a bottle of wine while I told her about my day. The irony of what we were doing was not lost on either of us. We were two ex-cons talking as though we were a pair of off-duty coppers. It was more than a little bizarre.

But for me it was cathartic. I desperately needed to express my thoughts and put into words how worried I was about where it was all going.

Scar, as usual, was a good listener and she clearly saw how confused and anxious I was.

I told her exactly what had happened in the cemetery with Neil Ferris's widow, then gave her a rundown of what Dewar had said about Benedict.

'I already knew that Benedict was working on a story about Strickland,' I said. 'What I didn't know was that Karina Gorski was helping him in some way. And she was seeing Strickland at the same time.'

'But what kind of information could she possibly have been giving him?' Scar said.

I shrugged. 'All we know is that he was willing to pay for it. Dewar said he signed over a total of four thousand pounds to her.'

'So perhaps she decided to use that money and go somewhere to start a new life.'

'It's not enough,' I said. 'She'd need a lot more than four grand.'

'Well, you don't know what she'd saved. Her brother told you the money rolled in after she joined the agency.'

'But I got the impression that she and her brother are close. So why wouldn't she have told him where she was going? And why not contact him at all in four years?'

'She might be running scared and doesn't want anyone to know where she is.'

'Or she could be dead,' I suggested.

I explained why I'd come to that conclusion. The facts were clear-cut, I said. Rufus Benedict had been digging up the dirt on Joe Strickland, a ruthless villain who hid behind a moody front of respectability. Before or during his investigation the reporter got involved with Karina Gorski, who he said was providing him with incriminating information against Strickland. At the same time Karina was apparently also involved with Strickland, which presumably gave her access to the information. Suddenly Karina disappeared and then a week or so later Benedict was murdered in a hotel room.

'So Strickland could have got wind of what was going on and had Karina killed by one or more of his henchmen,' I said. 'Then he set about planning Benedict's murder.'

'So why didn't he just make Benedict disappear as well?' Scar said. 'Why have him killed while he was with you? It was messy and risky.'

'Because he wanted to divert attention away from himself,' I said. 'Like I told you before, Strickland would have been the obvious suspect if I hadn't been framed.'

Scar pondered this for a few moments as she lit a cigarette. Then she said, 'It seems a bit extreme, doesn't it? I mean, even an immoral twat like Strickland would have had to have a good reason for murdering two people.'

'I agree, but then the story Benedict was pulling together with Karina's help might have been a serious threat to his empire and even landed him in prison. So he took drastic measures to ensure it was never published.'

'But even if it's true it'll be impossible to prove it,' Scar said. 'Especially without the cooperation of the police.'

As if on cue my mobile rang. DS McGrath's name popped up on the caller ID.

'I hope you're ringing to tell me you've arrested Sean Delaney,' I said, before he could get a word in.

McGrath was caught off guard. 'How the hell did you get his name?'

'That's my business, but I take it he's still swanning around the city while you lot do fuck all about it.'

He left it several seconds before responding.

'I'm calling to tell you that DCI Ash is spitting feathers,' he said. 'He can't believe you went to the paper after the warning he gave you. The editor of *The Post* has already been on. He said you're claiming that the police are part of a cover-up and that we're not taking the threats against you seriously.'

'Well it's true isn't it?'

'Leave it out, Lizzie. The boss and I have told you that you're wrong. The cover-up exists only in your head and you know full well that I'm investigating the attacks and threats against you.'

'Well, forgive me for thinking that what you're doing is just for show,' I said. 'I don't believe for a single second that you're taking it seriously. If you were, you'd be all over Sean Delaney and Joe Strickland.'

'We don't need you to tell us how to conduct an investigation,' McGrath said. 'We know what we're doing.'

A laugh erupted from my throat. 'Of course you do. You're letting Strickland and his cronies get away with murder. You know that Delaney beat me up in the alley and that Joe Strickland must have been behind it. Just like he was behind Benedict's murder and Karina Gorski's disappearance.'

'What do you know about the Gorski woman?' he said.

'I know that she was somehow involved in what happened four years ago. She was helping Benedict's investigation into Strickland's affairs and most likely fucking both of them at the same time. And then she vanished and you haven't been able to find her.'

'How do you know all this?'

'From Dewar at the paper and from her brother.'

'Well, it's true that Karina Gorski is listed as a missing person,' McGrath conceded. 'But we strongly believe she went back to Poland so that she could avoid talking to us.'

'Yeah, but you can't be sure, can you? Just like you can't be sure that she wasn't killed on Strickland's orders.'

'Oh, don't be absurd, Lizzie. This is Southampton, not Naples or New York. And Joe Strickland is a local businessman, not some Mafia don.'

I felt my blood heat up and screeched down the phone at the top of my voice.

'I'm fed up with you lot treating me like I'm an idiot and trying to gag me. What happened four years ago was not a straightforward case of murder, and I've got every right to do what I can to get at the truth. I don't give a flying fuck if Ash isn't happy or if it raises difficult questions for Hampshire police. The sooner you accept it the better.'

And with that I severed the connection and sat for a moment breathing in shallow gulps of air.

'I don't get it, Lizzie,' Scar said sharply. 'Are you trying to wind the cops up so they'll send you back to prison?'

I was taken aback. 'Why would you say that?'

'Why do you think? You've only just got out of prison. Yet you just keep pushing your luck. There was no need to talk to him like that, especially since you said he seemed like one of the good guys. It was deliberately provocative, and Christ knows how he's going to react.'

I was shocked. Scar had never raised her voice to me before. Her pallor dropped several shades and an angry glint settled in her eyes.

'Look, I'm really sorry, babe,' I said. 'But I'm wound up. I just wanted him to know that I'm not prepared to take their crap any more.'

'And that's the problem,' she said. 'You're just thinking about yourself all the time. We're together now. I love you and we've both got the opportunity to start over again. I don't want you to fuck it up.'

She grabbed her half-smoked cigarette from the ashtray on the table and pinched her lips tightly around the filter.

I could see her point and it made me feel bad. Scar had a lot to lose if I was put back inside.

'You need to give serious thought to what you're doing, Lizzie,' she said. 'Be realistic about what you can actually achieve. You're all excited because you've found out a few things about Benedict and Strickland that you didn't know before. But that's probably as far as you're going to be able to take it. And if you don't accept that then you're asking for trouble. If they don't bang you up again then you could get yourself killed.'

186

As she spoke, tears started to slide down her cheeks, and her lips trembled. I had never seen her so distraught and I felt a stab of guilt in my chest.

I put down my glass and moved to sit next to her on the sofa. She was shaking and sobbing, and her body collapsed against me.

'I can't help being scared and worried,' she said into my shoulder. 'I don't want to lose you and I have a horrible feeling that I will if you carry on.'

I didn't want to lose Scar either. And I didn't want to blow the chance of embarking on a long and meaningful relationship with her.

Deep down I knew I had set myself a near impossible task. And yet I'd told myself I should plough on regardless. Maybe Scar was right, and I should accept that there was only so far I could take it.

It was all very well seeking publicity and stirring things up. But how likely was it that I would elicit a confession or find concrete evidence to prove my case?

'I understand how you feel and why you want to get at the truth,' Scar said. 'And I've always been willing to help you. But I didn't realise how dangerous it would be. And I can't help thinking now that it's just not worth risking everything when the odds are stacked so firmly against you.'

I started crying too then, the sobs gushing out of me. And as I clung to Scar I suddenly came to a gut-wrenching decision.

'I'll stop,' I said. 'For all our sakes I'll let it go. It's over, babe. You don't have to worry any more.'

It was a rash decision made in the heat of the moment, and I knew I might come to regret it. But I also knew there was no going back.

Scar responded by shrieking with delight and telling me that it was absolutely the right thing to do.

I experienced a momentary flash of panic, but at the same time felt a weight lift from my shoulders.

'You'll come to terms with it, babe,' she said. 'I know it's hard, but at least we won't have to worry about you losing your freedom again.'

The emotion of the moment overwhelmed us both. We clung to each other as the tears flowed.

Then we opened another bottle of wine and talked about it. Scar's relief was palpable, although she sought constant reassurance that I was serious.

'Of course I am,' I told her. 'What you just said really hit home. I realise now how reckless I've been and how close I am to losing you and inflicting more pain on my mother and brother. I need to come to my senses and accept the reality of the situation.'

But it wasn't going to be easy. I knew that. I'd obsessed about it for so long and had been determined never to give up. I'd even convinced myself that I was making progress, that my tenacity was paying off.

But Scar was right. In all likelihood I wouldn't achieve my ultimate goal, which was to exonerate myself and expose those responsible for what had happened. And the mere act of pursuing it was increasing the risk of ending up in prison or even on a mortuary slab.

I felt mentally fried by the time we finished the wine and scoffed a couple of microwaved ready meals.

It was still only nine o'clock when we decided to slope off to bed. We were both too hyped up to sleep so we lay for a time in each other's arms talking about the future.

Scar's insecurity came to the surface, and she wanted to know if I was sure about committing myself to a relationship with another woman.

'I've never been so sure of anything in my entire life,' I said. 'I can't imagine being without you. And just for the record, I discovered long ago that dicks are overrated.'

We both laughed and I knew then that I had made the right decision. If I hadn't realised before that Scar was my future then I did now. I owed it to her to stay out of prison and to give our relationship a chance to blossom. I couldn't allow my obsession to get in the way. It would be another huge mistake to add to the mountain of errors that had screwed up my life.

Inevitably perhaps, we were both seized by the desire to make love. Scar made the first move by running her fingers over my breasts, causing goose bumps to spring up on the surface of my skin. And then she kissed me on the mouth, and I felt an immense flood of warmth wash into me.

It was sublime, as always, and so very different from the insensitive and often brutal encounters I'd had with the men who paid me for sex. Maybe that was why I'd become a late-blooming lesbian. My experiences as a prostitute had probably left a scar on my subconscious and caused a shift in my sexual orientation.

At least that was how I now chose to rationalise what was happening to me.

'I want to eat you,' Scar said as she put her face between my thighs and worked her magic so that I reached a mind-convulsing orgasm.

Then it was my turn to pleasure her and I savoured the sweet scent of her juices while she pulled at my hair.

Eventually we lay back against the pillows, sheened with sweat and gloriously exhausted.

Scar dropped off straight away and began snoring quietly and contentedly. But sleep eluded me. I couldn't help thinking about the decision I'd made and whether or not it meant I would never have peace of mind.

After a while I got up, slipped on my dressing gown and padded lightly out of the room for a cigarette and a cup of tea.

I'd just put the kettle on when I heard my phone buzz with an incoming text message.

The phone was where I'd left it on the coffee table in the living room. I retrieved it and saw that the message was from an anonymous caller.

But when I opened it up I was surprised at the identity of the sender and shocked at what she'd written.

Lizzie . . . I've decided to tell you everything. Come to my house right now before I change my mind. And come alone . . . Ruby.

17

To my eternal shame I decided to go to Ruby's house, despite what I'd said to Scar.

The invitation was just too tempting to resist. I didn't even think to ask myself why she'd had a change of heart, or indeed how she had got my mobile number. I was suddenly consumed by an overriding urge to find out what she had to tell me.

I checked the time. Eleven o'clock. I wondered fleetingly if I should wake Scar to tell her what I planned to do, but instantly decided against it. She'd quite rightly be furious and try to talk me out of it. And I didn't want to be talked out of it.

I took a moment to respond to Ruby's message. I tapped in the words *on my way*. Then I crept back in the bedroom to retrieve my clothes.

Scar didn't stir. I looked down at her half-covered face and prayed that she would forgive me for reneging on my word.

As I dressed in the living room, I wondered if I could get to Ruby's and back before Scar woke up. At least I would have time then to come up with an excuse before I was forced to explain myself.

I put on jeans, a light sweater and a leather jacket. I decided to walk to Ruby's because I'd had too much to drink to risk driving.

Before leaving the flat, I peeked in again on Scar. She was still fast asleep, and I felt pretty sure that she wasn't going to surface any time soon.

I fought off another rush of guilt and tiptoed to the front door, closing it quietly behind me.

It was dry outside and quite mild. A blurred moon hovered above the city and the air was thick with petrol fumes. I was surprised to see that there was still a lot of traffic on the roads at such a late hour. But then cities no longer went to sleep. They remained in perpetual motion, responding to the needs of their ever-growing and increasingly restless populations.

I walked as quickly as I could, hands in pockets, head down. I tried to tune out the sense of guilt that was weighing heavily on my mind. I told myself I had no choice but to find out what information Ruby wanted to impart.

I got to Ruby's street in no time and saw that the lights were on in her house.

When I walked up to the front door I was surprised to see that it was open a few inches. I assumed that she had seen me coming from one of the windows and had unlocked it.

As I pushed it open and stepped over the threshold, I called out her name. There was no response. The hall was in darkness but a shaft of light cut across it from the living room.

'It's Lizzie, Ruby. I'm coming in. Where are you?'

I shut the door behind me and called out again. But still there was no reply.

There was a light on at the top of the stairs and also in the kitchen at the end of the hall. But there were no sounds and no movement.

I walked up to the living room door and peered inside. Empty. So too was the kitchen, although I could smell fresh cigarette smoke.

I called out again and when I got nothing back I ventured up the stairs.

By now I was gripped by a creeping sense of unease. Why wasn't she answering me? Had she popped out, thinking it would take me longer to get here?

I reached the upstairs landing and the silence enveloped me. The light was coming from the main bedroom, the door of which stood open.

I stepped up to it and peered in. Another empty room, the large double bed unmade. But as I entered, I heard running water. It was coming from what I assumed to be an en-suite bath or shower room. The door was ajar, and there was a light on inside.

'Ruby! Are you there?'

No answer.

I crossed the room, pulled the door open.

And what I saw made me dizzy with disbelief.

Ruby Gillespie was lying on the tiled floor between the toilet pan and the shower cubicle. She wore a flimsy nightdress that was drenched in blood and the handle of a large kitchen knife protruded from her chest.

Her eyes were open and her deathly stare was fixed on the ceiling.

I felt a sickening wave of despair and closed my eyes to stem the bolt of panic. When I opened them again I had to lean against the doorframe to stop myself falling over.

Ruby Gillespie had been murdered, and since the blood was still oozing out of her chest it must have happened in the last few minutes or so.

Oh God.

I tried to swallow but my mouth was bone dry. Inside my head I started screaming and my heart beat so rapidly I thought it might explode.

Suddenly I sensed a presence behind me and heard a floorboard creak. I started turning, but before I could see who was creeping up on me I took a savage blow to the back of the head.

It shattered my senses and sent me spinning into a deep, dark pit.

18

God only knows how long I was unconscious. When I came to I was lying face down in the doorway. My head was throbbing and my vision was blurred.

Any hope that I was waking from a nightmare faded when I pulled myself into a sitting position and saw Ruby's blood-soaked body. It thrust me back into a hideous reality.

I stared at the knife in her chest, wishing it away. Then, to my horror, I realised that I was also covered in blood. It was smeared across my clothes and my right hand. I let out a cry of alarm and started struggling for breath.

But after a moment instinct took over. I hauled myself to my feet and turned to look in the bedroom. There was no sign of my attacker, the same bastard who had no doubt stabbed Ruby.

Was he or she still in the house waiting to have another go at me? I froze, not knowing what to do. My eyes were drawn back to Ruby who had been cold-bloodedly murdered.

I looked at my right hand. The blood was still wet and was smeared across the palm and between the fingers. Was it her blood or mine?

I used my left hand to feel the back of my head where I'd been struck by something hard. There was a slight, painful lump. But when I took my hand away there was no blood on it.

So how had I managed to get Ruby's blood on me? I didn't touch her before I was hit and . . .

It came to me then in a sudden blast of clarity that made the hairs on my neck quiver.

I was being set up. Just like before.

The body. The blood. The knife.

Jesus Christ, I'd walked into a trap, lured to Ruby's house by a message that might actually have come from her killer.

It would explain why I had been smeared with blood while unconscious. The killer wanted to make it look as though there had been a struggle. He, she or they had probably wrapped my hand around the knife handle in order to leave my prints all over it.

Fear filled my chest and pressed against my lungs. It was the perfect stitch-up, crudely similar to the scenario four years ago. Then it was Benedict's body on the floor of a hotel room. Now it was Ruby Gillespie sprawled on tiles in her shower room.

And here I was again, standing over the body with blood on me.

I clenched my fists and bit my tongue. A rush of nausea sent me stumbling into the bedroom where I vomited over the bed sheets.

My throat burned and my eyes watered. For a few seconds stinging tears blurred everything around me.

I straightened up and tried to steady my breathing. There was a bitter taste in my mouth and my throat hurt. I knew I had to somehow seize control of the situation and get my mind working before I was paralysed by terror.

I pushed down the impulse to take out my phone and alert the police. If they turned up now it would appear to them that I was as guilty as sin. Another open and shut case.

It was already on record that Ruby had been upset by my previous visit. How could I possibly make them believe that I hadn't killed her? There was the message asking me to come to the house. Her blood on my clothes. My prints everywhere.

Fuck, fuck, fuck.

I turned to have another look at the body and used every fibre of my being to stop myself screaming. I wanted to believe that it wasn't happening – that it was a bad dream from which I would soon wake up.

But of course it wasn't and I had to get my thoughts in gear if I was to work out what to do.

I took a deep breath and walked out of the bedroom onto the landing. There I stood and listened for sounds from downstairs. But I heard nothing.

I forced myself to look in the two other bedrooms and bathroom to make sure the attacker wasn't lurking behind a door. But the rooms were empty.

I walked downstairs on legs that felt fragile, half-expecting someone to jump out on me. But I was alone in the house. All the other rooms were empty as well.

In the kitchen I went to the sink, turned on the tap and splashed cold water on my face. Then I paced the floor, biting my lip.

If I wasn't going to call the police then I needed to come up with a plan. Would it be possible for me to fix things so that nobody would ever know I had come here in response to Ruby's text message? It was a tall order and would entail removing all the evidence of my presence. That included the knife, my prints, my vomit with its mass of DNA.

I was still thinking about it five minutes later when I heard the loud wail of a siren.

I rushed into the living room and turned off the light. The curtains were closed, and I pulled them open slightly to look out onto the street.

The sight of a police patrol car pulling into the kerb in front of the house chilled me to the bone.

I realised it was too late to do anything other than open the door or flee the scene.

It took me a split second to decide that if I stayed I'd be arrested and banged up for the rest of my life. I just couldn't see how I could convince the police that I hadn't murdered Ruby.

So blind panic sent me tearing back into the kitchen where an unlocked door gave access to the back garden.

I heard the front doorbell ring as I stepped outside. And as I sprinted across the lawn towards the rear fence I couldn't help thinking about the mountain of incriminating evidence I had left behind.

I ran like the clappers across the grass, arms pumping, legs pounding. A voice in my head roared: *Don't stop. Get away.*

The garden fence loomed about six feet high so I threw myself at it in a desperate bid to get a purchase. Luckily I did, which allowed me to pull myself up and over. I landed with a heavy thud on the other side, a narrow alley between the houses.

There was just enough light for me to get my bearings. I swallowed my racing breath and shook my head to clear the fuzziness.

I heard a dog bark in one of the gardens. Then the wail of another siren. I had to keep moving. No time to pause, not even for a second.

I moved off to the left where the alley came to an end about thirty yards away. I had no idea where to go or what I would do when I got there. All I could think about was putting distance between me and the police.

I reached the end of the alley, which opened out onto a side street. I stepped cautiously onto the pavement and looked both ways. There was no one about. I decided to cross the road.

But it proved to be a mistake. I was halfway across when I heard a shout. I turned and saw that a uniformed copper had come around the corner and was walking towards me with a torch in his hand. I guessed he was one of the officers who had arrived in the patrol car and had come to check the back of Ruby's house.

He lifted the torch, and the beam briefly touched my face.

Shit.

I broke into a run again, which prompted the copper to shout for me to stop. But I ignored him and moved as fast as I could along the street in the direction of the sprawling Southampton Common.

I crossed over several more roads and entered the south section of the Common through Cemetery Road. The cop was close behind me. Too close. If I didn't lose him quickly then his colleagues would join the chase and I wouldn't stand a chance.

I veered onto the first path which took me into the woods. The darkness enveloped me. There were no lights and I was running blind for much of the way.

At the same time my breath was laboured and my lungs were struggling to suck in oxygen. As the bushes petered out, I found myself bearing down on a pub that was set back from the road. I stopped short of the near-empty car park and stepped up behind a large oak tree, praying the copper hadn't spotted me.

I stood with my back pressed up against the trunk, holding my breath while listening for his footfalls.

And they weren't long in coming. Ten seconds maybe. But to my great relief he walked past the tree towards the pub, all the time speaking into his radio and telling whoever was listening that he had lost me.

He came within a few yards of the tree and the torch's beam washed over the ground around it. But then he quickly moved away, and I was able to let out a long, silent breath.

I waited until I couldn't hear him any longer and then peered out from behind the tree. I saw him walking across the car park towards the pub.

That was when I made my move and stepped backwards into the bushes.

Then I left the Common and legged it across The Avenue and down the road to the right of St Andrew's Church. I hugged the shadows as I hurried along several quiet, dimly lit streets. All the time I could hear the urgent clamour of police sirens heading towards Ruby's house.

But I didn't spot any more patrol cars or officers on foot. I did, however, pass several pedestrians who gave me strange looks and wide berths.

I headed south, skirting Bevois Valley and the Royal South Hants hospital, and after a while I found myself in an industrial area close to the river that meanders through the city. It was a quiet part of town late at night, and all the buildings were in darkness.

I came to one that looked as though it was derelict. Around the back, facing the river, there was a covered loading area which struck me as a good place to stop and take stock of my dire situation.

I sat on the cold, concrete floor up against a wall. My body was numb, my mind in utter disarray. Despair now consumed me like a black, suffocating cloud.

It was hard for me to take in what had happened and harder still to see a way out of the terrible mess I was in.

The voices in my head were at odds with each other. One was telling me that I shouldn't have fled the scene, that I should have opened the door to the police and told them exactly what had transpired from the moment I received Ruby's text message.

But the other voice was saying they would never have believed me – just like they didn't believe me the last time – so to have stayed would have been a huge mistake.

But by running away I was still in deep shit. It wouldn't take the police long to find out I'd been in the house, and the planted evidence would convince them I had killed Ruby.

It was only a matter of time before they caught me or I was forced to turn myself in.

My thoughts spun around, trying to work their way out of my head. I was too traumatised even to cry. So I just sat there, rigid as a tent peg, my body shivering despite the fact that the air felt warm.

I kept seeing Ruby's body on the tiled floor, the knife jutting out of her chest. The image looped in my head, making me feel sick.

Then suddenly I saw Scar's face and a sharp pain pricked my heart.

Oh God, what had I done?

I didn't dare try to imagine the pain and suffering she was about to experience. I'd let her down big time. If only I had ignored Ruby's message. Why the hell hadn't I stuck to my word?

Because you're selfish, Lizzie. And so fucking stupid.

It struck me then that I needed to talk to Scar. I had to tell her what had happened and warn her that the police would soon descend on the flat.

I didn't dare try to return there. I'd be too exposed, and the roads in that part of town would be buzzing with cop cars.

I fumbled for my phone and speed-dialled Scar's number. As I waited for the call to connect, I tried to work out what to say, but the words wouldn't come together.

The phone rang and rang and I prayed that she'd answer it. But if she was still asleep and the phone was in the other room, then she might not hear the ringing.

Pick up, babe! Please.

A recorded message eventually kicked in, and my heart tried to crack open my ribs. A terrible thought pulsed through me: what if I never saw Scar again? It was a horrid possibility, and it caused me to let out an anguished cry.

With a huge adrenaline rush, I jumped to my feet and tried to compose myself. The question facing me was what was I going to do? The short answer was: I had no idea.

But I had to do something. I couldn't walk around the city aimlessly for hours or even days on end.

I looked out across the river towards Woolston. Lights shone in hundreds of flats and I envied the people who were safely ensconced in their homes. Why couldn't I be one of them? Why did life have to be so cruel to me?

I was about to start walking again, because I couldn't think what else to do, when my phone rang.

It was Scar. I hesitated before answering.

'Lizzie! Is that you?'

I had to force the words out through the crimp in my throat.

'Something's happened,' I said. 'I need to talk to you.'

'What? I thought you were in bed. Where are you?'

I knew then that I had to see her. It wouldn't be enough just to explain myself over the phone.

'Get dressed as quickly as you can and come and meet me,' I said.

'I don't understand. What's going on?'

'Please don't ask any questions, babe. Just move your ass.'

'But you're scaring me. Why aren't you here?'

'I'll tell you when I see you.'

'Where are you, for God's sake?'

I had to think quickly. I didn't know exactly where I was so I needed to come up with a location.

'Shamrock Quay,' I said. 'It's down by the waterfront close to the football stadium. I'll be waiting at the entrance.'

'But Lizzie . . .'

'Just hurry, please. I need to see you before it's too late.'

I hung up then before she could ask any more questions. As I shoved my phone back in my pocket, my body convulsed with a violent shudder, and I threw up for the second time that evening.

19

I set out for Shamrock Quay, a busy marina and boat building centre by day, but a quiet spot at night after the restaurants close. I reckoned it would take me about ten minutes to get there if I didn't get held up along the way.

The streets seemed to close in on me as I walked. With every step I could feel the tension build and the fear grow. My heart was racing and pounding in my chest, limbs trembling uncontrollably.

Plus, I was having second thoughts about meeting Scar. Was it fair of me to involve her? The police would surely find out and accuse her of being an accessory, and that was the last thing I wanted.

But I still couldn't bring myself to go it alone. My emotions were spinning out of control and the panic was like a flaming ball inside me.

I was desperately scared, but it helped me to focus right now on just one thing: spending a few minutes with the woman I loved before both our worlds imploded.

I walked as fast as I could, but still Scar beat me to Shamrock Quay. It came as a huge relief because it meant I didn't have to hang around. I saw her car as I shuffled along the pavement towards the entrance. She was standing next to it looking out for me. The sight of her made my eyes sting and my heart jump.

It was gone midnight so the area was deserted. She'd parked in an unlit part of the street and I didn't see any CCTV cameras close by.

Scar spotted me as I dashed across the road, and as I approached her my insides knotted up.

'What the fuck is going on?' she yelled when I was close enough to hear.

'Just get in the car,' I said.

I opened the passenger door and slipped in and Scar got in beside me. The engine had been left running and the dashboard lights were on.

'We need to go somewhere secluded,' I said. 'We're too exposed here. I know a place not far away.'

She stared at me, her eyes bulbous and fixed, and I felt awash with shame.

'What have you done, Lizzie?' she said through tight lips. 'Please tell me.'

She looked terrified. Her hair was a ragged mess, her eyes streaked and bloodshot.

'When we get there,' I said. 'Please just drive.'

With some reluctance, she engaged gear and we pulled away from the kerb.

She sat in furious silence during the few minutes it took to get to an isolated spot in the shadow of the city's Itchen bridge. It was a small unlit parking area that served another waterside industrial complex, a short distance from the St Mary's football stadium.

205

When we pulled up she killed the engine and turned to face me. The silence was suddenly so profound that it roared in my ears.

'So come on, Lizzie,' she said. 'Where have you been and what have you done?'

Her eyes burned in a way I hadn't seen before. I wanted to cry, but I was afraid that if I started I wouldn't be able to stop.

'I've fucked up, babe,' I said. 'Really badly. And I don't know what to do.'

She continued to look at me, her fear clouded with confusion.

'But I don't get it. We went to bed together. We were both asleep.'

'You slept, Donna. I couldn't. So I got up to have a smoke. And that's when I got a text from Ruby.'

I started to tell her everything. But it wasn't easy. My words kept getting trapped by lumps of emotion.

Her features twisted in anger and disbelief as she listened, and when I was finished she said, 'You stupid, stupid woman. You told me it was over. You promised you'd let it go.'

She started sobbing then, deep anguished sobs that were distressing to hear. My body ached at the thought of what I had done and what I'd lost. My mind filled with sadness and pain and my chest became a symphony of agonising drumbeats.

'I'm so sorry,' I said, and I knew I sounded pathetic.

She stared at me through her tears, her brow furrowed, her glare intense.

'I can't believe it,' she muttered. 'Everything is ruined.'

My face flushed with shame and the ball of sadness expanded in my chest so much I felt it was choking me.

She squeezed her eyes shut as the tears rolled down her cheeks, and her nose began to run.

I leaned towards her and held her face in my hands. She opened her eyes and looked at me.

'I'll turn myself in,' I said. 'I realise now that it's the only option open to me. I just had to see you first.'

She took a large breath and shook her head.

'You can't do that, Lizzie. The police will never believe you. You'll go to prison for the rest of your life.'

'But I can't run away,' I said. 'I've got nowhere to go and they'd eventually catch up with me.'

Scar reached up and moved my hands away from her face, but she held onto them.

'I won't let them take you away, Lizzie. Even though you're a fool and a liar, I know you're not a murderer. And I also know I love you, and my life wouldn't be worth living if you went back inside.'

Her words sent a shiver down my spine. 'But what can I do? It won't be long before every copper in the county is looking for me. There's enough evidence in Ruby's house to get me convicted in a nanosecond.'

'Then it's a case of fight instead of flight,' she said. 'The people who did this to you will be thinking that they've solved their problem, that you'll soon be out of the way so they won't have to worry any more about being exposed. It means they won't be expecting you to go after them. But that's precisely what you're going to have to do. And it might not be as hard as you think because you at least know who they are.'

Relief squirmed in the pit of my belly. I could barely believe that Scar was prepared to stick by me despite the gravity of my current situation and despite my recent actions. Her words gave me a frisson of hope, even though the fear was still thick inside me.

She pulled me to her and gave me a hug, which ignited an almighty pang of guilt. I didn't deserve her forgiveness or her unconditional love, and I struggled to rein in the tears.

'We've got nothing to lose, Lizzie,' she said. 'We either go for it or you give up and accept that both our lives are over.'

I could see the desperation in her eyes and it moved me.

'Do you think we can do it?' I said.

She nodded. 'It's what we've *been* doing, Lizzie. Digging at the truth. Only now the stakes are much, much higher.'

She was right on that score. It was no longer just about avenging Leo's death and unmasking those responsible for stitching me up the first time. It was now about self-preservation. Survival.

But my head was filled with dark clouds and self-doubt. I felt stressed and vulnerable and I wasn't sure I had the resolve to take on the challenge.

'Think about *us*, Lizzie,' Scar said. 'And think about your mother and brother. If you go back to prison our futures will be a living hell.'

I swallowed hard and took a deep breath, then clicked my internal dialogue into the positive and told myself that it was still possible to expose the bastards and save my own skin.

'You've convinced me,' I said with a wavering smile. 'Let's do it.'

We stayed in the car to talk it through. We couldn't just drive off without a plan of action. Outside, a thin rain started up and we watched it weeping down the windscreen.

Scar removed a pack of cigarettes from her bag and we sparked up. I took a long, hungry drag, letting the nicotine get deep into my lungs. It eased the tension within me, but caused my voice to grate hoarsely as I spoke.

'So let's take stock of where we've got to,' I said. 'I've talked to all those who were on the list I drew up in prison. That's DCI Ash, Joe Strickland, Ruby Gillespie and Anne Benedict. Plus, the editor of *The Post* and the brother of Karina Gorski.'

'Don't forget the woman at the cemetery,' Scar said.

'That's right. Neil Ferris's widow, who I'm convinced is harbouring a guilty secret.'

'And then there's the lunatic with the tattoo.'

'Sean Delaney,' I said. 'It wouldn't surprise me if he's the one who killed Ruby and knocked me out.'

The mention of Ruby's name sent the image of her lying dead on the floor cartwheeling through my head.

'Why do you reckon she was murdered?' Scar said.

'Two reasons,' I answered. 'She became a liability after telling me she was made to lie in court about the knife. Also, the police knew I had a grudge against her and therefore it'd be easy to frame me for her murder.'

'And do you still think Strickland is behind both killings?'

'He has to be,' I said.

To me everything pointed to Strickland. He was at the heart of all that had happened, the eye of the vortex. All I had to do was prove it. It sounded so fucking simple.

'We should tell Tiny what's happened,' Scar said. 'He might be able to help us.'

I nodded. 'Good call. Maybe he can find out where Sean Delaney lives so that we can pay him a visit.'

'What about Strickland?'

'You've already got his address so we'll go there first.'

'If that's the plan then you need to be prepared to get rough. We can't hold back or pussyfoot around. If those guys won't open up then we have to make them.'

'I realise that,' I said. 'Which is why I'm glad you're with me. You've got experience when it comes to cutting off the testicles of men who upset you.'

I called Tiny, expecting him to be at home in Portsmouth. But he'd fallen asleep in his car outside my mother's house, and I woke him up.

He started to apologise but I cut in. 'That doesn't matter, Tiny. Everything has changed, and I need your help.'

I put the phone on speaker and told him that Scar was with me. Then I filled him in on what had happened and what we'd decided to do.

I thought he was going to try to talk us out of it, but instead he said, 'That's some fucking dilemma you're faced with. I can see why you're steering well clear of the police. They'll roast you.'

'My only hope is to get evidence to prove I didn't kill Ruby,' I said. 'Which means I have to go after those I believe to be responsible.'

'You mean Strickland and his team?'

'Exactly. We know where Strickland lives, but what I need from you is an address for Sean Delaney.'

'I told you before I don't have it,' Tiny said.

'But can you get it?'

'I could try.'

'Then please do. If he did kill Ruby then we need to get to him as quickly as we can.'

'Why not call the cops and steer them in that direction?'

'Because what happened tonight convinces me I can't trust them.'

'What do you mean?'

210

'Well, I didn't give my new mobile number to Ruby. Only you, Donna, my brother and the police had it. And yet a text message was sent to me from Ruby's phone.'

'So you think the police gave it to her?'

'More likely to her killer because I'm pretty sure he's the one who sent it.'

'Jesus, Lizzie. This gets worse by the second.'

'It was all part of the set-up to get me to go to the house and find the body,' I said. 'First the text, then Ruby's front door was left open, then I found the body and got clobbered. Finally the police patrol car turned up. I'm guessing they were meant to get me before I had a chance to scarper.'

Tiny was silent for a few moments, then said, 'I see where you're coming from, Lizzie, but you both need to be careful. What you're planning to do is bloody dangerous. A thousand things could go wrong.'

'I know that,' I said. 'But the alternatives are just as shitty. Hand myself in or go on the run. Either way I'm fucked.'

It wasn't until after I'd hung up on Tiny that I realised I'd drawn him into my mess as well. When the police eventually checked my phone the calls made on it would reveal that I'd been in contact with him.

It was another factor that added to my burden of guilt and made me feel like such a bad person.

20

All the information Scar had collected for me while I was still in prison had been kept in a file on her phone. So she was able to retrieve Joe Strickland's address as we drove away from the deserted industrial estate.

He lived in an upmarket area of Southampton known as Chilworth, where some of the city's most expensive houses were located.

The tension inside the car positively crackled as we drove there. I tried to keep calm, telling myself that we hadn't set ourselves an impossible task. It was achievable. We just had to be positive and hold our nerve. But that didn't stop my stomach from fluttering or my head from aching.

The roads were much less busy now, and that increased our sense of unease. We passed two police cars and I fully expected the second one to pull us over. Instead, it flew by with its blue light flashing and sped in the direction of Ruby's house.

A constant soul-destroying drizzle accompanied us across the city. We talked about what we were going to do when we got to

Strickland's place. But, of course, we couldn't be sure how things would unfold until we arrived. We'd have to play it by ear because we didn't know if he'd be alone.

His wife was probably with him and we felt sure we could handle her. But it would be more of an issue if he had a couple of minders on the premises for protection.

We were five minutes from Chilworth when my phone rang, and it made us both jump. I took it out of my pocket, but didn't recognise the number that appeared in the display window.

'Should I answer it?' I said. 'It isn't Tiny.'

Scar raised her brow. 'Then it could be the filth.'

'Shit.'

'Answer it anyway,' she said. 'If it is them we'll at least find out if they're already looking for you.'

I tapped the green key and my breath hitched in my throat when I heard DS McGrath's voice.

'Is that you, Lizzie?'

'Who is this?' I said.

'You know who it is, Lizzie. Where are you?'

'It's the middle of the night, for Christ's sake. What do you want?'

He pushed out a sigh. 'Don't play games, Lizzie. For your sake. Now tell me where you are so that we can come and talk to you.'

I felt the blood start pumping in my head and a cold sweat form on my brow. Scar reached out, put her hand on my knee, squeezed it.

'Why do you want to talk to me?' I said into the phone.

McGrath paused for a long beat and took a breath. 'A woman seen running away from Ruby Gillespie's house matches your description, Lizzie. We've also checked Ruby's phone so we know you went to the house, and we know what you did.'

'I didn't do it,' I said. 'She was dead when I got there.'

'So why didn't you explain that to the officers when they arrived?'

'It was another stitch-up,' I said. 'That's why the police went to the house just after I got there.'

'They were responding to a call,' McGrath said. 'Someone phoned in to report hearing screams in the house.'

'Well, whoever that was killed her,' I said. 'When I got there I was hit over the head and knocked unconscious. When I came to I had blood on me and you'll probably find my prints on the knife. But I didn't put them there.'

'Then you've got nothing to worry about have you? Let us bring you in, and you can tell us exactly what happened.'

'I don't think so,' I said. 'You've already made up your minds that I did it. Just like the last time.'

'That's not true, Lizzie. I'll make sure you're treated fairly.'

'Don't make me laugh,' I said. 'You'll do whatever Ash tells you to do and he'll take great pleasure in fucking me over.'

'But you can't just run away from this. You've got nowhere to go.'

'I'm already miles away from Southampton,' I said. 'And I know exactly where I'm going. It's somewhere you'll never find me.'

'You're making a big mistake. The further you run the guiltier you'll look.'

'But if I come back I know I'll never see the light of day again.'

'You can't be sure of that.'

'I can and you know it. I've been set up good and proper. Whoever is responsible has done a fantastic job. I've lost and they've won, and I hope they rot in fucking hell.'

I abruptly ended the call and switched off the phone so the signal couldn't be traced.

'How did I do?' I said to Scar.

She gave a thoughtful nod. 'You sounded really convincing. He probably thinks you're halfway up the M3 by now.'

Strickland's large detached house was set back from the road and surrounded by high, manicured hedges.

Scar pulled into the kerb across from it between two parked cars.

The street was wide and poorly lit, with neatly spaced trees and crew-cut verges.

She switched off the engine and in the silence that consumed us I could hear the nervous rhythm of her heartbeat.

'So how do we go about this?' I said.

There was no gate, just an opening between two brick pillars. Beyond it a short driveway led up to a two-storey Tudor-style property. A flashy BMW was parked in front of the garage.

Several lights were on inside, which was surprising considering it was past one in the morning.

'I suggest we walk straight up to the front door and ring the bell,' Scar said. 'When someone answers we barge right in and get down to business.'

I felt a strange dose of excitement because I knew I had nothing to lose. The prospect of getting my hands on Joe Strickland was a real incentive to take this diabolical risk.

I was psyching myself up with mindful images of Leo, Rufus Benedict and Ruby Gillespie.

We made sure the coast was clear before we got out of the car. The street was empty and the light drizzle persisted. I was pretty confident that no one saw us cross the road. Once we entered Strickland's property, we moved off the gravel driveway onto the wet grass and stepped up behind a large rhododendron bush. From there we were able to scan the front of the house. Two rooms downstairs had lights on and one upstairs. Curtains were pulled across the upstairs window, but those downstairs we could see inside.

To the left was the kitchen, and it appeared to be empty. The other window was much larger and gave us a view of the living room. We could see a figure inside moving around.

The rain made it impossible for us to see if it was a man or a woman, so we had to creep around the bush and move closer to the house.

Crouching low, we then stepped onto the driveway and sidled up against the BMW. From there we were able to see across the bonnet into the living room where it was clear that the figure was Joe Strickland and he was pacing the floor with a phone to his ear.

'I don't see anyone else,' Scar said, wiping a film of rain from her face. 'I'm guessing the wife is in bed, and there are no minders.'

'Then let's get moving,' I said.

But just as I took a step towards the front door, Scar grabbed my hand and jerked me back behind the BMW.

'Get down,' she gasped, and if I'd hesitated for even a fraction of a second I would have been caught in the glare of a pair of powerful headlights.

They belonged to a car that turned off the road onto the driveway. Its brakes squealed as it came to a stop a few feet from where we were crouching down behind the BMW.

The lights were extinguished, and we heard the car door open and then shut again.

Footfalls sounded on the gravel, and I couldn't resist raising myself far enough to see who was approaching the house.

But I caught only a blurred glimpse of a man's back before he disappeared inside the covered porch. He didn't have to ring the bell because the front door opened straight away, and he disappeared inside. A few seconds later, however, the visitor appeared as large as life in the living room. When I saw who it was my mind filled with red mist.

'You bent bastard,' I cursed aloud.

'I take it you know him,' Scar said.

'Damn bloody right I do,' I told her. 'That's my old friend Detective Chief Inspector Martin Ash.'

I saw Ash's appearance as proof that he was part of the whole ugly conspiracy.

He was Strickland's man on the inside, a corrupt copper who was without scruples. A man prepared to turn a blind eye to the most heinous of crimes.

It explained why I'd been so easily fitted up over Rufus Benedict's murder. Ash and Neil Ferris – as the lead officers on the case – had been in a position to manipulate the evidence and I was certain now that they did.

Why else was Strickland's involvement so readily dismissed despite him having had a motive for wanting Benedict silenced? And was it possible they had concealed or doctored vital security video that might have shown the two killers entering the hotel?

Now I wondered if Ash had also played a part in Ruby Gillespie's murder. Had he known it was going to happen? Maybe he had even suggested it as a way to solve two problems in one go: me and the woman who had decided to reveal a secret she'd kept for four years.

'We can't go in now,' Scar said, breaking into my thoughts. 'We should go back to the car.'

'He might not stay for long.'

217

'Or he could be here for ages, Lizzie. And I'm already soaked through.'

I turned to look at her. Unlike me she wasn't wearing a jacket, and her black T-shirt was plastered to her skin.

'You're right,' I said. 'I'm sorry. Let's go.'

We kept close to the hedge as we made our way back to the entrance. Seconds later we were seated in the car, and our wet clothes were causing the windows to steam up.

Scar put the heating on and we sat in silence for a few minutes. I had to blink back tears of rage and frustration that started to gather in my eyes.

'That was a close call,' Scar said, her voice barely raised above the sound of the rain on the windscreen. 'He must have come here to tell Strickland you're on the run.'

'Ash probably wants to make sure that all the angles have been covered,' I said. 'If I'm not in custody then things can still go wrong for them. If I had a gun I'd march in there now and confront them both. I'd soon get a confession out of them.'

'It's tempting, I know,' Scar replied. 'But without a gun or an army we're no match for them.'

I clenched my jaw and pushed my teeth together so tight it hurt. Nothing felt real to me any more. It was as though everything that was happening was part of a relentless nightmare.

I asked Scar for a cigarette and as she was reaching for her bag her phone rang. She checked it and said, 'It's Tiny.'

I stopped breathing while I waited for her to tell me what he had to say.

With the phone still to her ear, she said, 'He went to the Centurion bar and arrived just as Sean Delaney was leaving in his car. Tiny followed him home.'

'Where does Delaney live?' I asked.

'On a houseboat on the river at Bursledon,' she said. 'A secluded spot, apparently. Tiny's still there watching the place and wants to know what to do.'

'Get him to give you directions,' I said excitedly. 'It's too good a chance to miss. We'll go straight there and come back here later.'

21

The River Hamble runs along the eastern edge of Southampton and is famous for its marinas and boat yards. One of its lesser known features is a small community of houseboats along several tiny inlets. The boats are set back from the main river and surrounded by marsh and woodland.

I recalled seeing a news item about them on the local TV years ago when one of them was put up for sale for hundreds of thousands of pounds.

The spot was easy to get to. We took the main road out of the city and drove through the village of Bursledon, then followed a narrow lane over railway tracks to a small, deserted yard. From this spot a jetty zig zagged out across the marshland to where between eight and ten houseboats were moored.

Tiny was waiting for us in the unlit parking area. He seemed relieved to see us, but it was Scar he went to first, putting his arm around her shoulders and kissing her on the forehead.

'What happened at Strickland's house?' he asked.

'Detective Ash turned up while we were skulking in the front garden,' I said. 'So we had to retreat.'

'I really feel for you, Lizzie,' Tiny said. 'It must have been a terrible shock to find Ruby Gillespie like that.'

'It was,' I said. 'And I'm hoping that Sean Delaney will be just as shocked when we pay him a surprise visit.'

Tiny pointed to one of several other cars parked close by and said it belonged to Delaney.

'He came straight here from the Centurion. He left there with his cousin Ron Parks, who drove off in a different direction.'

'It could be that one or both of them went to have a drink and secure an alibi after leaving Ruby's house. Is Delaney alone now?'

Tiny nodded. 'I think so. I couldn't follow him all the way along the jetty, but from where I stood it looked as though he unlocked the cabin door once he was on board, and there were no lights on inside.'

'Well, show us which houseboat is his and you can leave us to it.'

'Are you kidding me?' he said. 'I'm coming with you.'

I shook my head. 'No, Tiny. I don't want you to get more involved than you already are.'

'And neither do I,' Scar said. 'It wouldn't be fair.'

'Forget it, ladies. No way am I letting you confront this guy by yourselves. He's a dangerous head case.'

Scar and I exchanged looks and she gave a barely perceptible nod.

'I suppose I would feel safer if he was with us,' she said.

I allowed the faintest of smiles to flick across my face, then patted Tiny's arm and felt a surge of gratitude flood through me.

'Okay, big boy,' I said. 'Welcome to the team.'

*   *   *

221

We followed Tiny through some trees to where the jetty began. Luckily there was a break in the cloud cover, and the moon's milky glow shone above the river and the winding creeks that led into it.

It took me a few seconds to pick out the dark shapes of the various houseboats. They looked like giant slugs resting in the mud. There were no lights on any of them.

'It's that one over there,' Tiny said, pointing.

It was over to the right at the edge of the inlet and separated from the others by about fifty yards. A prime position that must have commanded terrific views during the day.

The rain had eased to a light spray in the breeze, and the air was thick with the smell of the sea.

We walked along the jetty as quietly as possible, and when we got to Delaney's houseboat, the three of us stopped and listened for any sounds from inside. But all was quiet.

'I propose we just storm on board like it's a police raid and surprise him,' Tiny said. 'If we try the softy-softly approach he might hear us if he's not yet asleep.'

Instinctively, I reached out and held Scar's hand. It was warm and clammy.

'Are you sure you're up for this?' I said.

'Of course I am. Now let's just get on with it.'

The speed with which Tiny jumped on board took us by surprise. We were still clambering up after him when he kicked open the cabin door. A second later he was inside and there was a lot of noise and cursing.

By the time I followed him in he had Delaney pinned to the floor in the main living area. We learned later that Delaney had leapt out of bed on hearing a noise outside, but hadn't been quick enough to get the better of his unwelcome visitor.

When I switched on the light, Delaney was face down, and Tiny was sitting astride him. Delaney was naked and muscles bulged along every part of his body.

A chair had been knocked over along with a glass vase that had shattered into pieces.

'Who the fuck are you?' Delaney was yelling. 'What do you want?'

Tiny put a hand against the back of his head and pushed his face into the carpet.

'Keep quiet and still or I'll break both your arms,' he warned him.

Scar and I walked further into the cabin and looked around. It was an open-plan set-up with a sofa and armchair at one end and a kitchen with a dining table at the other.

'We need to find something we can use to tie his hands,' Scar said.

We found a ball of string in one of the kitchen drawers. I used a carving knife to cut off a length that Tiny wrapped around Delaney's wrists.

Tiny then hauled him up and pushed him into one of the chairs. He started to struggle, but Tiny whipped an arm around his neck and squeezed, causing Delaney to choke and splutter.

'You're going nowhere, creep, so behave yourself,' Tiny said.

When he was still, Tiny let go of his neck, and Delaney sucked in a couple of ragged breaths, his face flushed red.

He suddenly didn't look so tough and threatening with his small, flaccid penis hanging between his thighs. My eyes zoomed in on the pit bull tattoo on his chest and it brought back the painful memory of what he'd done to me in the alley.

Having neutralised our victim, all three of us stepped in front of him and I aimed the knife at his face.

223

Alarm shivered behind his eyes when he saw me. His mouth fell open and a thin line of saliva stretched between his upper and lower lips.

'We're here to find out all you know about the murders of Rufus Benedict and Ruby Gillespie,' I said. 'But please don't spill your guts too soon because I've got a lot of anger that I need to work out of my system first.'

I felt like I was possessed by a demon – but not against my will. The rage and hatred that stirred inside me was a welcome sensation.

Sitting before me was the man I believed to be one of the architects of my downfall. The same man who had beaten me and my brother and in all probability had murdered Ruby Gillespie.

He was a cold, sadistic creature and he deserved all the pain I intended to inflict.

'I don't know about any murders,' he said. 'So don't waste your time or mine.'

Heat rose in my face. I put the knife in my left hand and lashed out with my right fist, striking a solid blow against his nose, which started spurting blood.

Through gritted teeth he called me a bitch and sprang to his feet. But Tiny shoved him back on the chair and then stood behind him with a firm grip on his shoulders to stop him moving again.

'I recognise you,' Delaney said, flicking his head backwards and his eyes sideways. 'You used to work for Joe.'

'Is that right?' Tiny said.

'Yeah, it is. I never forget a face and I'll make sure you bloody well pay for this.'

That was my cue to strike him again, and it gave me great pleasure to give him a fierce kick in the shin. His face twisted up in pain and blood vessels bulged out of his temples.

He glared at me defiantly and was about to say something when Scar stepped forward and gave him three sharp slaps around the face.

'That was for beating up my girlfriend and threatening to rape her, you bastard,' she said, her voice remarkably calm in the circumstances.

I was reminded of the time in prison when Scar and I had launched a joint attack against a notorious bully named Thelma Lamb who had threatened to kill us both for refusing to do her bidding.

It was the last threat she ever made against us because she was transferred to a hospital, and we learned later that she suffered two fractured ribs, a broken nose and a dislocated jaw.

So the pair of us were far from squeamish when it came to resorting to violence when we felt it was necessary. It was something Sean Delaney was about to discover.

'So let's start with the easy questions,' I said. 'Why did you attack my brother and me?'

His expression remained defiant, and he spat at me, the dollop of phlegm landing on my jacket.

'Go fuck yourself, bitch,' he yelled. 'I'm not telling you anything.'

I couldn't help smiling because I wanted so much to hurt this man and I just needed the excuse to do so.

'I'll ask you again,' I said evenly. 'Why did you attack us?'

His mouth twitched at the corners and he shook his head.

'You don't scare me, bitch. And you don't fool me either. I know you haven't got what it takes for this stuff.'

Without warning I slashed the blade of the carving knife across his chest so it left a line of blood between the eyes of the pit bull. He let out a fearsome scream and stared down at himself in disbelief.

'Way to go girl,' Scar said and gave him another savage slap around the face for good measure.

Tiny let out a low whistle and said, 'Jesus. Remind me not to get on the wrong side of you two psychos.'

I was on a roll now, in the grip of a primal urge to inflict pain on this sorry excuse for a man.

I slashed him again with the knife, this time across the forehead, leaving a gash about five inches long.

He moaned and threw his head back, the veins in his neck bulging outwards.

'Now start talking,' I said, spacing my words out and speaking slowly. 'I promise you that this won't end until you've told us everything.'

There was uncertainty in his expression now as blood spilled from his forehead into his eyes.

I found it hard to control the disgust I felt for him. I knew that whatever I did to him it wouldn't impact on my conscience. My rage was a result of four years of torment, anger and frustration.

'If I was you, Delaney, I'd start telling her what she wants to know,' Tiny advised him. 'If you don't then I hate to think what state your body and mind will be in at the end of this little party.'

Delaney lowered his head, shifting his gaze to the floor. Blood dripped from his face onto his thighs.

'Go to hell,' he murmured.

His words sliced through me like a rotor blade, releasing a surge of raw anger. I reacted by stamping down hard on his left

226

foot. I heard the crack of bone as the heel of my shoe crushed his toes.

I then did the same to his right foot and to stop him from screaming Tiny put a hand over his mouth.

'Not so tough now, are you?' I said. 'Do you really think Joe Strickland will appreciate what you're doing? Don't you realise that by the time we've finished with you, you'll be a fucking cripple and Strickland won't have any use for you?'

Tiny removed his hand and Delaney breathed in deeply through his flared nostrils.

I could see that we were getting to him. He must have understood by now that we were serious, that we weren't going to leave until we got what we wanted. I couldn't afford to anyway. This was in all probability my last desperate throw of the dice. I needed him to open up and tell us what had been going on. I wouldn't get another opportunity like this with the net closing in around me.

'Why did you attack me?' I said again. 'Did Joe Strickland tell you to? And did he also get you to kill Ruby Gillespie and Rufus Benedict?'

He shook his head, spraying blood over himself. And then he looked at me with dead eyes, but said nothing.

'This is ridiculous,' Scar said and suddenly snatched the knife from my grip.

She bent over and with her free hand lifted his limp penis and pressed the tip of the knife against the base of the shaft. It drew a spot of blood and on seeing it sheer terror transformed Delaney's expression.

'I went to prison for cutting off a bloke's balls,' Scar said. 'So believe me when I say that I won't hesitate to slice off your pathetic little cock if you don't start coughing up.'

The threat of losing his manhood was enough to weaken his resolve.

'Okay, okay,' he spluttered. 'I'll tell you. Just take that fucking knife away.'

Sean Delaney actually began to cry, big drops of tears streaming from his eyes. When he started to speak, his face twitched and contorted, but none of us felt inclined to make it any easier for him. We just stood there hanging on to his every word.

'Joe told us to rough you and your brother up,' he said. 'He wanted to stop you making trouble for him. He thought it'd be enough.'

'What's he so worried about?' I asked.

He tried to blink away the blood that was gathering in his eyes and mixing with the tears. It didn't work and his discomfort gave me a perverse thrill.

'He learned a couple of weeks ago that your friend here was asking questions around town on your behalf,' he said, flicking his head towards Scar. 'So he assumed you were gonna dig up the Benedict business, and he didn't want that.'

'Was it you who left the note on our car at the hotel?'

He frowned. 'What note? I don't know anything about a note.'

'Are you sure?'

'Positive.'

I didn't know whether to believe him or not, but I didn't want to hold him back now that he had started to talk. So I let that one go for now.

'Okay, so let's go back four years,' I said. 'Why did you kill Rufus Benedict? And please don't bother to deny it.'

He squeezed his eyes shut and held his breath. His face got darker, and every muscle in his body tensed up.

'Answer the question,' I said.

He opened his eyes, moistened his lips and managed to shake his head.

'I . . . I . . . can't.'

Which prompted Tiny to pummel a fist into the back of his head, causing a wheezing gulp of air to explode out of his mouth.

'You fucking can and you fucking will,' Tiny seethed. 'So stop pissing about and get on with it or my friend here will cut off your cock.'

Delaney started to foam at the mouth and for a moment I thought he might pass out. But instead he lifted his head and looked at me, his eyes thin and unfocused.

'You already know why Benedict had to die,' he said. 'He was working on a story that would have brought Joe down. So Joe had to sort him out.'

I felt a dark and seductive urge to stab Delaney through the heart. It took a huge effort to resist.

'So it was you and an accomplice who came to our hotel room that night,' I said. 'You drugged us with the champagne, killed Benedict and made it look like I did it.'

He squinted at me, but didn't say anything. He didn't have to.

'So was the other man Ron Parks, your cousin?'

He let out an involuntary groan and nodded.

I felt Scar's hand grip my arm. I turned to look at her, saw that her face was ashen, drained of blood. She forced out a smile and squeezed my arm reassuringly.

I turned back to Delaney and made a sneering shape with my mouth.

'Tell me why you killed Ruby Gillespie,' I said.

His chest muscles contracted beneath the blood that covered much of his torso, and his breathing became harsh.

'She couldn't keep her gob shut,' he said. 'She told you that we made her lie to the police about you and the knife. Big mistake. We knew then we couldn't trust her not to tell anyone else. So Joe decided to kill two birds with one stone and get you both out of the way.'

Even though it was what I'd suspected it came as a massive shock. I felt a violent surge of hostility towards Sean Delaney. I wanted to kill him for what he had done to me and to his other victims. But I knew I had to keep him alive so that he could tell his story to the police and clear my name.

It was Scar who spoke next, her voice low and quivering.

'What did Karina Gorski have to do with all of this?' she said.

Delaney struggled to get the words out. 'I don't know. I wasn't told.'

'Was she in a relationship with Strickland?'

'He had a thing with her. It was just paid-for sex. She often stayed overnight in his flat.'

'Where is this flat?'

'Down at the marina. He uses it to entertain and for some business meetings. It's close to his office and his wife knows nothing about it.'

'And Karina went there regularly?'

'That's right.'

'So what happened?' Scar said. 'Did she find out something about him? Is that why he got you to kill her too?'

'We didn't kill her,' he said. 'She disappeared. No one knows where she is. One day she was on the scene and the next day she wasn't. I have no idea why.'

Was he telling the truth about that? I wasn't sure. But having confessed to killing Benedict and Ruby I couldn't see why he would lie about it.

'What about the police?' I said. 'How involved have they been in the cover-up?'

'I'm not sure.'

'Come off it, Delaney. DCI Ash is as bent as they come. And so was Neil Ferris. Joe Strickland must have called in favours to influence the investigation and to keep his name out of it.'

Delaney was struggling to respond now. He could barely keep his eyes open, and the loss of blood from the two knife wounds was making him weak.

I was worried he might lose consciousness and we'd have to get him to hospital.

'I need . . . some water,' he uttered. 'And please . . . wipe my eyes.'

He actually looked like he'd just stepped off the set of a horror movie. The blood covered most of his face and body and was even pooling on the chair between his legs.

'I'll sort it,' Tiny said.

What happened next I didn't see coming. None of us did.

As Tiny moved towards the sink, Delaney lowered his head and started to sob. I chose that moment to turn to Scar to see how she was holding up.

And that's when Delaney leapt from the chair with the speed of a striking panther.

He lifted his right knee and thrust it into my stomach. I stumbled back, winded, and dropped the knife on the floor.

Delaney then started shaking himself and struggled to free his hands from the string that tied them together behind his back.

He managed to do it before any of us could react, and he quickly bent over to pick up the knife.

Scar threw herself forward to try to prevent him reaching it, but she was too late. He was grasping the knife in his right hand as she fell against him and to my horror I saw him plunge the knife into her body.

I screamed and instinctively reached out to stop her falling, but her weight sent us both crashing to the floor.

I heard Tiny cry out, and in the same instant I saw Delaney staring down at me, still brandishing the knife with Scar's blood on it.

It looked as though he was going to stab me next. But he had difficulty staying upright on shattered feet and this gave Tiny the precious seconds he needed to launch himself across the room and get to Delaney before he could do any more damage.

Tiny rammed into him with brute force, narrowly avoiding the knife that was aimed at his chest.

They both stumbled against the dining table and then collapsed onto the floor in a grappling heap.

Delaney, despite the beating he'd taken, was still a force to be reckoned with, and managed to hold onto the knife which he thrust towards Tiny's throat.

Tiny seized his wrist and they rolled across the floor, leaving a trail of Delaney's blood on the polished decking.

I took my eyes off the pair for a second to look at Scar. She was on her back now and clutching the wound in her side, her face creased up in pain.

Oh God, please don't let her die.

'You bastard!'

It was Delaney's voice, and it drew my eyes back to the struggle that was happening just a few feet away.

Tiny had succeeded in pushing the knife away from his own throat, and the tip of the blade was now only inches from Delaney's face.

They were locked in a battle of strength and my heart froze as I watched Delaney open his mouth and growl like an attack dog.

But it was the last sound he made because at the same time his arm went limp, and the blade shot straight between his teeth and deep into the back of his throat.

22

My immediate concern was for Scar. I hunkered down next to her and panic threatened to overwhelm me when I saw the state she was in.

Blood was oozing from the wound in her left side, and her T-shirt was already soaked. But she was still conscious, thank God, and her eyes were open.

I bent over and touched her cheek.

'Stay with me, babe,' I said. 'We'll call an ambulance. You'll be okay.'

She moved her head. 'No ambulance. Too risky. Take me to the hospital.'

Tiny came and knelt beside me. He lifted her T-shirt to look at the wound. I was shocked to see there were actually two wounds – one where the blade had entered her body and the other where it had exited. They were only a couple of inches apart.

'That's a relief,' Tiny said. 'The blade went straight through the fatty tissue below the ribcage. It hasn't damaged any vital organs. But we need to stem the blood.'

He fished a white handkerchief from his pocket and placed it over the wounds, applying pressure to slow the rate of bleeding.

Then he told me to look for a first-aid kit. I found one in the cupboard below the sink.

He took out some gauze and bandages to dress the wounds.

'As a doorman I took a first-aid course,' he said. 'I've treated stab wounds before.'

I dropped to the floor again, held Scar's hand and told her that I was sorry.

'Not your fault,' she said, grimacing from the pain. 'We under-estimated him.'

I stroked her forehead. It was cold and wet, and her skin was white as bone.

'She's going to be all right,' Tiny said. 'But you need to get her to the hospital fast.'

'What about you?'

He tossed his head towards where Delaney lay on the floor.

'I need to clear up this mess. It'll take a while.'

'Is he dead?'

He nodded. 'For sure. And we can't let anyone find him like this.'

'Jesus Christ,' I said. 'What a fucking disaster.'

'I didn't mean to kill him, Lizzie. But it was him or me. I'm sorry.'

'What about? You had no choice.'

'I know. But you needed him alive. Now he can't tell the police what he told us.'

It was true, but worrying about Scar had made me overlook the fact. Now I felt a whole lot worse. I looked over at Delaney's blood-soaked corpse. The knife was still embedded in his mouth and the sight of it caused a tightening in my throat.

'So this was all for nothing,' Scar said and her words hit me like steel arrows.

I had to breathe in through my nose in order to fill my body with oxygen.

It was a total mess. A tragedy. Scar was seriously wounded, and Sean Delaney was dead. The police would add him to my list of victims, and Scar and Tiny would be in trouble too. I couldn't believe it had gone so wrong so quickly.

'That's all I can do for now,' Tiny said. 'I'll help you get her to the car. Go straight to A and E. Make up a story that she was attacked in the street or something.'

'What will you do?' I said.

He shook his head. 'I'm not sure yet. I can't just leave this like it is. Our prints are all over the place, along with some of Donna's blood. And I need to get rid of the knife.'

We lifted Scar to her feet, but she couldn't stand up so it was a real effort getting her off the houseboat.

Then Tiny carried her in his arms along the jetty and I followed. It had stopped raining but the clouds obscured the moon so it was pitch dark. It meant that even if we were being watched by someone they surely wouldn't be able to identify us.

When we reached the car I opened the doors and Tiny put Scar on the back seat. She was still awake and in a lot of pain.

'Take her phone from her bag,' Tiny said. 'I'll call you on her number. And don't worry. It's not as bad as it looks and it's not as serious as it could have been.'

He leaned inside to kiss Scar on the cheek, and I jumped in behind the wheel.

'Are you going to be all right?' I said to him.

'I'll be fine. Just get our girl to the hospital as quickly as you can.'

*   *   *

236

I drove like a maniac to the General Hospital and crashed through two red lights. I kept talking to Scar to keep her awake, but halfway there she lost consciousness.

I stopped the car in a panic and checked that she was still breathing. She was, and the dressings Tiny had applied to the wounds were still in place and holding back the blood.

As I drove I could feel the guilt colonising my thoughts, jabbing at my conscience. I blamed myself for Scar's condition and Ruby's murder. Neither would have happened if it hadn't been for me.

I was right back in my own personal hell, wading up to my neck in shit. Images from the last few hours were flying around in my skull and my resolve had turned to jelly.

Sean Delaney's confession should have cheered me up, but he might as well not have given it. With him dead there was still no way I could prove that Joe Strickland was behind both murders.

And as if that wasn't bad enough, the three of us had Delaney's blood on our hands.

Tiny may well have shoved the knife into his mouth, but in the eyes of the law we were all culpable.

I replayed the scene on the houseboat every which way, but I kept coming back to the undeniable conclusion that we had fucked up. And now we faced dire consequences.

At the hospital I brought the car to a screeching halt outside the emergency department. I climbed out and started yelling for help. Within seconds a couple of paramedics were lifting Scar out of the back seat, and I was telling them that she'd been stabbed.

They put her on a trolley and wheeled her inside. This woke her up, and she reached for my hand.

'We're here now, babe,' I said. 'The doctors will sort you out.'

Inside a trauma team surrounded us and questions were fired at me. I told them her name and said she was my girlfriend. I explained that she'd been attacked in the street by a man who had demanded money.

'There was a first-aid kit in the car,' I said. 'I used it to stop the blood.'

'She's a very lucky lady,' one of the doctors said after giving the wounds a cursory examination. 'The angle of penetration is such that the damage was confined to the fatty tissue at her waist. The loss of blood is not life-threatening and that's partly thanks to you and the good job you did. We'll stitch up the wounds and treat her for shock.'

The relief pounded through me and brought tears to the surface.

'Are you all right yourself?' the doctor said. 'I can see there's blood on your clothes.'

'It's not mine,' I said. 'It's Donna's.'

'Well, why don't you go and grab a coffee from the machine over there while we set your friend up in a cubicle? You look like you need it.'

'I will, thanks.'

'Did you call the police, by the way?'

I shook my head. 'There was no time.'

'Well, not to worry. A nurse is doing that as we speak. We're obliged to report knife wounds. They'll be here shortly so you can tell them what happened.'

The fear and dread grew inside me. It felt like a wire was tightening around my head.

What the hell was I going to do?

I walked trance-like along the corridor. There was a patient toilet next to the vending machine. I went in and closed the door behind me. It was a single cubicle so I was alone.

I was shocked at the sight of myself in the mirror. I looked like I'd been dragged through ten hedges backwards. My hair was a wet mess, and my face a sickly pallor. Even when things were really tough in prison I had never looked this bad.

I stared hard at my reflection and watched the tears slipping out of my eyes. Suddenly nothing seemed real any more. My mind was completely numb, as though it had been blasted with anaesthetic.

After a few moments I dropped my head in my hands and started to cry. The sobs poured out of me.

It was several minutes before I was able to pull myself together. I lowered my jeans and knickers and used the loo, then washed my hands and face in hot, soapy water. It did nothing to improve the way I looked, but it did reignite my thoughts so that I could put them to work on the immediate problem facing me: the imminent arrival of the police.

The stark choice was to stay and let them arrest me or leave Scar and run for it. I felt paralysed by indecision.

I told myself I needed a coffee to help stimulate my brain cells. Luckily I had enough change in my pocket for the vending machine. I opted for strong and black and I felt my blood warm as it swam through my body. I was still drinking it when a young nurse appeared to tell me that Scar was waiting for me.

'I'll show you where she is,' she said with a pleasant smile.

'Is she okay?'

'She's doing well.'

'That's great.'

'I've been told the police will be here in a few minutes. A room's been set aside so that they can talk to you in private.'

I felt an unbearable pressure building up in me. I sucked in chunks of air in a desperate bid to slow my galloping heart.

When I saw Scar I had to fight back another flood of tears. She was lying on a bed with her head raised on a pile of pillows. An IV line ran into her arm and a monitor pulsed away above her head.

The nurse explained to me that the wounds had been cleaned, and the doctor was preparing to apply the stitches. She'd been given medication to offset the effects of the shock and she was holding up well.

The nurse left us alone, and I stepped up to the bed and held Scar's hand, caressing the fingers.

'Thank Christ you're going to be all right,' I said. 'I've been so worried.'

She managed a smile. 'There's no need to worry about me, Lizzie. You have to look after yourself. Go before the police get here.'

'I can't leave you,' I said.

'You must. They'll arrest you and I don't want that to happen.'

'It's going to happen sooner or later,' I said. 'We both know it. I'm in a hole and I'm not going to pull you down it with me.'

'But there still has to be a chance to expose Joe Strickland. Tiny will help you.'

I squeezed her hand. 'I don't think so, babe. We had our chance and we blew it. I can't see us extracting any more confessions.'

'Then just go away. Abroad. Anywhere. When you're settled contact me and I'll come and be with you.'

I shook my head. 'That's not possible. I don't have a passport for one thing.'

'You can get round that. I know people who can help. Surely it's got to be better than spending the rest of your life in prison. Make no mistake, Lizzie, that's what will happen if you hand yourself in.'

Every word she spoke sent beats of sadness through me. I feared that whatever I did next would lead to the end of our relationship. How could we possibly have a future together after what had happened?

'Please just go, Lizzie,' she pleaded. 'For my sake if not your own. At least give yourself time to think it through before you wreck our lives.'

At that moment the nurse reappeared to inform me that the police had arrived.

'They're waiting for you in the office at the end of the corridor,' she said.

I thanked her and said I was on my way. Then I leaned over the bed and kissed Scar on the lips.

'You win,' I said. 'But please don't hate me when it ends in disaster.'

'I could never hate you, Lizzie. I love you more than anything. And that's why I don't want it all to come to an end here and now.'

'I'll call the hospital to check on you,' I said.

'My phone's in the car. It'll be safer if you use that.'

I kissed her again and then with great reluctance I slipped out of the cubicle before my emotions could overwhelm me.

I looked along the corridor towards the office where the police were waiting, then took off in the opposite direction.

I walked out of the emergency department without drawing attention to myself and was relieved to see that the car was where I'd left it.

I got behind the wheel and drove away from there, before the coppers who were waiting for me realised I wasn't coming and raised the alarm.

23

I drove around aimlessly for a while, sliding around the streets, trying to compose my thoughts. It was 4 a.m., and I felt empty inside.

The city was still pulsating with the sound of sirens, but they weren't all involved in the search for me. I saw two fire engines steaming through the streets to yet another emergency, either a blaze or a serious road accident, I supposed.

I eventually pulled over to the kerb in a quiet side street so I could have a smoke to calm my nerves. I found the ciggies in Scar's bag and checked her phone at the same time. There were no missed calls or messages from Tiny.

I scrolled to his number on the phone and pressed speed-dial. I wanted to update him on Scar's condition and find out where he was and what he was doing. But to my dismay the call didn't connect. No ringing and no tone.

Shit.

I puffed on the fag and closed my eyes. An image of Scar and me in bed back at the flat flashed unbidden into my mind. I saw myself in her arms, her lips on mine, and it evoked a deep sense of loss.

Would we ever sleep in the same bed again? Would we ever make love or go shopping together or share a meal?

I couldn't bring myself to believe that we might somehow emerge from this deep, dark tunnel and go on to survive as a couple. Too much had happened. There was little doubt in my mind that Scar would now be better off without me.

With me there was only misery and pain. A lifetime on the run from the law or years of having to watch me rot in prison. It wasn't fair and she didn't deserve it.

As I thought about this a silent rage built up inside me. I could feel the blood vessels throbbing at my temples, my fists clenching involuntarily.

I realised suddenly that if my life was about to plunge over a cliff then I wanted to take the person who was ultimately responsible with me. It wasn't enough that Sean Delaney was dead. He'd been a mere cog in the wheel.

Joe Strickland was the man who had created my nightmare. He was the one who had caused all the suffering. He had got his minders to kill Ruth Benedict and Ruby Gillespie. And he had probably done something terrible to Karina Gorski.

He had also framed me for a crime I didn't commit and ensured I wasn't there when my son needed me most. And to cap it all he had destroyed my only chance of happiness with the woman I loved.

And all the while he thought he was untouchable. Money and influence kept him safe.

But there was no way I could let him get away with it. If my life was finished then I wanted to make sure that his was too.

I threw the stub of my cigarette out the window and started up the engine.

I now knew what my next move was going to be and it gave me a sense of purpose.

I was going to drive straight over to Joe Strickland's house and tell him exactly why he didn't deserve to live.

And then I was going to kill him.

The house in Chilworth was in darkness and the only car on the driveway was Strickland's BMW. By the time I got there I felt so wired it was as though I was plugged into the electricity mains.

I had abandoned all hope of getting out of the mess I was in and had convinced myself that killing Joe Strickland could not possibly make things any worse. I was going down and determined to take the bastard with me.

I parked across the road and looked around to make sure there was no one about. The street was empty, no sign of any cop cars. But that did not mean the property wasn't under surveillance. For all I knew there were security cameras I couldn't see that would be monitoring my every move.

But my state of mind permitted me the luxury of ignoring the risks. I was in a place I'd never been before – resigned to a gruesome fate while at the same time detached almost from reality. It was like being spaced out on drugs.

I climbed out of the car and walked across the road and onto Strickland's driveway. It was then that it dawned on me that I really hadn't thought this through. I didn't have a weapon and I had no idea how to gain access to the house.

Did I just ring the doorbell and attack him with my fists when he answered it? Or did I make him suffer first like I'd made Sean Delaney suffer? And what was I supposed to do if someone else answered the door? His wife? Or his daughter? Jesus, it was getting complicated.

I reached the BMW and paused to draw a breath. My legs felt like spaghetti and there was a dull, deeply embedded ache behind my eyes. But while standing there an idea came to me. The BMW would almost certainly have an alarm. If I set it off then it was bound to draw Strickland outside.

I tried opening one of the doors. It was locked, and the alarm didn't go off. I then resorted to kicking the side of the car as hard as I could, and it did the trick. The car exploded into life, lights flashing, alarm blaring.

I hurried over to the big rhododendron bush and stood behind it as the lights went on in the house. Then I watched as the front door opened and Joe Strickland appeared wearing a dressing gown and carpet slippers. He looked around before walking over to the car and silencing the alarm with a key fob. Then he shook his head and strode back towards the front door.

I waited until his back was to me and broke cover. I sprinted across the grass and reached the door just as he was about to close it.

I shoved him as hard as I could, and he went tumbling forward onto the hall carpet. I pushed the door shut behind me and then let fly with an almighty kick that landed smack in the middle of his face.

He went out like a light, and I stood there looking down at him, rigid with shock and astonished that he was already at my mercy.

As I stared down at Joe Strickland I felt that I was losing my mind; my sanity was slipping away.

It made me realise why people snap and carry out atrocious acts of violence. They're driven to it by events they have no control over.

That was how I'd come to be here inside the house of the man whose life I was about to end. He was responsible for unleashing my demons, the demons that lie dormant in every human being from the moment of conception.

I had been pushed too far, and they'd emerged to seek retribution on my behalf.

Bless 'em.

Strickland only remained unconscious for a few seconds. Blood dribbled from a cut my shoe had opened up below his bottom lip.

I watched as his eyes fluttered open, and a groan escaped from his mouth.

I knew I had to act quickly before he came to his senses so I reached down, grabbed the collar of his dressing gown and rolled him onto his front so his left cheek was pressed against the carpet.

Then I snatched the car key from my pocket and stuck the pointed end against the back of his neck.

'Can you hear me?' I said.

He didn't answer, but he did groan a few more times.

'It's me, you bastard,' I said. 'Lizzie Wells. Can you hear me?'

He moved his head so that he could see me.

'What do you think you're doing?' he managed to utter.

'I'm holding a very sharp hunting knife against your neck,' I said. 'If you don't do exactly as I tell you then I'm going to shove it right in up to the hilt.'

'Are you fucking crazy?'

'Right at this minute I am. And it's because of you. So trust me, I won't hesitate to do it.'

He closed his eyes while his mind processed what I'd told him.

I wasn't sure what I was going to do if he called my bluff. I could only hope the key felt like the tip of a knife and that my sudden appearance had shocked him into submission.

'What do you want?' he grunted.

I want to kill you in the most painful way imaginable.

'I just want to talk to you,' I lied. 'There are things I need to know.'

In other words I want to hear you confess before I send you to fucking hell.

'This is insane,' he said. 'You shouldn't have come here.'

'I tried talking to you at your bar,' I said. 'But you called the police.'

'I told you, I've got nothing to say.'

'Well I have because I know everything now.'

'Is that so?'

'I know you got Delaney and his cousin to kill Benedict and Ruby Gillespie. And for the second time you fixed it so that I was in the frame.'

He started to respond, but I told him to shut up. I needed to concentrate on how to get him into another room, preferably the kitchen, where I could get my hands on a real knife. Here in the hall there wasn't much I could do except stab him with the car key.

'Get up,' I said.

I kept pressing the key against his neck and pulled on his dressing gown. He struggled up and I made sure he had his back to me when he was standing.

'If I apply slightly more pressure the blade will go through your neck and cause a lot of damage,' I said. 'So don't give me a reason to if you want to live through this.'

The hall was short and bright, with painted walls and a plush brown carpet. There was a staircase and three doors leading off it.

'Where's the kitchen?' I said.

'The door at the end.'

'Is there anyone else in the house?'

'No.'

'What about your wife?'

'She's at her mother's until tomorrow.'

I prayed he was telling the truth because I was in no position to take him on a tour of the house to make sure. The longer I carried on bluffing with the key the more likely it was I'd come unstuck.

'Lead the way,' I said.

The kitchen was large and spacious, with a breakfast bar between the fitted units and a dining area.

My eyes were drawn to a wooden block on the breakfast bar containing a selection of kitchen knives with stainless steel handles.

I pushed him towards the table and got him to sit in one of the chairs with his back to the breakfast bar.

Then I took hold of a handful of his hair with my left hand and with the other I pocketed the key and reached for the biggest knife in the block.

My confidence shot up as I flashed the blade in front of his face before pressing it against his throat.

'You fucking whore,' he said. 'You weren't even armed.'

'Well, I am now,' I said. 'And I want you to be in no doubt that I'll slice your throat wide open if you don't talk to me.'

'I don't believe you.'

'So try me and find out. You see, you've pushed me too far, Strickland. I no longer have anything to lose. You've taken everything away from me, including my son. Now the police believe I killed Ruby Gillespie, and they're going to put me back inside.'

'It's where you fucking belong.'

I jerked his head back and sliced the blade across the bridge of his nose to show him I meant business. He yelped in pain as the blood ran down his face.

I put the blade back against his throat and said, 'I know that whatever you tell me now you won't repeat to the police. You'll just deny everything, and I doubt I will ever be able to prove it. But I want to hear you confess. It's the only thing I've got to look forward to.'

And I want to hear it before I slit your throat wide open.

'I had nothing to do with any murders,' he said.

I shook my head. 'That's not good enough. You tell me the truth and you get to live. I'll walk away and you'll never see me again. But if you keep on shitting me I'll kill you.'

His body stiffened, and his eyes almost popped out.

'I've told you I didn't . . .'

I moved the blade and pushed the tip into the flesh beneath his chin. Blood rushed out and the bastard shrieked like a baby.

'Oh, Jesus, no. Please.'

'The truth then,' I said.

He closed his eyes and tightened his jaw. Then after a few agonising beats, he said, 'I couldn't let Benedict ruin me. He found things out. He was going to put them in the paper so he had to be stopped.'

'So you sent Delaney and his cousin to the hotel?'

'Yes.'

'How did you know we were there?'

'Ruby told us. I'd asked her to let me know when Benedict was shagging one of her girls.'

'Did she know what you were going to do?'

'No.'

'But you got her to lie in court about the knife.'

249

'Of course. She knew that if she didn't go along with it she'd also end up dead.'

'So why frame me?'

'That's obvious, surely. You said so yourself. I would have been the prime suspect because I had a strong motive for wanting to stop Benedict publishing his story.'

'And it didn't matter what happened to me?'

'You were collateral damage. No one gave a fuck about you.'

I squeezed the handle of the knife until my knuckles turned white.

'And then you decided to kill Ruby because she broke her silence and told me what she did,' I said.

He nodded. 'It gave me the opportunity to sort you out at the same time. It wouldn't have happened if you'd heeded the warnings and just got on with your life.'

'So now tell me what happened to Karina Gorski,' I said.

'She vanished. I had nothing to do with it.'

'That's a lie. She was helping Benedict. She gave him information about you. So you decided to get rid of her.'

'You're right about the information. She was screwing me over and feeding Benedict. Then she tried to blackmail me with the information. But I swear I didn't get her killed. Someone got to her before I did.'

'Really? Who was it?'

He didn't get to answer the question because just then there was a noise behind us and I snapped my head towards it.

My heart slammed against my chest when I saw a woman standing in the doorway. It was the same blonde woman who had been with Strickland in the bar. His wife.

She was wearing silk pyjamas and staring at me through large, fearful eyes.

'Please don't hurt him,' she said in a voice that trembled. 'Just put the knife away and leave before the police get here.'

'The police!' I said.

She nodded. 'I knew there was something wrong when Joe didn't come back to bed. Then I heard him cry out so I called the police from the bedroom. Told them we had an intruder. You've got a couple of minutes at most.'

It's now or never, I thought. All I have to do is whip the knife across Strickland's throat and he'll be dead in minutes.

So why was I hesitating?

'Please don't do it,' his wife said as she stepped into the kitchen. 'Just go. I beg you.'

'It's what I came here for,' I said. 'Do you know what your husband has done to me?'

'I heard what he just told you, but it's not true. He was telling you what you want to hear.'

'And you really believe that?'

'I do. I know my husband. He's not a monster.'

I swallowed hard and bile stung the back of my throat.

'Your husband deserves to die, Mrs Strickland. He's a sick, immoral bastard and you must know it.'

Her eyes flared hot. 'You've got it wrong. Please don't hurt him. Leave while you still can.'

Those eyes shot through me like a thousand volts, and her words melted my resolve. I felt my heart drop into my stomach.

I wanted to ignore her and rip her husband's throat wide open. But I suddenly realised I wasn't strong enough. Or ruthless enough. When it came down to it I couldn't commit cold-blooded murder.

It didn't mean that I wasn't disappointed in myself, though. I felt gutted that I was weaker than I thought I was.

251

I took the knife away from Strickland's throat, and he exhaled loudly.

'You owe your life to that woman,' I said, and stepped back from the chair.

He leapt to his feet, swung round and fixed me with a glacial stare.

'You can say what you want to the police,' he said. 'But I guarantee they won't even listen to you. And my wife's right. What I told you is a pack of lies. I'll never admit to anything I didn't do.'

'I don't expect you to,' I said. 'But we both know that what you told me is the truth. You're a scumbag.'

He gave me a perfunctory smile that made me regret letting him live.

'Why don't you join me for a glass of wine?' he said. 'We can continue our chat while we wait for the police to arrive. It'll probably be the last drop of booze you have for years to come.'

I looked at his wife. Her eyes dropped like lead weights to the floor. Her shame was evident in that simple gesture and it gave me a tiny crumb of satisfaction.

I turned back to Strickland and said, 'Your time will come, mate.'

'Of that I have no doubt,' he said. 'But it won't be for a long time yet.'

His smug expression filled me with a feral rage. I threw the knife across the room because the urge to use it returned with a vengeance.

Then I wrenched my gaze away from him and headed for the door. His wife kept her eyes down as I walked past her.

A shot of adrenaline propelled me forward and I ran out of the house like a sprinter leaving the blocks.

I heard the police siren as I was getting into the car, but I was away from there before they arrived on the scene.

I felt no sense of relief or self-satisfaction, however. I just felt like I was the loneliest person in the world.

24

Within minutes of leaving Strickland's house my sense of isolation deepened. I pulled into a side street, parked up and called the hospital to check on Scar.

I was put through to the emergency department where a nurse insisted I give my name. When I did she asked me to wait and a few seconds later a man came on and identified himself as a police officer.

'You need to give yourself up, Miss Wells,' he said. 'Tell me where you are and we'll arrange to come and get you.'

I ended the call and smacked the palms of my hands against the steering wheel. Blood vessels throbbed at my temples and a sob stuck in my throat.

I waited a couple of minutes and then tried to reach Tiny's number again, but the call wouldn't go through. I wondered if he'd switched his phone off or maybe he'd lost it?

I closed my eyes and sat back, feeling emotionally depleted. I was alone now and in deep, deep trouble. The police were hunting me for killing Ruby Gillespie. And it was likely they would also pin Sean Delaney's murder on me.

Tiny had said he was going to clean up the houseboat and get rid of the evidence. But he might not have been able to do it. Perhaps something had happened to him. Maybe that was why his phone was off.

I couldn't see how I could escape from the mess I was in. Not unless Strickland had a change of heart and made a full confession. But that wasn't going to happen.

My despair was compounded by the fact that there were still unanswered questions that were bugging me.

Who had put the note on the car windscreen when we parked it at The Court Hotel the day I came out of prison?

What had happened to Karina Gorski, assuming Strickland and Delaney were telling the truth when they said they didn't know?

And what was so explosive about the information that Karina had sold to Benedict and used to try to blackmail Strickland?

I opened my eyes and stared out through the windscreen. It was dawn already, and a tinge of purple was creeping into the sky.

I decided I needed a smoke and some fresh air. I lit up in the car and got out after switching off Scar's phone so the police couldn't home in on it.

There was a slight chill in the air and the clouds were breaking up. It looked like it was going to be a reasonable day.

I was in the suburb of Portswood, and it was just shaking off its slumber. As I turned into the high street I caught the aroma of fried bacon and saw it was coming from a greasy spoon café that had just opened up.

My stomach gurgled like an old boiler but at the same time the smell fed my underlying nausea. I knew I wouldn't be able to eat anything, but I was gasping for a big, hot mug of coffee. The place was called Milo's Eatery and the frontage looked new or refurbished.

I went in and discovered I was the first customer of the day. The proprietor, a grizzly old guy with rough skin and a heavy accent, gave me a funny look. I held my arms in front of me to cover the blood on my clothes and ordered a strong black coffee.

A TV was fixed to one of the walls so I chose a seat with a view of it.

I watched the morning news while I waited for the coffee, but I didn't take it in. My mind was struggling with something far more important.

I had to decide whether to go to prison or go on the run. It was a hellish choice but there were no other options open to me.

My coffee arrived and it tasted good, better than the weak dishwater I'd had in the hospital. But I almost choked on it when I saw myself staring out of the TV screen. It was the prison mugshot I was all too familiar with. The commentary that accompanied it came as just as much of a shock.

'*Police have issued a photograph of the woman they want to question in connection with the murder of Ruby Gillespie. Lizzie Wells, who's twenty-seven, was released from prison only a few days ago and is believed to have known the victim whose body was found last night in her home. She'd been stabbed to death.*'

I stopped breathing as they ran video footage of the front of Ruby's house. White-suited Scene of Crime officers were milling around looking for forensic evidence. When the reporter signed off, the show's presenter linked to another Southampton story.

'*Meanwhile the fire brigade are still at the scene of a blaze that destroyed a houseboat late last night on the River Hamble at Bursledon. A fire brigade spokesman has just confirmed that one person's remains have been found at the scene. The cause isn't yet known, although it's believed the fire might have been started deliberately.*'

They cut to a shot of Delaney's houseboat which had been reduced to a black smouldering hulk.

I allowed myself a private smile. The fire must have been Tiny's work. He had delivered on his promise to clean up the mess we'd left behind. From the look of what was left of the boat the coppers would struggle to find any evidence linking us to it.

It was a small positive but it didn't really change anything.

I finished the coffee and glanced over at the proprietor to signal for another. He was holding a phone to his ear and giving me another strange look. I met his gaze, and he turned away guiltily.

I didn't need to be told what he was doing. He must have seen my picture on the news and was alerting the police.

Bugger.

I slammed the mug down on the table and ran from the café without paying.

The experience had a profound effect on me. By the time I got back to the car I knew that I didn't want to spend years evading the police and hiding in shadows. I would always be looking over my shoulder, terrified of being spotted. A couple of women I met in prison had gone down that road and had told me what a nightmare it was.

Having made up my mind, I was thrown off balance. I had to light another ciggy to stop myself shaking. And then I sat there infecting my lungs for another fifteen minutes as my head filled with feelings of sadness and loss and pain.

Finally I plucked up the courage to key the ignition. But I didn't plan on driving straight to the central police station.

First I had to say goodbye to Leo.

25

I got to the cemetery long before it opened, but I had no trouble getting in. Part of the perimeter included a low brick wall and I was over it in a flash.

I trampled between the headstones as the rising sun cast deep, shifting shadows around them.

My breathing was hard and laboured, my body a mess of tightening knots. But when I came upon Leo's grave I felt an odd sense of peace and finality.

This is where it ends, I told myself. *This is where I have to accept defeat.*

I bent down, kissed his headstone, ran my fingers over the inscription.

'I have to go away again,' I said. 'I'm so sorry. Please forgive me for being such an awful mother.'

The emotions swamped me and I fell to my knees and cried. It felt like I had failed him all over again, and the pain was like a sword through my heart.

During my time in prison I had been so determined to avenge

his death. And after my release I'd been so full of hope. But I realised now that I'd been stupid and naïve. I hadn't really stood a chance against the forces that were lined up against me. Now I had to face up to it and accept the consequences.

After a while I reached out to tidy up the flowers in the vase and wondered if Pamela Ferris would continue to bring them. Or had I scared her off?

Pamela Ferris.

The woman had slipped from my mind in all the excitement of the last day and night. But I still didn't know why she had come here week after week or why she had run away when I'd confronted her.

'It's a strange thing for her to do, Leo,' I said aloud. 'She didn't know us and she's the widow of one of the detectives who arrested me. Yet for some reason she felt compelled to keep bringing you flowers.'

I realised then that I couldn't go to prison without knowing why she had done it. Did she feel guilty about something? And did it have anything to do with her late husband?

I had one last opportunity to find out before I handed myself in, and I decided to take it. After all, I was in no great hurry to bring my freedom to an end.

I gave my son's headstone another kiss and mouthed a silent prayer.

I promised him I'd be back one day and that I would always be thinking about him.

Then, through a deluge of tears, I said goodbye and hurried back to the car.

I knew from my earlier internet search that Pamela Ferris used to live with her husband in Water Lane, Totton. I was familiar with the area but not that particular road.

So I went online with Scar's phone and found it using Google maps. I was working on the assumption that she probably still lived there, and that she hadn't left for work since it was still only 7.30 a.m.

I didn't have her house number but I'd recognise her black VW when I saw it.

And I did see it, as soon as I drove along the short, inauspicious street. It was parked on the driveway of a terraced house with a pebble-dash façade.

I pulled over to the kerb a few doors down and walked back. I kept my head down and tried not to look like a desperate murderer on the run from the police.

I went straight up to the front door and was relieved to find that the curtains were closed across the windows.

I rang the bell and a pulse pounded in my head as I waited for it to open. I stood slightly to one side so she couldn't see me through the peephole.

A full minute passed and I was about to ring again when the door opened, and there she was. She froze when she saw me, gasping involuntarily.

'Hello, Mrs Ferris,' I said. 'I've come to have a little talk with you.'

Her jaw went slack and she stared at me with giant eyes. She was in her dressing gown and her hair was wet, but she'd already applied her make-up.

I put my hand against the door before she could close it.

'I'm coming in whether you like it or not, Mrs Ferris. I strongly advise you not to scream or resist.'

She was clearly too afraid and too traumatised to do anything other than step back and let me enter.

'Are you alone in the house?' I said.

She nodded.

I could smell the shower gel in her hair and the fear emanating from her pores.

I closed the door behind me and said, 'I don't want to hurt you, Mrs Ferris. But believe me I will if you don't answer my questions. Your late husband's friends on the force are about to arrest me. So I'm scared and desperate, and that makes me highly dangerous.'

She licked her lips and found her voice.

'They're saying on the news that you're wanted in connection with a murder.'

'I know what they're saying, Mrs Ferris. But I didn't do it. It's a stitch-up. I don't expect you to believe me, but it's the truth.'

Her expression hardened suddenly, and her eyes seemed to turn in on themselves. I watched her closely, fearful that she might scream or even attack me. Instead she made a tight slit of her mouth and breathed out a pitiful sigh.

I got the impression that something she had been bottling up for a long time was about to be released. It caused my heart to do a little somersault.

'The thing is I do believe you,' she said after a long pause.

Her words jolted me because they were so unexpected, and I felt my eyebrows spike.

'Are you being honest?' I said.

She nodded again and her eyes slid away from me as though out of embarrassment.

'But why?' I said. 'I don't understand.'

She fixed her gaze on the wall to her left and said, 'This is the second time they've done it to you and I know I can't just stand by and say nothing.'

It was like being hit full-on by a shockwave. Every nerve in my body became taut and I had to blink away a rush of dizziness.

'Come into the kitchen,' Mrs Ferris said, facing me again. 'I think you need a cup of tea.'

I breathed deeply as I followed her along the corridor, desperately trying to take the tremble from my lips.

The kitchen was small and bland, with old units and cluttered work surfaces. Mrs Ferris gestured for me to sit at a glass-topped table before she started making the tea.

With her back to me, she said, 'Why are the police saying you killed the woman?'

'Because I knew her,' I said. 'And she sent me a text asking me to go to her house last night. Only when I got there she was dead and the police arrived a few minutes later. So I panicked and ran.'

She turned around to face me and I noticed for the first time that she looked pale and tired. Red veins spoiled the whites of her eyes.

'You need to tell me everything, Mrs Ferris. How you know I'm innocent and why you've been tending my son's grave since your husband died.'

But she wasn't going to be hurried. The kettle boiled and she poured the teas.

She put the mugs on the table and sat opposite me. Her eyes glistened with tears that were trying to come out.

I waited with mounting frustration for her to speak, but I decided not to push her in case she had second thoughts.

After what seemed like an eternity, she said, 'Neil was a good husband and father. He loved me and I loved him. But four years ago he suddenly changed. He became distant and depressed. I didn't know what was wrong with him until after he committed suicide and I found the note.'

'But the papers and the police said he didn't leave a note.'

'Well, he did, along with a DVD recording of himself. I just didn't tell anyone because I was too ashamed of what he revealed.'

'What did he reveal, Mrs Ferris?' I asked gently.

She ran a tongue over her teeth and looked down at her hands resting on the table.

'He told me that he'd done a very bad thing and that he'd been struggling to live with the guilt,' she said. 'That was why he was depressed.'

'Did it have anything to do with me?' I asked.

She nodded. 'He knew all along that you didn't kill Rufus Benedict. On the DVD he confessed to helping another officer manipulate the evidence to make sure you were convicted.'

I felt a sudden rage. 'I knew the police must have been involved. Bastards.'

'I'm afraid my husband lost his way, Miss Wells. He had a gambling problem, you see. Built up heavy debts. So when a colleague encouraged him to sell his soul to Joe Strickland he did. Strickland paid money into a bank account that I didn't even know existed.'

She paused for a few moments to compose herself. Beads of sweat had popped out on her forehead and her hands were shaking.

'It continued to play on Neil's mind and his depression got progressively worse,' she said. 'Then a year ago he read in the papers that your son had died. And as you probably know he went to the funeral. I told him it wasn't a good idea. He found it very upsetting, and it pushed him over the edge. That's when he decided to take his own life.'

'So he jumped in front of a train because he felt guilty about what he did to me?' I said.

'That was partly it. But it wasn't the only reason.'

'Oh?'

'On the DVD he said he also couldn't stop thinking about the girl. It was torturing him.'

'What girl?'

'The one he killed,' she said, almost in a whisper. 'Her name was Karina Gorski, and she was Polish.'

Detective Neil Ferris had killed Karina Gorski!

That was what his widow had just said and it left me completely shell-shocked. I couldn't speak for several seconds. The silence in the kitchen became so intense that I could hear the hum of the freezer, the tick of the boiler.

Mrs Ferris picked up her mug and sipped at her tea. Her face was the colour of chalk and her pupils were wildly dilated.

'The police told me Karina simply disappeared,' I said. 'They said she probably went back to Poland.'

Mrs Ferris put the mug down and shook her head. 'She didn't just disappear,' she said, suddenly finding renewed strength. 'My husband murdered her. They then hid her body and pretended it never happened.'

I was confused as well as shocked. This was a hard thing to process.

'And you found this out only after he died?' I said.

She nodded. 'From the DVD. Neil wanted me to make it public. I know I should have, but I told myself I couldn't live with the shame. I also wanted to spare our daughters. I didn't want them to know what their father had done.'

'So you kept it to yourself?'

'I'm afraid I did. That's why I felt I had to put flowers on your son's grave, Miss Wells. You see, if I'd let the police see the DVD you would have been released from prison a year ago. But for purely selfish reasons I held it back, and the flowers went some way towards assuaging my guilt.'

The anger that coursed through me caused my chest to contract like a fist.

'I can't believe you did that,' I said, my voice tremulous and vengeful. 'That was despicable.'

'I'm so sorry,' she said. 'But I couldn't bear the thought that Neil would be labelled a murderer. It would have destroyed all our lives.'

'What about my life?' I said. 'I spent a year in prison when I didn't have to.'

She started to cry then, black rivulets of mascara staining her cheeks.

I was furious, fit to explode. I had to slow down my breathing to get air into my lungs.

'For what it's worth it's made my life a misery,' she sobbed. 'I kept telling myself I should take the disc to the police, but I couldn't bring myself to do it. After I saw you at the cemetery yesterday I felt terrible. I suspected it was you who phoned the office and I knew you'd track me down. I've been agonising over what to tell you. Then your face appeared on the news this morning, and I had a feeling it was happening all over again.'

I squeezed my hands into fists, so hard I was digging small crescents in the palms with my fingernails.

'So tell me why your husband killed Karina,' I said. 'And what part he played in bringing me down.'

She drew herself upright, wiped her eyes with a tissue she fished from her pocket.

'I think it'd be better if you watch the DVD,' she said. 'It's upstairs. I'll go and fetch it.'

She invited me into the living room, which was austere and impersonal. The furnishings were hard edged and colourless, the walls devoid of pictures.

265

The television rested on an ugly glass stand above a DVD recorder and a Sky box.

She switched it on and slipped the disc into the player. I sat at one end of a big brown leather sofa and she sat at the other.

Before she pressed play on the remote she looked at me with her red, puffy eyes.

'I hope that after you've seen it you can find it in your heart to forgive me,' she said. 'What I did was cruel, and I want you to know that I'm prepared to see that justice is finally done. I'll talk to the police, tell them everything.'

'It's a bit late for that, isn't it?' I said.

'I'm sure it will help in the present circumstances, Miss Wells. At least it should make the police think twice before charging you with that woman's murder.'

Her words cut through the rage and produced a glimmer of optimism. Had my luck changed? Was the widow woman going to get me out of the mess I was in?

I pushed the thought to one side because I didn't want to build my hopes up.

'Let's get to it,' I said.

I stared at the screen as she pressed play. The opening shot was of an empty chair in this very room.

'He recorded it while I was at work,' she explained.

After about ten seconds Neil Ferris stepped into shot and sat in the chair, but I almost didn't recognise him.

He was a shadow of the man he was four years ago. His face was gaunt and hollowed out, his eyes huge and haunted. Hard creases framed his mouth and when he spoke his voice cracked hoarsely.

'*If you're watching this recording, my love, then I'm already dead. I've been thinking of taking my own life for months. Seeing that poor woman standing next to her son's grave made me realise that I couldn't go on any longer.*

'*The feelings of guilt have overwhelmed me. Lizzie Wells did not kill Rufus Benedict and yet I helped falsify the evidence to get her sent to prison. I thought I could live with it because she was just a nobody, a prostitute. And I thought that if we charged her with manslaughter instead of murder it would be less bad. But I was wrong.*'

I glanced at Mrs Ferris. Her eyes were glued to the screen, and her body was stiff with tension. I wondered how many times she had tortured herself by watching this, and why she hadn't destroyed it.

'*But framing Lizzie Wells wasn't the worst thing I did three years ago,*' Ferris said. '*The worst thing I did was kill a young woman named Karina Gorski. It wasn't meant to happen. We were only supposed to extract some information from her. Except I lost my temper because she wouldn't open up. I punched her so hard in the face that she fell and cracked her head on a slab of concrete.*'

He stopped talking and closed his eyes. His jaw went tight, and the tendons in his neck stood out.

As he tried to compose himself I felt the blood flowing into my face. It was so hard to take in. I had just been declared innocent by a dead man. If his wife hadn't suppressed his confession the world would have known about it a year ago.

Ferris opened his eyes and continued speaking.

'*You need to know how it all came about, Pam. So I'm now going to tell you. And then I want you to take the disc to the Chief Superintendent so that Lizzie Wells can be freed from prison. I know it's going to be hard for you and the girls to live with the knowledge of what I've done, but it's necessary. I desperately want to right this wrong.*'

In a faltering voice he laid it all out like a defendant giving evidence at his own trial. He said he was one of two corrupt officers based in Southampton who were on Joe Strickland's payroll. They helped ensure the smooth running of his illegal empire by giving him advance warning of raids and turning a blind eye to his activities.

But things got messy just over four years ago when Rufus Benedict got involved with Karina Gorski, who was an escort. He became one of her most regular clients and one night she let slip that she was also Joe Strickland's favourite tart. She often slept overnight at Strickland's city centre flat and he took her away for the occasional weekend.

This gave Benedict an idea. For years he'd been trying to write a story for his paper exposing Strickland's operations. Getting the information had always proved impossible, though.

But somehow he managed to persuade Karina to help him by installing a hidden video camera and two electronic bugging devices in the flat, which Strickland used for private meetings away from his office.

The surveillance equipment was there for a month and during that time picked up a wealth of incriminating material – and not just against Strickland. Ferris and his accomplice, as well as corrupt local government officials and drug dealers, often appeared on the recordings.

The video footage and the tapes included dodgy deals being made, conversations about drug and people trafficking, as well as graphic sequences showing Strickland having sex with Karina.

'*Benedict was planning to put it all into his story,*' Ferris said. '*But he didn't count on Karina getting greedy. She knew the recordings were dynamite and realised that Strickland would pay a lot of money to get his hands on them.*'

'*So she showed him some of the video footage and tried to black-mail him. She wanted half a million pounds and said if he didn't pay up it'd be sent to the police.*

'*Strickland told us about it and wanted to send his henchmen Sean Delaney and Ron Parks to sort her out and get the tapes. But we offered to go and see her first, thinking we'd have more success getting the material from her and finding out exactly what Benedict had.*'

Ferris went on to say that they picked Karina up from outside a pub and took her to one of Strickland's empty building sites. There she stood her ground and refused to back down, even when they threatened to fit her brother up for a crime and get her sent back to Poland.

'*She just kept telling us that if she didn't get the money we'd all be exposed,*' Ferris said. '*She tried to convince us that she had all the material and was looking after it for Benedict. Of course, we didn't believe her. She was so full of herself and I don't think she realised how serious it was.*

'*That was when I lost my rag and punched her. She hit the concrete slab and died instantly. It was a freak fucking accident, but we knew we had to cover it up. So we put her body in the car and took it into the New Forest. We buried her in a shallow grave in woods behind The Crown pub at Ashurst.*'

Ferris said they then carried out a search of Karina's home, telling her brother they were looking for clues as to her where-abouts. During the search they found a box under the bed. It contained video and audio recordings from Strickland's flat.

Their attention then shifted to Benedict and Strickland told them he was going to arrange for the reporter to be dealt with. But there were two problems. Firstly they didn't know if Benedict had his own copies of the tapes and secondly Strickland didn't want to come under suspicion himself because everyone knew that Benedict was working on his story.

So they put Benedict under surveillance, followed his every move for about a week after Karina vanished and finally got lucky when he led them to a safety deposit box at a local bank. They used an official search warrant to get a look inside and found a cache of tapes which they removed.

Strickland then decided it was safe to kill Benedict to get him off his back and stop him from making too much noise over Karina's disappearance. So he started making arrangements.

'*He asked us to make sure we got involved in the murder investigation,*' Ferris went on. '*It wasn't difficult and so we were able to interfere with the hotel security footage and make sure that Lizzie Wells carried the can. Once she was put away everything got back to normal.*'

My mind was reeling. I was astonished at the amount of detail Ferris had put into his confession. It was clear that he'd thought it through carefully and planned exactly what he was going to say.

But there was one thing he didn't reveal until almost the very end, just before he again told his wife that he was sorry and said goodbye to her.

It was the name of the other bent copper who had been involved from the start, the person in fact who had encouraged him to sign up with Strickland in the first place.

When I heard the name I felt a surge of angst. It was another thing I knew I was going to have trouble coming to terms with.

I turned to Mrs Ferris and said, 'I want you to make a phone call for me. I want you to call DCI Ash at the central police station. Ask him to come here straight away because you have something important to say relating to Lizzie Wells. And tell him to bring

DS McGrath with him. It's important they both come. If Ash asks you what it's about just tell him you can't say over the phone.'

When she looked at me her eyes were curiously vacant, and it seemed like she had lapsed into a state of shock.

'I know the number of the station by heart,' she said. 'I'll get the phone.'

26

While we waited for the two detectives to turn up, Mrs Ferris went upstairs to get dressed.

I was pacing the living room when she came back down. She'd put on a black corduroy skirt and thin blue sweater that clung to her fragile frame.

'I've got to call the office,' she said. 'Tell them I won't be coming in.'

I watched her make the call and wondered if she fully realised the implications of what she had done by letting me view her husband's confession. Her life was about to crash into the buffers and there was even a chance she would go to prison for withholding information from the police.

After she'd spoken to her boss, she went to the front window and pulled back the curtains. The morning light seemed to reshape her face, and she suddenly looked much older.

'Where are your daughters?' I asked.

She turned to face me.

'Laurel is at uni and Clare is on holiday in Ibiza.'

'Your husband mentioned them to me a couple of times while I was being questioned,' I said. 'It sounded like he was very proud of them.'

'He was. They've been hard work like all teenage girls, but Neil doted on them. We were a happy family back then, or so I thought.'

'Did you have any idea that he was taking bribes from Joe Strickland?'

She shook her head. 'None whatsoever – I'd never even heard of Strickland then. Neil always seemed so devoted to his job.'

'You said he gambled. Did you know about that?'

'Not the extent of it. I knew he bet on the horses and played poker occasionally with his colleagues, but I didn't realise he was running up big debts. We had to take out a loan to pay some of them off.'

Despite the fact that this woman was also a victim I couldn't bring myself to feel sorry for her, not after what she had done to me.

'You know you'll probably be arrested,' I said.

She nodded resignedly. 'It's no more than I deserve. In a weird way it'll be a relief. Deep down I've known this day would come and that's probably why I kept the disc. But it's the girls I'm worried about. They're going to be devastated.'

Neither of us spoke again until Ash and McGrath arrived some ten minutes later. Mrs Ferris saw them from the front window and said, 'They're here.'

'Then you'd better go and let them in,' I said.

She showed them into the living room and when they saw me they both came to an abrupt halt.

Ash said, 'What the fuck are you doing here?'

I tried to remain calm. 'I've been waiting for the pair of you to arrive.'

His small dark eyes flickered to Mrs Ferris and then back to me.

'Have you got us here so that you can hand yourself in?' he said. 'Is that it?'

I grinned. 'Actually no. You're here to watch some telly.'

The pair exchanged glances, and I felt smug because I knew that the tide had now turned in my favour and I was intent on enjoying the next few minutes.

'Have you lost your fucking marbles?' Ash said. 'You're wanted for questioning in connection with a murder, one which you so obviously committed. Your prints are on the weapon and you were seen running from Ruby Gillespie's house.'

'I was framed,' I said.

Ash rolled his eyes. 'Here we go again. The little whore is the victim of yet another conspiracy.' He turned to Mrs Ferris and asked her. 'Are you all right, Pam? Has this mad woman threatened you?'

Mrs Ferris shook her head. 'No, she hasn't.'

'So why did you get us to come here? You said you had something to tell us.'

'I asked her to call you,' I said.

Ash wrinkled his brow. 'Is that right? So am I missing something here? What the hell is going on?'

'I've already told you,' I said. 'There's something I want you both to see on Pam's television. It's a production featuring her late husband.'

That drew another confused look from Ash. But the expression on McGrath's face was altogether different. He suddenly looked worried.

It was Ash who spoke first. 'I don't understand. Is this some kind of sick joke?'

Mrs Ferris responded. 'I lied to you, Martin, when I said that Neil didn't leave a suicide note. He did, along with a DVD on which he made a confession. I didn't want anyone to know about it, especially the girls.'

Ash was dumbfounded. 'Are you serious? I don't believe it.'

'Well, it's true,' I said. 'I just watched it. And guess what. Your dead colleague reveals who really killed Rufus Benedict and what happened to Karina Gorski. He even tells us where she is buried.'

As I spoke, I kept my eyes focused on McGrath's face and the shock was evident. I could tell he knew the game was up and was weighing up his options. But I wasn't going to give him time to come up with a way out. I was already holding the TV remote so I pressed play, and the screen flickered into life.

The two detectives stood like statues as Neil Ferris started talking. Neither of them moved a muscle, until it came to the part where Ferris revealed the name of his partner-in-crime. Then their faces suddenly became animated. Ash's mouth fell open and his eyebrows shot up. And McGrath shut his eyes and mouthed a swear word under his breath.

'*I want my colleagues on the force to know how sorry I am*,' Ferris said. '*Especially DCI Ash who I worked with on the Benedict case. I deceived him into thinking I was doing my job when I was really colluding with Paul McGrath to get a conviction against Lizzie Wells, even though we both knew she was innocent.*

'*Unlike me, Paul has shown no remorse. That's why I want to name and shame him. He's a bad apple and I blame him for getting me involved with Strickland in the first place.*

'*He'll probably say I'm lying and if he does then just check out his bank accounts and mobile phone records. He's been taking bribes from Joe Strickland for years. There might even be traces of his DNA on Karina Gorski's remains.*'

When the four-minute disc had run its course the tension in the room was thick enough to slice with a knife. Ash turned to McGrath and said, 'What have you got to say for yourself?'

McGrath swallowed a lump and tried to speak, but the words refused to come out.

I crossed the room and stood in front of him, close enough to smell coffee on his breath.

'It was you who left the note on our car,' I said. 'You're the mystery man wearing the cap on the CCTV. You knew I was being released that day so you must have followed us from the prison. And it must have been you who gave my number to Strickland so they could send a text message to me from Ruby's phone. No one else had it.'

McGrath remained silent. His mouth became a taut wire, and sweat glistened on his forehead. His eyes were filled with a mixture of fear and hatred.

I looked at Ash. 'I thought you were the one I couldn't trust. McGrath here was always so nice and helpful. Now I know why. The fucker was just as keen as Strickland to stop me stirring things up.'

Finally, McGrath opened his mouth to speak, but I didn't want to hear some lame protestation of innocence. So I shoved my knee into his groin and he doubled over.

'That was for the part you played in getting me convicted,' I said.

Then I punched him as hard as I could on the back of the head, and he dropped to the floor like a heavy sack.

'And that was for trying to do it to me a second time.'

The pent-up anger and frustration exploded out of me and I rained more blows on McGrath's head as he tried to get up off the floor.

Ash pulled me away before I could cause any real damage, but at least I had the satisfaction of knowing I'd hurt the bastard.

As soon as McGrath was on his feet, Ash let go of me and seized him by the arm.

'You need to sit down while I call this in, Paul,' he said.

He forced McGrath onto the sofa and looked him square in the eyes.

'These are serious allegations that have been levelled against you, and they need to be investigated,' Ash said.

'It's all bollocks,' McGrath responded. 'Ferris was lying.'

'Why would he do that?'

'Well, apart from the fact that he was off his trolley, it was his way of getting back at me. We never did like each other. He was a pathetic tosser. I told him that to his face more than once.'

'So you're not bent?' Ash said.

I saw the jut of his jaw. ''Course not. But I always suspected that he was on the take. He was desperate for money all the time because he kept pissing away his wages on the horses. He was a loser and I wasn't surprised he topped himself.'

Mrs Ferris suddenly pushed me out of the way so she could stand in front of McGrath.

'How dare you say that?' she screamed at him, her face just inches from his. 'It was you who talked him into going down that road. He wasn't a bad man, and he wasn't pathetic.'

'He was a corrupt twat and you must have known it,' McGrath sneered. 'Is that why you didn't tell us about the DVD? You wanted to protect your own reputation as well as his?'

I thought for a fleeting moment that she was going to spit in his face. Instead she reached out and grabbed a pen that had been sticking out of the top pocket of his suit jacket.

Neither I nor Ash realised what she was going to do with it until it was too late.

So we watched, horrified, as she raised it above her head in a stabbing motion and then plunged it straight into McGrath's right eye.

Ash immediately pulled her away and wrestled her to the floor. Her screams were drowned out by the inhuman sounds coming from Paul McGrath.

He was lying back on the sofa, pressing his fingers against the unsightly mess that was his eye socket. Blood was spurting out of it like water from a garden sprinkler.

The damage was extensive, but as he writhed in agony I found it hard to keep from smiling.

Everything that happened after that was a bit of a blur. My eyes misted over and my brain struggled to take it all in.

McGrath screamed until he passed out and Ash did a lot of shouting into his phone.

This was followed by flashing lights and the plaintive wail of sirens.

Mrs Ferris sat on the sofa, her mouth pinched and drawn in tight. She didn't speak and she didn't seem to regret what she'd done. It was as if she'd gone into a trance.

Eventually the room filled up with police officers and paramedics. McGrath was carried out on a stretcher, and Mrs Ferris was led away in handcuffs.

When it was my turn to be carted off, Ash put his hand on my shoulder and asked me if I was all right.

'I feel like a bomb has gone off inside my head,' I said. 'But I'm also relieved that you now know the truth about Benedict. And at some point I'll expect a grovelling apology from you and everyone else.'

He shook his head. 'Don't get too far ahead of yourself, Lizzie. We still need to ask you questions about Ruby Gillespie's murder.'

'But you don't really believe I did it, surely.'

'I don't know anything for sure right now. This is a real mess and it's got to be sorted.'

'Are you going to arrest Joe Strickland?'

'Officers are on their way to pick him up now, along with some of his people.'

'Does that include Sean Delaney?'

He narrowed his eyes at me. 'Why do you ask?'

'You know why. Delaney and another bloke attacked my brother and me.'

He pursed his lips. 'Yeah, well, we think Delaney's dead. There was a fire on a houseboat at Bursledon last night – *his* houseboat. A body was found in the wreckage. It's not yet been identified, but it's probably him.'

'Can't say I'm sorry,' I said. 'The man was an animal.'

'Were you by any chance out Bursledon way last night?'

'I was too busy staying one step ahead of your lot. Besides, how would I have known he lived on a boat?'

He gave me an arch look. 'You've got a point there, I suppose.'

A thought jumped into my head and I said, 'Why did you go to Strickland's house last night?'

His brow peaked. 'How do you know I went there?'

'I saw you. You arrived just as I did. I hid behind his BMW and then left when you went inside.'

'Well, I gather you went back later. He called a short time ago to tell me you barged in and attacked him with one of his own kitchen knives.'

'It was the only way I could get him to admit that he was behind all three murders – Benedict, Ruby and Karina. His wife was there. She heard him.'

'Was your girlfriend also a witness?'

My eyes widened and I didn't know how to respond, so I didn't try.

'That's another thing we need to talk about back at the station,' he said. 'I was at the hospital an hour ago. We know you took her there, but what we're not sure about is who stabbed her and why.'

'She must have told you.'

'She said she was attacked when she went to pick you up from outside Shamrock Quay.'

'That's right. Some bloke appeared out of nowhere and wanted money. When we told him to fuck off he pulled a knife. Donna got stabbed in the struggle.'

'So what happened to the guy?'

'He ran off.'

'Can you describe him?'

'I'm afraid not. It was too dark and it happened too quickly.'

He didn't seem convinced. 'So why didn't you call the police?'

'Because I was in too much of a state. I started tending to Donna's wound with the first-aid kit in the car and then I rushed her to the hospital.'

'Well, your girlfriend was bloody lucky. She could have been killed.'

'How was she when you spoke to her?'

'She's been patched up, and it seems she's more worried about you than she is about herself.'

'I'd like to go and see her.'

'I'm sure you would. But that can wait.'

Ash signalled for one of his officers to take me away. But as I was led towards the door I turned back to him and said, 'You didn't answer my question. Why did you go to see Strickland last night?'

He simply shrugged. 'I thought it was only fair to warn him that you'd been seen running away from a crime scene. I had a feeling you might turn up on his doorstep, and I was right.'

So it still wasn't over for me. I faced awkward questions about the attack on Scar and I was still suspected of killing Ruby.

Strickland and McGrath would no doubt deny any involvement in Ruby's murder. And it was a fair bet that Delaney's cousin Ron Parks would be busy constructing an alibi.

The thought that I remained in the frame filled me with dread.

On the way to the station my thoughts turned to Scar and Tiny. I hadn't heard from them in ages, and I wanted to tell them what had happened.

I turned on Scar's phone and saw that I'd had five missed calls from an unidentified number.

I wondered if Tiny had been trying to get through so I phoned his mobile, but once again it failed to connect.

This time I left Scar's phone on, and it was a good thing I did because it rang just as we were approaching the central police station.

I answered it and my heart jumped when I heard Tiny's voice. 'Thank God I've got you,' he said.

I told him I'd been ringing his mobile, but he said he'd dropped it in the mud while running away from the houseboat.

'I'm at the hospital, Lizzie. They just let me in to see Donna and she's doing well, so don't worry. But I need to tell you what to say to the police about last night, assuming I'm not too late.'

'I'm not sure,' I said, keeping my voice low so the officers in front couldn't hear me. 'They know I was with Donna when she was stabbed.'

'That's okay because it's also what she's told them. She said she went to meet you at Shamrock Quay after you phoned her. She parked in a poorly lit part of the street and got out of the car. When you came along some bloke suddenly appeared and demanded money. It was dark and neither of you got a good look at him. When you told him to bugger off he pulled out a knife. There was a struggle and Donna was stabbed. He ran off and you rushed Donna to the hospital.'

'That's basically what I've told them,' I said.

'Good. And don't admit to going to Delaney's houseboat. You probably know there's nothing left of it.'

'I saw the news. You did a good job.'

'It wasn't hard. There was a can of paraffin on board and plenty of matches.'

I filled him in quickly on what had happened, but as he started to ask questions we arrived at the station, and I was ordered out of the car.

'I've got to go,' I said. 'Give my love to Donna.'

27

They put me in a cell and I was glad because I was completely wasted.

The events of the past twenty-four hours had sapped every last drop of energy from my body.

When I stretched out on the hard, smelly mattress my brain felt like a dead weight. Even the adrenaline that rampaged through my body couldn't keep me awake.

I dreamt of blood and knives, and bodies being buried in shallow graves. And I saw a stream of faces, all soaked in tears. Scar. Leo. Ruby Gillespie. Pamela Ferris. Anne Benedict. Karina Gorski.

When they woke me up I was covered in sweat and my mouth felt as rough as sandpaper. I was astonished to learn that I'd been asleep for no less than eight hours.

Ash had apparently told his people to leave me alone while they carried out various inquiries.

I was given a cup of tea and a bacon sandwich, which I demolished in minutes.

Then I was escorted to an interview room where Ash and another officer I didn't know asked me a bunch of questions. They were polite rather than aggressive and I began to believe that maybe the worst was over.

I told them what had happened from the time I received Ruby's text message to the moment Ash and McGrath walked into the Ferris house. The only part I left out was the visit to Delaney's houseboat. I had to go through the knife attack on Scar and I twice, presumably so they could be sure that my account matched the one she'd given them. Ash told me there were no CCTV or traffic cameras near the spot where the attack took place and I realised that if there had been our story would have collapsed.

It was only after they were satisfied with my statement that Ash started to tell me what had happened while I'd been asleep.

'McGrath is in hospital still and I'm told he's serious but stable,' he said. 'Unsurprisingly he's lost the use of his right eye. But given what happened I'd say he's lucky to be alive. We'll hopefully start to question him tomorrow.

'Meanwhile, we've already had a peek at his bank statements and phone records. There's no question that Ferris was telling the truth about him being on Joe Strickland's payroll. He was bent all right.'

'What's happened to Pamela Ferris?' I asked.

'She's in a cell and about to be charged with GBH and withholding vital information from the police. She's also in a bit of a state so we'll be giving her a psychiatric assessment.'

'Have you talked to Strickland?'

'Indeed we have. But he's naturally denying everything.'

'So is he likely to get away with it?'

Ash allowed himself the luxury of a smile. 'I very much doubt it. We obtained a warrant to search his house and flat and we've checked his phones. Turns out he's been in regular contact with McGrath and Ferris over the past four years.'

'So you've got him banged to rights?'

'No question about that, but we've also got something else that should cheer you up even more.'

'Oh?'

Ash pushed a large brown envelope across the table towards me. 'Have a look in there.'

I took out a black and white photograph of a car that appeared to have been taken at night.

'It's a traffic camera shot of a Mazda heading towards Ruby Gillespie's street just before she was murdered. It belongs to Ron Parks. You can just about see two people in the front seats. We believe Sean Delaney is the second person.'

'So does this prove to you that I didn't kill Ruby?'

'Not by itself it doesn't,' he said. 'But the killers were careless, no doubt because they assumed that once we'd collared you we wouldn't put too much effort into the investigation.'

'What do you mean by careless?'

'We arrested Parks three hours ago. Just in time I think, because it looked like he was about to take off. Anyway, he was wearing the same shoes he had on last night and one of them had a trace of blood on the sole that is a match for Ruby's.'

'Jesus.'

'I reckon it's only a matter of time before he cracks and starts talking. We'll chivvy him along with some empty promises.'

'What about Delaney?' I said.

'We've confirmed through dental records that it was his body on the houseboat. The fire officer's provisional report suggests it was arson.'

'So someone killed him.'

'Either that or he killed himself. It's probably one of those cases we'll never get to the bottom of through a total lack of evidence.'

There was something in the way he looked at me that left me in no doubt that he knew I'd been involved.

I began to feel uncomfortable, so quickly changed the subject.

'Have you talked to Karina Gorski's brother yet? He'll want to know what Ferris said on the DVD.'

He shook his head. 'Not yet. But we've started searching the wood near the pub in Ashurst where Ferris said she was buried. As soon as we find something we'll inform him.'

There was a long, heavy silence during which tears welled up in my eyes.

'I think it's safe to assume that you won't be charged with Ruby's murder,' Ash said. 'And we've got enough evidence already on Strickland, McGrath and Parks to hold them in custody. As soon as one of them starts to blab the whole thing will collapse like a house of cards.'

Now I did start to cry. I couldn't hold it back.

'I've done you a terrible injustice, Lizzie,' Ash said. 'On the Benedict case I jumped to the wrong conclusion and failed to realise that two fellow officers were manipulating me along with the evidence. I should have been more on the ball. On top of that I've said some vile things to you since then. I apologise whole-heartedly. I'll do whatever is necessary to see that you're well compensated for the time you spent inside.'

There was no way I was prepared to accept his apology, and I wasn't going to pretend I did just to make him feel better. In fact I suddenly couldn't bear to look him in the eyes.

'So am I free to go?' I said.

'Of course. For your information the appropriate authority will be in touch about having your conviction quashed.'

It was small consolation for having lost a son and so many years of my life.

'I also called your mother to put her in the picture,' he said. 'I hope that was okay. There's been a lot of news coverage, and I felt it only fair to let her know how things stood.'

'How did she react?'

'She sounded pleased and relieved, especially when I said we'd uncovered evidence proving you didn't kill Rufus Benedict.'

I felt guilty because I hadn't thought to call her. I made a mental note to go and see her as soon as I got the chance.

'There's a driver downstairs waiting to take you home,' Ash said.

I shook my head. 'I'm not going home. I'm going to the hospital, but I need to pick up my car outside the Ferris house first. So the driver can drop me there.'

28

There were more tears when I finally got to the hospital. Scar and I shed them as we clung desperately to each other. In fact Scar got so emotional that I feared her stitches would burst open.

'You did it, babe,' she said. 'I'm proud of you.'

'But I couldn't have done it without you by my side,' I said. 'You stuck by me when most people would have run a mile. I won't forget it.'

'We're a team, Lizzie. Have been since the day we started sharing a cell.'

'Turns out that was one of the luckiest days of my life,' I said.

She smiled. 'I love you so much, babe.'

'And I love you more than you can ever imagine.'

Tiny cleared his throat to get our attention.

'So what about me, girls? Can I be part of this little lovefest?'

We both laughed and I gave him a big hug.

'You'll be my friend for life, Tiny,' I told him. 'I can never thank you enough for what you did for me.'

I thought he might have a little cry too, but being a man he naturally managed to hold it in.

I gave them the good news about no longer being a murder suspect and then quickly ran through everything that had happened to me – from my encounter with Joe Strickland to Neil Ferris's filmed confession.

They were relieved that I was in the clear and I was relieved that Scar was looking so much better. The doctors were keeping her in one more night for observation, but she was already on the mend.

I stayed at her bedside for an hour and then told her I had to go home to change.

Before leaving I asked Tiny to step outside into the corridor. There I gave him another hug and thanked him for what he'd done.

'I'm sorry you were drawn into this,' I said. 'Especially for what happened on the houseboat.'

He smiled. 'Best we don't ever mention that again, Lizzie.'

I smiled back. 'Agreed.'

I didn't go straight home. Instead I drove to my mother's house. As soon as she opened the door I could tell that she too had been crying. Her eyes were raw and her make-up smudged.

It was also immediately evident that her attitude towards me had changed. There was a warm glow in her expression that hadn't been there before.

'My God, you look dreadful,' she said. 'I'll make you something to eat and run you a bath.'

'I'd rather have a cuddle,' I said.

She enfolded me in her arms and I felt her tears on my face.

'I'm sorry I didn't believe you, my love,' she sobbed. 'And I'm sorry for the way I acted towards you. I feel deeply ashamed. Please forgive me.'

'Of course I forgive you,' I said. 'You're my mum. And there's no need to be ashamed. I've always been a crap daughter and I've caused you a lot of pain over the years. I was to blame for the fact that we never got on. And you were right when you said that I was ultimately responsible for what happened to Leo. I should have been here for him and for you.'

'The way I treated you was wrong, Lizzie. But I want you to know that despite what I did and said I always mentioned you in my prayers and asked God to look out for you.'

I felt my heart miss a beat.

'I didn't doubt that for a minute, Mum. But as far as I'm concerned that's all in the past. This is the start of a new and happier phase in our lives.'

My brother appeared in the hallway suddenly, looking confused.

'I've been worried about you, sis.'

I broke away from my mother and embraced him. 'I'm on top of the world, Marky. So there's no need to worry.'

'Where's your friend? I like her. She said she'd be coming back.'

'And she will. I'll bring her round tomorrow. In fact you'll be seeing a lot more of her from now on because we're an item.'

'I thought as much,' my mother said with a smile that I really appreciated.

'Are you shocked?' I asked her.

The smile turned into a chuckle. 'Don't be daft. In fact I've got a feeling that she'll make you happier than any man ever would.'

It was probably the nicest thing my mother had ever said to me, and it sent a tingle down my spine.

Suddenly I was filled with a deep sense of elation. For the first time in my life I felt optimistic about the future.

I really did believe that my luck had changed and the bad times were behind me.

EPILOGUE

A month later Karina Gorski was laid to rest in a proper grave. It had taken the police a week to uncover her remains in the New Forest using ground penetrating radar equipment.

Scar and I attended the funeral, which took place in the same cemetery where Leo was buried. As we stood with the other mourners I could see my son's headstone in the distance.

No trace of McGrath's DNA was found on what was left of Karina. But that didn't matter because after days of intense questioning he had finally confessed to being involved in her death, claiming it was a tragic accident.

He had also owned up to being on the take and had implicated Joe Strickland. Strickland was facing a number of charges ranging from bribery to conspiracy to murder.

Strickland's main nemesis was Sean Delaney's cousin Ron Parks, who had been charged with murdering Ruby Gillespie and Rufus Benedict. He'd told the police that the killings were carried out on Strickland's orders. He had also admitted attacking me and my brother.

So it had been a busy month, during which my picture had appeared in all the papers and on various television news programmes.

But I didn't mind because for a change they'd all been saying nice things about me.

And telling their readers and viewers that Lizzie Wells wasn't a cold-blooded killer after all.

Coming Soon . . .

The Alibi

Bev Chambers is the best crime reporter in London.
She comes from a family of villains herself – and she isn't
afraid to bend the rules in order to get a story.

Megan Fuller, former soap star, has been stabbed to death at
her home in South London. Media is rife and the pressure
is on to expose the killer.

Danny Shapiro, the notorious gangster, becomes the
prime suspect because of his stormy relationship with
the fallen celebrity.

But Danny has a watertight alibi, so the police can't touch him.
But that doesn't stop Bev. She's suspicious and makes it her
business to pursue the story.

A story which ends in tragedy and heartbreak.

The
ALIBI

JAIME RAVEN

To Lyanne, Ellie and Jodie – my three wonderful daughters.

PROLOGUE

'Don't look at me like that, you pathetic bitch. You brought this on yourself.'

The words fell out of his mouth on the back of a ragged breath.

Through the tears that blurred her vision, Megan Fuller watched him straighten up and step away from her. She wanted to plead for her life, to beg for forgiveness, but she couldn't speak because her mouth was filled with blood and fragments of broken teeth.

She had never known pain like it, not since she was robbed of her virginity as a child. Back then she had at least known that she wasn't going to die. But now she feared that she had only seconds to live. From the demented look in his eyes she could tell that he had completely lost it. The red mist had consumed him. He was in the grip of a dark rage, and not for the first time. She'd seen it happen before and had likened it then to someone being possessed by the Devil.

He gave her a look of sneering contempt as he stared down at her, his face tense, jaw locked, blue veins standing out on his neck.

'I warned you,' he yelled. 'It didn't have to be like this.'

Every molecule in her body was screaming, and hot tears spilled from her eyes.

She should never have let him in. It had been the mother of all mistakes. He was fired up before stepping over the threshold, intent on making her regret what she had threatened to do to him.

After slamming the front door behind him, he had launched into a furious rant, accusing her of being a money-grabbing whore. She had tried to calm him down by offering to make him a cup of tea.

But it wasn't tea he was after. He wanted her to tell him that she was backing down and that he didn't have to worry. But her refusal to do so had wound him up to the point where he'd snapped.

He'd smashed his fist into her face. Not once but twice. The first blow struck her mouth and stopped her from screaming. The second blow broke her nose and sent her sprawling backwards onto the kitchen floor.

Now she was at his mercy, unable to cry out as she watched him reach towards the knife block on the worktop. He withdrew the one she used for cutting vegetables. The sight of it paralysed her with fear.

'You were a fool to think I'd let you get away with it, Megan. The others might cave in, but I fucking won't.'

His voice was high-pitched and filled with menace, and his chest expanded alarmingly with every breath.

Panic seized her and she tried to push herself up, but he responded by stamping on her right arm.

There was no stopping him now, she realised. Even if she could talk he was too far gone to listen to reason.

'You've always been a frigging liberty taker,' he fumed. 'But this time you've overstepped the mark big time.'

The knife was above her now, and as he squeezed the steel handle the blood retreated from his knuckles.

She tried again to scream but it snagged in her throat and suddenly she couldn't even draw breath.

At the same time he lowered himself until his knee was pressed into her chest and his weight was threatening to crush her breastbone.

Face clenched with murderous fury, he moved his hand so that the tip of the knife was pressed against her windpipe. She could actually feel the adrenaline fizzing through her veins like a bolt of electricity.

A voice in her head was pleading with a God she had never believed in.

Please don't let him do it.

Please make him see sense.

She managed to swallow back the blood in her mouth and let out a strangled sob. But that was about all she could do.

'I can't let you live, Megan,' he said, and the harsh odour of his breath caused her nostrils to flare. 'I realise that now. If I do I know you'll make it your business to destroy me.'

She arched her body, desperate to throw him off, but he was too heavy and too determined.

Suddenly all hope took flight and she felt herself go limp.

Then she closed her eyes because she couldn't bear to look at his face as he plunged the knife into her throat.

CHAPTER ONE

BEV CHAMBERS

I jolted awake to the sound of my mother's voice and the earthy aroma of instant coffee.

'You need to get up,' she said. 'The paper phoned and they want you to call them back straight away.'

I forced my eyes open and felt a throbbing pain at the base of my skull, made worse by the harsh sunlight streaming in through a gap in the curtains.

'Oh, Jesus,' I groaned.

'Let me guess,' my mother said, placing a mug on the bedside table. 'You've got a hangover.'

I rolled on my side, squinted at the flickering numbers on the digital clock.

'Bloody hell, Mum. It's only half-eight.'

'That's right,' she said, her tone disapproving. 'It's also Saturday – one of only two days in the week when Beverley Chambers gets to spend quality time with her daughter.'

'I hadn't forgotten,' I said. 'Is she still in bed?'

'You must be joking. She's been up for an hour. I've washed

and dressed her and she's having breakfast. She thinks you're taking her to the park.'

I felt the inevitable wave of guilt wash over me. It had been a mistake to drink so much last night. But then how else would I have got through what had been such a tiresome ordeal?

'How bad is it?' my mother asked.

I closed my eyes, held my breath, tried to assess the level of discomfort.

'On a scale of one to ten I'd say it's an eleven,' I said.

My mother exhaled a long breath. 'Then sit up and drink some coffee. It'll make you feel better.'

I hauled myself up and placed my back against the headboard. I had to close my eyes again to stop the room from spinning. When I opened them my mother was still standing there looking down at me. Her arms were folded across her ample chest and she was shaking her head.

I sipped at the coffee. It was strong and sweet and I felt it burn a track down the back of my throat.

'When did the office call?' I said.

'A few minutes ago,' my mother said. 'I answered your phone because you left it in your bag – which you left on the floor in the hallway, along with your coat and shoes.'

I couldn't resist a smile. It was like going back to when I was a wayward teenager. Most weekends I'd roll in plastered, barely remembering what I'd been up to. My poor mum had put up with a lot in those days and even now, aged twenty-nine and with a kid of my own, I was still a bit of a handful. Still cursed with a reckless streak.

'So how did it go?' she said. 'Was this one Mr Right?'

I shook my head. 'I should be so lucky. Suffice to say I won't be seeing him again.'

She gave a snort of derision. 'I told you didn't I? The only blokes you'll meet on those internet dating sites are losers and cheats. It's a waste of time and money.'

And with that she turned and stepped back out of the room.

'Can you get my phone for me?' I called after her.

'No I can't,' came the reply. 'If you want it you'll have to get up.'

I took a deep breath and let it out in a long, tuneful sigh. It was becoming increasingly difficult not to accept that she was probably right about the dating thing. Last night had been awful. Another date, another disaster. The guy's name was Trevor and in the flesh he looked nothing like his profile picture. Most of his hair had vanished since it was taken and he'd also grown a second chin. He said he was an IT consultant, and I believed him because he spent the whole time talking about what he did with computers.

It became obvious early on why he was still single at the age of thirty-five. And if it hadn't been for the fact that he'd gone to the trouble of travelling all the way across London to meet me I would have left sooner than I did. But that would have been impolite, perhaps even a little cruel. So I'd stuck it out while knocking back the Pinot in an effort to numb my senses.

Over the last five months I'd dated seven men through online dating sites and Trevor was the dullest. He'd been even less entertaining than Kevin the chiropodist who had offered on our first date to examine my feet. When I wouldn't let him he went into a sulk and accused me of being a snob.

But no way was I a snob. When it came to men I'd always been happy to cast a wide net. I'd never discriminate against race, colour or class, and I accepted that most guys around my age had baggage from a previous relationship. I just wanted someone who was honest, open, reasonably intelligent and with a sense of humour. It would help, of course, if there was also an instant physical attraction. But so far those I'd met online had lacked most or all of those qualities.

'I suppose it's time I called it a day,' I said aloud to myself, knowing I didn't really mean it.

The trouble was I missed being in a relationship. The divorce was two years ago and I hadn't slept with anyone since. But it wasn't just the sex. I missed being part of a couple. I missed the companionship, the intimacy, the stream of pleasant surprises that were part and parcel of a burgeoning relationship.

Of course, being a single mum with a full-time job kept me busy. In fact I had hardly any time to myself. And that was essentially the problem. I wanted more fun and a touch of romance in my life. I wanted to fall in love again and maybe have another child. I wanted a home of my own and to share it with someone who'd get to know me as well as I knew myself.

My mother didn't really understand me, or so she said. She reckoned I was being selfish, that I should forget about men and focus on bringing up Rosie.

'You already work far too many hours,' she told me when I first joined the dating scene. 'You haven't got time for a boyfriend or a husband.'

But then she had her own reason for wanting things to stay as they were. As long as I remained unattached she got to have us living with her. Not that I'd ever complain. If it wasn't for my mother I'd probably find it impossible to look after a three-year-old *and* continue to work as a journalist.

Thanks to her I didn't have to pay for child minders or meet the high cost of living in London. Whilst married, my husband and I had shared the exorbitant rent on a property in Dulwich.

But Mum owned outright this three-bed terraced house in Peckham, and my contribution to the outgoings was relatively small.

She was also on hand to take care of Rosie. That was important, given the fact that my job entailed horrendously unsocial hours.

Take this morning, for example. I had a horrible feeling that the news desk wanted me in on my day off. Why else would the office call me at this hour on a Saturday morning? Had something happened? Was there a breaking news story they wanted me to get across?

There was only one way to find out, of course, and that was to get up and phone them back. But it was the last thing I wanted to do. My head was hurting and I felt more than a little nauseous. Plus I didn't want to have to tell my daughter that I might not be taking her to the park after all.

As if on cue the bedroom door was flung open and there she was, the apple of my eye, looking absolutely gorgeous in a yellow dress, her long fair hair scraped back in a ponytail.

'Mummy, Mummy,' she yelled. 'Nanny said you have to get up. You're not allowed to go back to sleep because if you do you'll be in trouble.'

People have told me that Rosie is the image of her mother. And it was true up to a point. We both had blue eyes and hair the colour of wheat. Our noses were small and pointed, and we each had a slight lisp.

But Rosie had her father's facial bone structure and also his smile, which was one of the things I'd loved about him in the beginning. That was before I realised he used it as a distraction, a way to make me believe that he was a caring, faithful husband instead of a cheating scumbag.

'Hurry up, Mummy,' Rosie said excitedly. 'It's sunny and I want to go to the park.'

She stood next to the bed, pulling at the duvet, her big round eyes pleading with me to get up.

'Slow down, sweetheart,' I said. 'It's still really early and Mummy's got a headache.'

'I can kiss it better for you.'

The words out of my daughter's mouth never failed to lift my spirits. I put the mug back on the bedside table and reached over so that she could peck me on the forehead.

'I feel much better already,' I said.

Then I pulled her close to me and gave her a cuddle. She felt soft and warm and smelled of shower gel.

'Go and tell Nanny to make me some more coffee,' I said. 'I'll be out as soon as I've been to the loo.'

She skipped out of the room, repeating my words to herself so that she wouldn't forget them.

I then dragged myself out of bed, only to be confronted by my own reflection in the wardrobe mirror.

I usually wear silk pyjamas at night but I'd either forgotten to put them on or I just hadn't bothered. I couldn't remember which. But anyway I was naked except for my watch and a going-out necklace.

As always I cast a critical eye over my body. And as always I felt a pang of disappointment. Despite all the diets, gym sessions and yoga classes, I was still very much a work in progress. My breasts were not as firm as they used to be, my thighs were riddled with cellulite, and my tummy looked as though it was in the early stages of pregnancy.

But I did have my good points, thank God. My hair was full-bodied and shoulder length and I never had to do much with it.

I was just over five seven in bare feet and had a face that most people considered attractive. In fact, my ex went so far as to tell me that I reminded him of the actress Jennifer Lawrence. It gave my ego a huge boost up until the day I discovered that he was incapable of being truthful.

I shook my head, annoyed that I'd allowed that deceitful toe rag to invade my thoughts this early in the morning. But then it wasn't as though I could distance myself from him. For all his faults – and there were plenty of them – he adored Rosie and made a point of seeing her twice a week as part of the custody arrangement. It meant we remained in contact, and in all honesty it wasn't as bad as it had been at the start. I was over the shock and humiliation of his betrayal, and all the feelings I'd had for him had evaporated.

I was now civil to him whenever we met and that made life easier all round. There were never any arguments over maintenance payments and he was usually willing to help out when I needed certain favours.

Naturally my mother hated him with a vengeance, and when he called at the house she made a point of retreating to her bedroom to avoid seeing him.

But it wouldn't be an issue today because he'd taken Rosie out on Thursday and wasn't due to see her again until Wednesday when he'd pick her up from the nursery.

Today it was my turn to spoil her – if I didn't have to go to work. And that was a bloody big if.

I turned away from the mirror, picked up my robe from the chair next to the bed and peered through the curtains. The sun was shining just as Rosie had said. It made a change since we were in the middle of one of the wettest and coldest Novembers for years.

My bedroom was at the front of the house and the view was

of a row of almost identical terraced houses opposite. All of them were worth in excess of half a million pounds, which seemed extraordinary to me given that Peckham used to be one of the grimiest and most dangerous parts of South London. But having undergone massive regeneration and steady gentrification, the area was now considered a trendy place to live, attracting families and city workers alike.

For me, Peckham was both familiar and convenient. The house was a short walk from the railway station and from there it was just a ten-minute train ride to London Bridge and the offices of the *The Post*, the evening newspaper that served the capital. I'd worked there for the past five years.

Peckham Rye Common was also close by and that was where I'd planned to take Rosie today. I really didn't want to disappoint her because Mum was right about me not spending enough quality time with her. I definitely needed to make more of an effort, put Rosie before everything else and stop jumping to the tune of the news desk.

I came to a decision suddenly. If the news desk asked me to go to work I'd tell them it wasn't possible. I'd say I'd already made plans and they couldn't be changed.

They'd no doubt be surprised because I loved the job and could usually be relied on to come in at short notice. But this time they'd just have to call up someone else, assuming they hadn't done so already.

'You took your time getting back to me,' Scott Granger said. 'I was about to get someone else to cover a story that we've just got wind of.'

'I'm afraid that's what you'll have to do, boss,' I said. 'It's my day off and I've made plans.'

'Well I suggest you change them or else you're going to be sorely disappointed. This is huge.'

'That's what you always say when you're short of people.'

'I mean it this time, Bev. You've got first call on this because you're the paper's crime reporter. So I want you on it from the start. And trust me it's right up your street.'

Granger was *The Post's* senior news editor and an expert in the art of manipulation. He was an old-school newspaperman who knew there was one sure way to get a reporter – any reporter – to do his bidding, and that was to dangle the carrot of a cracking yarn.

'So, just out of curiosity, what's the story?' I said.

I could imagine him smiling on the other end of the line, thinking he'd got me hooked and that all he had to do was reel me in. He'd been my mentor after all. Had helped nurture my career since I got the job at *The Post*. He was also the one who had nicknamed me The Ferret, because of my uncanny ability to ferret our stories.

Three years ago he appointed me to the position of the paper's first ever female crime reporter. And in the pub afterwards he told me: 'You got the job because, like me, the news is embedded in your psyche, Bev. It's part of your DNA. You can't resist the excitement that comes from being the first to tell people what bad things are happening all around them. It's like the rush you get from a sniff of the white stuff.'

He'd been right, of course. From an early age I'd been fascinated by the news and how it was covered and disseminated. Before I left school I knew exactly what career path I wanted to follow. It wasn't easy, given my background, but I'd managed to pull it off, and like every other hack I knew I was now addicted to the chase.

311

'There's been a murder,' Granger was saying. 'And the victim is none other than Megan Fuller.'

It took a second for the name to register.

'Do you mean the actress?' I said.

'Yep, although as you know that's not her only claim to fame. As well as being a former TV soap star she was also the ex-wife of a well-known London gangster.'

'Christ,' I blurted. 'Danny Shapiro.'

'That's right,' Granger said, as though he'd scored a point. 'Danny fucking Shapiro – the villain with the film star looks who took over a huge criminal empire after his notorious father got banged up.'

I felt a surge of adrenaline. Granger wasn't far wrong in saying the story was huge. Danny Shapiro was one of the country's highest-profile criminals. His gang operated south of the Thames and was involved in drug trafficking, prostitution, extortion, money laundering and even kidnapping. He and Megan Fuller had been tabloid fodder throughout their four-year marriage which had ended in divorce fourteen months ago.

'Megan was found stabbed to death at her home in Balham earlier this morning,' Granger said. 'We had a tip from a paramedic who attended. So we've got the jump on everyone else.'

I was suddenly oblivious to the ache in my head as my mind filled with a flood of questions that I doubted Granger would know the answers to. I was certain the story would have created a buzz in the newsroom. The headline writers would already be focused on the paper's early edition front page, and the online team were probably about to publish something on the website. Then it'd be out there, leading to a full-blown media firestorm.

'So do you still want me to pass the story on to one of your colleagues?' Granger said. 'Only I can't piss around. We need to move on this.'

From where I stood in the kitchen I could see Rosie at the table in the adjoining dining room. She was busy drawing pictures on a pad with big colourful crayons. My mother sat next to her, but her eyes were on me and her brow was scrunched up in a frown. I could tell she knew what was coming.

I felt my resolve dissipate and the guilt rear up inside me again as I turned away from them and said into the phone, 'Okay give me the details and Megan Fuller's address. I'll get right on it.'

'That's my girl,' Granger said. 'I knew you wouldn't disappoint me.'

CHAPTER TWO

ETHAN CAIN

The girl had said she was eighteen, but Ethan Cain wasn't sure he believed her. She looked younger. Much younger.

It hadn't stopped him spending the night with her, though. She was mature enough to know exactly how to please him.

And even if she was underage there was no danger of anyone in authority ever finding out. The girl would be too scared to let slip that she'd been shagged by a thirty-four-year-old man at his flat in Wandsworth.

She was still asleep on the bed and she hadn't stirred when he'd got up just now to have a piss. It didn't surprise him. Last night she'd consumed copious amounts of vodka and had sniffed at least five lines of coke. So she'd probably be comatose for a while yet.

But that was okay because he wasn't in a hurry to get shot of her. It was Saturday and he didn't have to go to work. Besides, he was already aroused at the prospect of fucking her again, maybe a couple of times this morning if he could manage it.

After emerging from the en-suite bathroom, Cain sat naked in the armchair next to the bed and lit his first cigarette of the day. It was always the best, the most satisfying, and he savoured the acrid warmth that filled his throat.

He could see himself in the stand-up mirror and decided that it wasn't a pretty sight. He looked far better with clothes on. At least they concealed his paunch and the man boobs that had begun sprouting up after he'd stopped working out. He wasn't grossly overweight, just bigger and softer than he wanted to be.

He switched his gaze back to the girl. The duvet had been pushed aside to reveal her lying spread-eagled on her back. She looked good enough to eat and it was all he could do not to get back on the bed and feast on her bare flesh.

She had lush black hair, small pert tits and skin as smooth as porcelain. It struck him that she was a picture of innocence. But this made him smile because she was far from innocent.

Ania Kolak – if that was her real name – was among the thousands of Eastern European sex workers who had poured into London in recent years. She was Polish and had told him that she hoped one day to embark on a career as an actress.

He'd heard it all before. Most of them believed that selling their bodies was a means to an end and that after a few years they'd have enough money saved to be able to fulfil their dreams. But in most cases that never happened. Instead they ended up as drug addicts or pathetic zombies drained of every last drop of self-respect.

Not that he gave a toss. As far as he was concerned it served them right. They didn't deserve his or anyone else's pity.

He did have some sympathy for those who were forced into sex slavery, though. Their plight was indeed tragic. But all the women and girls he'd been with had clearly become prostitutes out of choice. Many of them had told him they actually enjoyed being on the game. It meant they had enough cash to live well in one of the world's most expensive cities.

It still amazed him how much some of them earned. The high-class escorts who worked the West End often raked in thousands of pounds in a single night.

Ania wasn't in that league, not yet anyway, and her fee for an entire night was five hundred pounds. Cain was just glad he didn't have to pay her and the others out of his own pocket. He would never have been able to afford it.

As it was he was lucky. The girls and drugs were the perks he enjoyed for being on Danny Shapiro's payroll. Danny, like his father before him, ran the biggest prostitution racket this side of the Thames. But it was only part of his empire, an empire that stretched across the whole of South London.

He was, without doubt, the shrewdest villain in the capital and the most feared. Even the Russians, who controlled the West End, and the Albanians who ran most of North London, knew better than to try to muscle in on his territory. They did attempt it a couple of years ago and quickly came to regret it. Two of their top people were shot dead outside their homes in Kensington, and one of the casinos they operated up west was set on fire.

It was widely accepted that Danny was just as ruthless as his old man, Callum Shapiro, who was doing a twenty-five-year stretch for a raft of convictions including murder.

Cain's relationship with Danny was purely professional. He didn't actually like the man, let alone trust him. But the arrange-ment they had was mutually beneficial. And, to be fair, Danny had always treated him with a modicum of respect – unlike Frankie Bishop, Danny's second-in-command and the gang's most brutal enforcer.

Bishop, a career criminal, had earned his ferocious reputation on the South Coast where he was groomed by a gangster named Joe Strickland. He'd managed the security arrangements at Strickland's pubs and clubs in and around Southampton. One night he attacked a punter who ended up with a fractured skull and ruptured spleen. For that he went down for three years. While in prison he met a couple of Danny's lads and they urged him to move to London if he wanted to see more action and more money. So after his release he dropped in on Danny and offered his services. And Danny jumped at the chance to take him on.

It was Bishop who handed Cain his monthly cash retainer and supplied the girls and drugs. But dealing with him was never a pleasant experience. In the underworld he was known as 'The Nutter' because it was obvious to everyone that he was a grade-A psychopath. Still, Cain reckoned it was a small price to pay to indulge his passion for sweet young things like Ania. A passion that he'd never been able to control and which had led to the collapse of his marriage to a woman who had been devoted to him. A woman who gave birth to his child on the same day he was screwing a young colleague he was having an affair with.

Now, of course, he didn't have to worry about his wife finding out. He was divorced and so he could do as he pleased, have as many women and as much coke as he wanted.

And so that was what he did because it helped him to forget how much his addictions had cost him.

Ania was still out cold, her chest rising and falling with every breath. It occurred to him that he ought to take one of his little blue pills so that he could make the most of her before she left. It would take at least thirty minutes to kick in so he decided to wash it down with a cup of tea.

He crushed what was left of his fag in the ashtray on the floor and rummaged in the bedside drawer for a pill.

In the kitchen he opened the blinds and reached for the kettle to fill it with water. That was when he noticed his mobile phone on the worktop next to the sink.

As soon as he picked it up he saw that he had two unopened text messages and three missed calls.

'Shit.'

At some point last night he'd put the phone on silent and had forgotten to take it off. It had been careless of him. Downright stupid.

He checked the times of the messages and the calls. They had all come in during the past hour, which was a relief. He would say he was asleep in bed and hadn't heard it ringing.

It wasn't until he phoned the office that he discovered why they were anxious to reach him. And it was bad news.

He wasn't going to have a day off, after all. And there would be no time for even a morning quickie with Ania.

Cain didn't know what to make of it. Megan Fuller had been murdered in her own home in Balham.

Jesus.

He had never met the woman but he knew all about her. She'd appeared in a soap that had aired on the BBC for about five years, playing the glamorous wife of a cantankerous factory owner. In real life she'd been married to Danny Shapiro and, by all accounts, it had been a tumultuous relationship.

The word on the street was that she'd fallen on hard times since the Beeb dropped her from the soap over a year ago as part of a character shake-up. She'd been struggling to find other work ever since and had recently been threatening to write a tell-all book about her life.

Danny was among a number of people who were apparently

not happy about it. He feared she might reveal a bit too much about their life together in order to secure a lucrative publishing contract.

As Cain stood under the shower, he realised that Danny would most likely be in the frame for her murder because the book thing meant that he had a motive. And if so then things could get tricky. He thought about phoning Danny to find out what he knew, if anything. But he decided against it. Maybe later when he had a better idea about what was going on.

After the shower, he towelled himself dry and had another go at waking Ania. She hadn't responded to the first attempt, but this time her eyes flickered open and she looked up at him.

'I said get your arse out of bed and get dressed,' he told her. 'Something's come up and I have to go out.'

She licked her lips and cleared her throat. 'Can't you just leave me here? I'm tired and I don't feel well.'

'Like I give a shit,' he said. 'Your clothes are over there. Put them on and scram. I've left a thirty-quid tip on the chair.'

He was suddenly no longer interested in her. He was in such a hurry to get going he didn't even look at her as she got out of bed and sauntered naked into the bathroom to use the toilet.

By the time he'd put on his grey suit and a white shirt he was flustered. He didn't bother with a tie because he hated wearing them.

He told Ania she would have to have a shower when she got home and while she put on her clothes he called her a cab.

'Charge it to my account,' he told the operator. 'The name's Cain. Detective Inspector Ethan Cain.'

After hanging up he grabbed his wallet and warrant card from the dressing table and slipped them into his pocket. Then he checked himself in the mirror one last time and decided that nobody would guess he'd been up half the night shagging a teen prostitute and snorting coke. That was a relief. It meant he was ready to report for duty.

He checked his watch. Seven forty-five. Balham was only a couple of miles away and with luck he could be at Megan Fuller's house in less than half an hour, traffic permitting.

CHAPTER THREE

DANNY SHAPIRO

'We're getting reports that the British actress Megan Fuller has been found dead at her home in London. Police say she was stabbed late last night. Her body was discovered this morning. Scotland Yard has confirmed that murder squad detectives are at the scene. We'll bring you more when we have it.'

Those words from the BBC newsreader hit Danny Shapiro like a cattle prod. His eyes snapped open and he struggled to focus on the TV screen fixed to the wall in front of his bed.

For a few seconds it was just a blur. And by the time his vision cleared the newsreader was talking about the war in Syria. But the caption scrolling across the bottom of the screen told him that he hadn't been dreaming.

Breaking News: Soap star Megan Fuller found murdered in her home.

Danny sat bolt upright and shuddered from a fierce intake of breath. He had turned the telly on twenty minutes ago to help him shake off his slumber before getting up. Since then he'd been dozing on and off and hadn't taken any notice of it.

But now he was wide awake and the morning news had his full attention.

Megan Fuller. His ex-wife. Murdered. Stabbed. In her own home.

Jesus Christ.

Surely it can't be true, he told himself. It must be a ghastly mistake or some sick joke. After all, he was at her house last night and she had been very much alive. As spiteful and as mouthy as ever. They had argued and there'd been a shouting match. He remembered threatening her and recalled the fear on her face as she'd backed away from him in the kitchen.

She had really pissed him off with her crude ultimatum, and he'd told her that he wouldn't allow himself to be blackmailed. But she'd laughed in his face and had said he would have to pay up or suffer the consequences.

Afterwards he'd come straight home and had drunk himself into oblivion because he'd been so angry. That was why his head was bunged up now and there were things he couldn't remember: such as whether he'd given her a slap – or worse – before storming out. If he had then it would have been the first time. During three years of marriage he'd never once laid a hand on her, even though he'd come close to it on numerous occasions.

He was sure he would have held back last night too, whatever the extent of the provocation. But right now he couldn't be a hundred per cent certain. He closed his eyes briefly, cast his mind back to last night, saw himself inside Megan's house, yelling at her, threatening her.

But the picture kept fading, which came as no great surprise. Although he enjoyed the booze, he wasn't a heavy drinker and when he did get rat-arsed he often suffered partial memory loss the morning after. Usually the memories surfaced eventually, but sometimes they didn't.

He was reminded of the time he got into an argument with a stranger who got lippy with him in a nightclub. The next morning he remembered the argument, but had no recollection of punching the bloke in the face and then stamping on his head. Luckily Frankie Bishop had been with him in the club and had told him what had happened.

'I wouldn't worry about it, boss,' Bishop had said. 'Most of us don't remember everything we do when we're hammered. And I reckon that's a good thing. It's just a shame we can't blank out some of the stuff we do when we're sober.'

But Danny *was* worried. Not knowing exactly what had happened last night sparked a twist of panic in his gut.

He opened his eyes, grabbed the TV remote from the bedside table, switched over to Sky News.

And there was Megan's face filling the screen, her eyes staring right at him. He felt the air lock in his chest and was gripped by a sudden anxiety.

It was a photograph he had seen hundreds of times before, one of the professional publicity shots distributed by the BBC. It showed Megan at her most stunning, before her life became a train wreck. Her long brown hair framed an oval face with soft, delicate features. Her smile was warm and engaging, and for a split second he remembered why he'd fallen in love with her in the first place.

His mind carried him back six years to the night they met. It was at a New Year's Eve bash in a club his father had just taken over in Camberwell. She'd come along with a group of luvvie friends from television and he'd been there with Bishop and some of the crew.

Danny had introduced himself and had given them two bottles of champagne on the house.

'It's my way of thanking you for coming to the club,' he'd said. 'I do hope it's the first of many visits.'

It was Megan who asked him to join them at their table to welcome in the new year. And from that moment he was beguiled by her beauty and the fact that she was a celebrity.

At the stroke of midnight they'd kissed, and he would never forget how good it felt and how his heart raced. It was the start of a passionate relationship that most people – including his father – predicted wouldn't last. And they weren't wrong.

Callum Shapiro never did like Megan, and he told Danny he was a moron for getting involved with someone in the public eye.

'Are you off your fucking trolley?' he said after Danny proposed and Megan accepted. 'You're a villain and you need to keep a low profile. You've let this celebrity thing go to your head and it's a big mistake. On top of that you and her are from entirely different worlds. She'll be trouble, son. You mark my words.'

But Danny didn't listen. He loved Megan and he enjoyed the thrill of being in the limelight and going to film premieres and celebrity parties. And he lapped up the attention and the way the tabloids described him as the playboy son of the reputed gangland boss Callum Shapiro.

Four months after he met Megan they got married on Danny's twenty-seventh birthday. But then, two months after the wedding, his father was arrested and the lawyers warned them he was facing a life sentence.

So it fell on Danny to take the reins of the organisation, which made his life more complicated and put an enormous strain on the marriage from the start.

If Megan had conceived during that first year then maybe things would have been different. But she put her career before a family and at the same time Danny found that being the boss meant a bigger commitment than he'd been prepared for. So the odds were stacked against them from the beginning. It didn't help that Megan found it tough coping with pressure and suffered bouts of depression, which she blamed on an unhappy childhood and low self-esteem.

'Miss Fuller was thirty-three and married for several years to Danny Shapiro, the man who has repeatedly denied any involvement in organised crime in London.'

Now his own face stared down at him from the TV screen as the newsreader relayed background information relevant to the story.

Danny's unease mounted as he watched and listened with a hawkish intensity.

'The couple split up three years ago and were divorced fourteen months ago. Shortly after that Miss Fuller was dropped by the BBC from the long-running soap. A close friend has told Sky News that this – coupled with mounting debts – caused her to become clinically depressed.'

Danny had known all about the state she got herself into. She'd phoned him often enough to tell him it was his fault for being a shit husband and cheating on her with a string of women. Out of guilt and pity he had given her a large sum of money as part of the divorce settlement, plus two properties – the house in Balham and the cottage in the New Forest.

But he'd refused to accept responsibility for the fact that she blew the money on high-living and a business venture that went tits up. She'd been forced to re-mortgage the house and put the cottage on the market.

On the TV the newsreader was saying that Megan's body was discovered by her own father when he called at the house this morning.

'Mr Nigel Fuller apparently looked through the kitchen window when he got no response from ringing the front doorbell. He then saw his daughter's body lying on the kitchen floor.'

Danny's mind conjured up an image of the scene that would have confronted Nigel Fuller. It caused the muscles in his jaw to tense and brought a lump to his throat. It also made him realise that deep down he still had feelings for Megan despite the friction that had developed between them. And for that reason he was saddened by the manner of her death.

He started to go through the events leading up to last night again in his head. Megan had called him on his mobile early in the evening. She'd wanted to give him the news that her agent had secured a publishing deal for her autobiography.

'So here's the thing, Danny Boy,' she'd said. 'If you want to stop me dishing the dirt about you and your business then you'd better sort out the money fast. Half a mil buys my silence.'

She'd severed the connection before he could respond, leaving him fuming. He'd tried to ring her back but her voicemail kicked in. Out of frustration he'd thrown his phone across the room, smashing it against a wall.

And that had been a mistake. It meant he couldn't cancel a business meeting he was due to have in Clapham with a couple of Turks who had opened up a new drugs supply route into the UK from Istanbul. He'd been in no mood to go but their number was on the phone so he'd been forced to.

But he was glad he had because over a plentiful supply of booze they'd struck a good deal. The Turks had access to some high quality coke and heroin, and they were now going to be one of the firm's main suppliers.

But as he left the flat Danny's thoughts switched back to Megan. And because he was tanked up he decided to go to her house to confront her. But his anger grew because it was pissing down outside and all the taxis were occupied. Luckily he hadn't been suited up and was wearing jeans and a fleece with a hood. He'd even had a fold-up brolly with him.

He'd walked about a mile from Clapham to Balham, and by the time he got to Megan's house he'd sobered up slightly but was still fit to explode. . .

'A police source has just confirmed that there are no signs of a break-in at Miss Fuller's house. This leads them to believe that she may have been murdered by someone she let in – someone she might have known.'

The newsreader's words seized Danny's attention again and pulled him back to the present. And that was when alarm bells started going off inside his head, and he realised that he had a serious problem.

It didn't matter that he was convinced he didn't kill Megan. Unless it was obvious to the cops who did then he was going to be their prime suspect.

They'd probably find out that she phoned him earlier in the day, even though he used an unregistered mobile. They would know he was worried about what she would write in her forthcoming book. They'd probably drum up CCTV footage of him walking from Clapham to Balham. And he couldn't be sure, of course, that he hadn't been seen entering or leaving the house.

Fuck.

His heart started booming in his ears and a hole opened up in his stomach. He told himself to stay calm, not to panic, but he had to fight back an urge to scream.

This was bad. Really bad. The cops would jump at the chance to pin Megan's murder on him and once they discovered he'd been to the house they'd have him bang to rights.

Fuck.

What he needed was an alibi and he didn't have one. He also had no idea what to tell the Old Bill when they eventually turned up. He needed to think, to get his mind around the problem and see if he could find a way out.

A coffee would help, he decided. And then a hot shower. He had to flush the booze and the sleep from his system so that he could start firing on all cylinders.

He threw back the duvet and swung his legs over the edge of the bed. And at that moment the landline started ringing in the other room. His heart froze in his chest and his body flooded with adrenaline. Only a few people had the number to the house phone – his father, his lawyer, his accountant and Frankie Bishop.

He had no idea which one of them it could be or whether he should answer it. He didn't want to speak to anyone until he knew what he was going to say. So he listened to the ringing for about thirty seconds. And after it stopped he didn't move. He just sat there, his mind whirring, as he tried to think of a way to save himself.